The Sin Eaters

By the Author

Strange Saint

Andrew Beahrs

THE SIN EATERS

The Toby Press

The Sin Eaters

First Edition, 2008
The Toby Press LLC

POB 8531, New Milford, CT 06776-8531, USA
& POB 2455, London W1A 5WY, England
www.tobypress.com

Cover credit: Dulle Griet (Mad Meg) 1564 (oil on canvas) by Pieter the Elder Bruegel (c. 1525–69) ©Museum Mayer van der Berg, Antwerp, Belgium/Giraudon/The Bridgeman Art Library Nationality/copyright status: Flemish/out of copyright

ISBN 978 1 59264 236 6, *hardcover*

A CIP catalogue record for this title is available from the British Library

Typeset by Koren Publishing Services

Printed and bound in the United States

For my sisters, and Virginia.

Prologue: Sarah

Jamestown, the Virginia Colony. 1621.

At last it is summer. Dawns now bring a red sun, heavy with the promise of heat; in afternoon, swamps and gardens and tobacco fields warp under a sultry blaze. Many an evening carries wind and rain to us. Then forest and plantation strive to stand before the hot storms that thud thundering up the broad channel of the James River. In my old home, the slow surge of the seasons was well known to me, as evident as words on a page. But this is a new country. A new manner of summer.

I have found many things in Virginia to love, and to wonder at. When the rains do not come, dusk fills with the scream and flash of insects that light the underbrush like lost stars. The taste of roast venison is no longer a luxury. And even now, men paddle a canoe into sight around the first point of marshland, towing a sturgeon nearly as long as the craft they pilot. All these things are worth my love. But no matter how many years the Lord may grant me, no matter how

I may come to relish this earth, the wet air and red clay of Virginia will keep me from ever truly feeling it a home.

My home will always be Monkshead, the village in the English Midlands that I came to with my husband many tens of years ago. Home is where I lost my children, none of them old enough to have shed their swaddling. Home is where I found solace for my losses in helping others bear children of their own. Home is where I passed my days with Henry until he was taken from me, and where I had thought to stay until I died myself. Home is the place I at last was driven from. Or abandoned, as I sometimes tell myself.

Until Virginia dropped her chains of summer heat about my shoulders, binding me to shade trees and the so-slightly cooler riverbank, I often went outside the settlement. I would crutch to the forest or to the edge of the wetlands, seeking out new plants. Not caring what men might think of a lone, old woman searching the swamp, I rooted up pasty bulbs, plucked petals, and wrestled with thorny bushes. Once the poisoned sap of a creeper-vine covered my arm with red, running blisters. So fierce a thing! Fiercer than thorns. Though it marred my sleep for a week, I came to revel in the horrid itch, as much as I did in the curious accent of the Powhatan man who bade me seek out goldenrod, or in the relief that paste of the goldenrod brought. All were ways of coming to know this place.

Yes, there are things in Virginia to love. But how can I think it a home, when even the breeze sweats? When every breath seems filled with a swamp wounded and left bleeding into the wind?

Below me the James River has gone red under the sunset, its swollen flood now the color of rose petals. The canoe holds three men, their paddles flashing brightly in the sunset light on the water. Always night seems to come first to the James.

Even paddling slowly, the men strain; behind them the barely-sunken sturgeon sends up ripples in the riverwater. Such fish may be found and taken in the shallows on the far side of the marsh, where the warm water lulls them nearly to sleep. Drowsing so, they can be harpooned with fishing-darts, or even caught with a loop of rope slipped cunningly around the tail. One of the canoeing fellows is a Powhatan, and practiced in such things.

I find that I am touching my face with my palm. For years I have adorned my cheeks and chin with a small constellation of stars cut from black felt. In my youth the fashion began among wealthy folk, who sought to cover scars and craters left by pox. My own stars and moon remain, though my skin has aged beneath them. My hair, once the color of oak bark, now hangs in loose gray strings.

My owl, Henry my husband would say, when, during love, my eyes went wide as hope. I laughed at the name, and took it silently to heart. For his owl is what I felt myself to be. His bird, who could at any time fly if she chose. Thus every day with him was a new dedication.

Sky, I think. *Skin. Hair. Age.* There are times that these things feel a mask. There are times I rejoice to think that none here can see the woman it covers.

Were I to learn the stories of the men here, very likely I would find some to mirror mine, like different clothes draping on a single drying-frame. In recent years some tales have been common throughout the English midlands. *Our village had lands*, a fellow might say. *Common lands. All our folk used them and worked on their upkeep. There were shared pastures where a man might graze his cows, shared wastelands at the edge of the royal forests where he might gather wood. But our landlord decided he could get more profit selling wool than collecting rent. He hired fellows to build fences around the pastures, and to guard the fences. Then he ordered them to raise sheep inside the fences—sheep for his profit alone, on pastures we villagers had all shared. Some of my people stayed. I left.*

So it was in my old home. Most of my congregation fled before the changes, leaving for America, leaving me alone among the thieves who legally stole our lands.

The canoe bumps gently against the dock. Men gather there, carrying ropes and landing-hooks to help raise the sturgeon. So many men, so far from their first homes. How truly could any of them tell their own stories? Once I thought I had a strong hold on the tale of my own life. But the more I clutched it to me the more it changed, shifting as surely as the face aging beneath my stars.

It took unmooring from my old home to make me question

the truth of the story I told myself for so long. It took abandoning my home, my solid place, and a long flight across a country I have now left and lost. I have fled through forest, and down river, and over lake. A monastery has sheltered me, and a barn's sweet straw. I have lived in hope of purity and in fear of murder. I have met good men and bad men, and I have met evil. And I have returned to the best and worst place of my life, learning that what I thought were nightmares were only veiled memories.

My mind falls back and back: across a wind-swept ocean, to lands beloved and despised. It rests, at last, upon the English morning that saw the end of my old home and the beginning of my wanderings. Almost I can taste iron, feel the singe of fire, smell the choking smoke.

Many, hearing my tale, would think it was the cruelty of others that drove me from my village. And surely the cruelty of Monkshead's new masters was a part of it.

But I know that what truly made me leave, on that April morning, was memory. Memory, conjured by a word.

One: Sarah

The black moon fell from my face, drifted to the page. I'd been reading and the felt crescent lay on the paper like a babe's gummy grin, blocking a neat curve of text.

I touched my cheek where the moon had been. Though the skin there was still sticky with sap, the sap would need freshening if it were to hold the felt patch until night. And it must hold, if I were to leave my house. I'd not choose to have any man see part of my sky fall away. Keeping patchwork planets and moons on one's face is an old, old fashion, one never much seen near my village even when popular. I have my reasons for keeping it. None of them allow for having the stars fall away by chance.

I pushed myself up, my knee treacherous and cracking out the chill of morn. I shuffled to the corner beside the chimney, where my herbs hung like scarves above a small drawer-table. Gently crushing the bundled plants would loose healing scents of rosewater, smoke, and honey, that would wrap illness softly as a dressing of hare pelt. Boiled, they'd bring forth colors gaudy or plain. I only brushed fingers lightly over a stem as I bent to open the drawer. In it was a small wooden box carved with the face of a grinning monkey or landlord, filled with my sewing stuff and a good store of sad-colored felt. Also there was a wooden ball, which I had rolled over cracks in the bark of scrub-pine until it bulged with sap. I unwrapped it from the damp cloth meant to keep it from drying into a profitless lump of stone.

I felt for my constellation's remaining points. One star on my temple. One on my cheek, one on my chin. Only the moon was gone from beside my nose. With all four patches there, fixed by sap to the planes and curves of my face, I could make a constellation in whatever form I wished. Often I formed a letter that mirrored my mood. *Q* might stand for *Quiet*, *F* for *Fortunate*. You might say it would be difficult to form a *Q*, or an *F*, with a scant three stars and a moon. But I say that the stars in the sky look not very much like a plow, nor a giant, nor a lion. It's all in how you imagine the lines between the stars cornering and curving.

And in truth I did not want my letters to be clear to all. I liked thinking that Sam Ridley did not know he was being mocked when I went to him marked with an accusing *B*, for *Bastard*, or *C*, for *Cunt-beard*, or *S*, for *Sower of a Crooked Woman's Woe*. To me, each was as clear as a banner ordering him from town. But only to me.

The moon I'd been using was still a fine logwood black, not yet gone gray under springtime sun. With a pinch and press of sap by my nose it again held fast. I had been thinking of Ridley, who I'd doubtless see that morn; thus I imagined that the moon completed an *I*, for *Ignorant*.

I returned to my bench, lifted my skirts, and began rubbing oil of chamomile on my knee. As I rubbed I imagined the herb calling aid from the turn of Venus and a distant, desert wind. The joint warmed quickly. But through the smell of sweet oil and herb came a thin, sharp scent of rot. I looked up past rafters to the vault of my roof. Spring's rains had fallen hard even before the last snowmelt was gone, and there was a good deal of water in the bound thatch. Probably it should have been stripped away and replaced a season or two before. A lost sparrow flitted between beams, perking her head whenever she landed. My windows were only greased paper, not nearly clear enough to let in the light of morning, and the sparrow was barely visible in the dark beyond my candle.

But my mind was still on Sam Ridley, leader of the vagabonds who seized the village lands after my congregation departed. Strange, that he had such a hold over me that morning. Most days I was able to think only of my own home, the small needs of belly and hearth, until I was so unfortunate to see the vagabonds in the flesh. That morning something kept Ridley creeping around the edges of my mind and heart.

It was the sin-eater, I realized. Though it had been some days since he came to Monkshead, on that morning the thought of him harassed me, like the sickness from yesterday's bad water. Ridley's cruelty towards the sin-eater was a reminder of just how much things in Monkshead had changed. My old congregation would not have countenanced sin-eating; but neither would they have chased a simpleton from town, with axes and thrown clods of turf, as Ridley and his crew had. As long as the man left swiftly, my congregation would have let him do so at his own pace, without forcing him into humiliating flight.

It is rare to see a sin-eater. Many have never heard of the profession. But it is a simple calling, that fills a simple need. When all England was still Catholic, a grieving family could rest easily, knowing that their dear one had confessed all sin to a priest, and so been absolved before going to meet the Lord. Now the English Church has renounced confession, taking away that small comfort, spilling out the old, washing waters. Now a father may fear that his son goes to the next life sullied with sin—a daughter may fear for her mother, a husband for his wife. Any woman who has been party to a pig-killing will know how badly one can want water to wash away blood from her hands. How much more will she desire a cleansing basin for her family, when they pass on from this slaughterhouse life?

And so, many refuse to see a loved one face the Lord uncleansed. Instead they leave bread and wine on the corpse through the night, imagining that sin will thus pass from the body into loaf and cup. Then they find a fellow so simple, poor, or hopeless that he is willing to take on another lifetime of trespass for a few coins. He eats the sin-soaked bread, he drinks down the cup of crimes. Perhaps he is grateful for the meal.

This new practice seems to me cold, cruel, and useless. I do not believe that we can do anything to cleanse ourselves before the Lord; our sins are our own, and He will not be blinded to them. He will only forgive if He so chooses. And though the old way of confession was an error, at least it wronged no other man. Feeding a fellow your sins is a sin itself. How prideful, to imagine that you might so easily mask the gaze of the Lord!

I'd seen the sin-eater only from behind, his limbs lank as a water-strider's as his clumsy, shambling run carried him from town, Ridley and his mob screeching behind like cranes. I heard later that the fellow had asked Ridley artless questions about our recent dead. A sin-eater should not be so trusting; he should take care when choosing who he reveals himself to. Those who believe that he absorbs sin, storing it within himself, will not abide his presence for long.

Whether or not Ridley truly believed that a man could eat another's sins, he had seen a chance for sport. When the yelling drew me from my house, already the vagabonds had chased him down the road, axe-handles and coppice-poles raised overhead like the wings of a raucous flock. At least they had not beaten him. I never saw his face, but I'd hated the manner of his going. I hoped he'd had food enough to last until the next town.

My knee warmed and loosened. Even in the dark I could feel the village about me; its air and water and earth. I knew them as well as I did my own body. I knew the way high clouds swirled and tussled, I knew the way streams hissed deep beneath us, and how they could be heard by one who knew how to listen. I knew the heralds of flood and storm. Once, such knowledge was only knowledge—useful as a means of growth or healing, but no more appreciated than is the use of one's own fingers before they begin curling with age. Now any knowledge of my old village, useful or not, was a solace. I much needed a set, solid place, as my home seemed to sink away beneath me.

I breathed deep, trying to find a calm foundation in things known, and things remembered. But that foundation was soon destroyed by the vagabonds, running their sheep past my door.

Past the open, sunny doorway they rumbled, two and three

sheep at a time, each small group accompanied by a trotting or stumbling man. Many of the latter carried long, curving crooks. There was bleating, shouting, laughter; I heard herdsmen whooping and, I could have sworn, the glug of swilled ale and huffcap.

I went to my own ale butt, lifted the lid, and drank a bitter ladleful for assurance of heart. Then I went out into the brightening spring morning.

For many years, I had found the familiar view from my dooryard comforting. Now, even without the running sheep, there were a hundred small signs of what I'd lost. Past the village road and the stream beside it, the old snake fence jig-jagged its way up a far pasture slope gone wild; spring grass, feverfew, and bushy charlock were overtaking the violets and pale yellow lady-smocks of earliest spring. Here and there a railing had fallen from the fencing, leaning askew among the dandelions and primroses. Once, dozens of cows would have grazed down the pastures, but now there were only four left, among them my own old, mottled missy. I've always loved a meadow, but the sight of that field gone over entirely to flowers left an ache in my heart.

On the ridge above the few cows, stood the tiny mill we'd always depended on at harvest, standing now like a child spread-eagled before the sun. Its sail-frames would stay naked this year; the grain fields on the other side of the village were to be cleared by sheep instead of scythes.

In my very dooryard a yearling ewe stood among the rosemary and greening fennel, tilting her head to reach the tender leaves of a newly sprouting bear's breeches. The plant had trouble enough with caterpillars; I kicked the ewe out from my garden as two more sheep dragged the vagabond Merchant past me. Merchant lay on his back, gripping each sheep by its fat tail, kicking clumsily to aid them, scraping a skewed path. A crowd of idiots followed coughing behind. They danced, they shouted, they joyfully broke wind. Hurriedly I twisted my moon and slid a star, making my *I* into an *M. Masterless men*, I thought. These fools were not masters of their own selves.

The dust of the passing flock damped the smell of fresh spring growth. Vagabond Kelly came grinning from the stream, wet to the waist, golden kingcups and trailing watercress clumped on his boots and trousers. A lamb struggled in his arms, her head jerking sharply as a sprung trap. Kelly jumped twice, a gesture both mocking and oddly carefree, then dropped her hard to the ground.

For a moment my vision filled with crimson—a bright, bleeding, cock's tail red. A cloak, past me almost before I saw it.

"You, Sam Ridley. Ridley!" I called. He glanced back. His eyes always reminded me of a painting I once saw of a gurge whirlpool; they seemed at one moment fixed in place, at the next to turn curiously. Leader of the band, he'd taken Midge Thomas' fine home for his own. That made him my closest neighbor, a circumstance I preferred not to think about overmuch. His comportment was merry, his chin well kept, and like all the newcomers he wore an odd mix of old rags and new stuff bought with landlord's gold. His boots were black leather, his cloak the dragon-scale red one might expect at court; but his trousers and jerkin were coarse cloth, patched with loose stitching, and deerskin, and rabbit pelts. When his cloak blew open the furs made him look like an animal playing at being a man.

He gave a happy wave. "God speed you well," he called, and turned away. Silently I cursed the back of his head. *God speed* is the proper greeting to give a woman standing hard before death's door. Though aging, I was not so old as that, nor was I ill. Courtesy required that he offer me *Well met.* I had despised him from the first for such slights, great and small.

Now, I've been vagabond myself, and my Henry a vagabond with me, in the years before he called upon his cousins' goodwill and we came to Monkshead to stay. There is no shame in being a vagabond. I understand the longing for a home one feels when on the rolling road. But understanding a man does not mean you must like him. Sometimes, the more clearly you can see a fellow, the more his faults come to seem hard as nuts. I had already seen that Ridley was willing to force others to wander. I knew that to better his own station he would give grain fields to sheep, forcing the old farmers into vagabondage themselves. And I knew that he would play at being lord of the town, chasing out sin-eaters and other harmless drifters. Ridley seemed to have no care for any beyond himself, unless they were willing to raise him high. I swore, and followed his parade of sheep and idiots.

John Jacobs fell in beside me, his hunched shoulders those of a man making his uncertain way through mud. His beard tapered to a point and he pinched it absently, as one might hold down washing in a breeze.

"Well met, John," I said.

He looked at me as though waking up. "Sarah. Well met. Do you know what they intend with the sheep?"

"I do not," I said, for we had already passed the footbridge that led over our little river and thus to the overgrown cow pastures. Probably they would put the sheep there until cowslip and clover had time to grow in the grain fields. I'd never have imagined that I might long for the hardy fumitory that sprung up in a normal year wherever a furrow was plowed. Now the memory of tearing aside its pink-and-red flowers to make room for barley was a poignant one; clearing fumitory was a task of a new springtime, that spoke of a harvest to come.

Two weeks before, the vagabonds had begun erecting an oaken pale around the grain fields to hold their flocks. When I first saw those boards set, solid as dying, around fields that gave bread to generations, for an instant I'd envied the most of my congregation the journey to America. Perhaps they'd been right that no righteous community could be so cut off from the earth and yet survive. It was a weak and shameful moment for me; I'd made my choice and would live with that.

Jacobs' mind was also on the fence. "They'll finish the enclosure soon enough," he said. "So many of them, so few of us left."

"Where's your wife?" I asked sharply. That was a bit of a slap. I hate to watch a man lie down before a fight that needs fighting; I wanted him to realize that he still had something worth struggling for. But with a squeeze of his lips he again drew inward, hating to see his home so turned and too much a coward to stand against it.

The crowd came to rest before John Stradling's slumping house. I pushed my way through, often blocked by some fool until he saw that it was an old woman behind him and not some drunken companion he could happily brawl. The pain in my knee was slowly returning, a slight clicking begun in every step.

The vagabonds formed a corral like a half-circle, each end touching against John Stradling's old house. Ridley stood in the center beside the gray hump of the village beehive oven. Surrounded by bleating, stamping sheep, he looked like a dwarf clinging to a tide-swept rock.

John Stradling's house was the oldest, and largest, in the village. It had needed to be big, for when first built it had housed animals and men together, each with their half of the dwelling. But for many years it had served our congregation as a meetinghouse, with only a slight fall in the floor marking where the stable had been. Under the morning sun it had a closed-up, tired, finished look, the small glass windows clouded as though palms pressed against them from within.

I did not honor all that happened in that house, nor in our meetings there. But when Ridley made his way to the door and opened it with a flourish, then kneed in the first reluctant sheep, my heart twitched like a cocoon popping open. At last I knew why the vagabonds had brought their animals to the village center. The future was not enough for them—they must also have our past. And how better to seize it than to steal our most important place, making a sheepfold where we'd worshipped?

"That's no place for a beast," I shouted.

From across the flock Ridley's eyes seemed swirled with pleasure. "It was built for beasts," he said. He booted a second sheep through the door; it vanished as into a sea-cave.

I struggled through the bleating flock. They were still frantic from their run and they jolted my legs, making me sway uneasily. To my right, Merchant rose from among the woolen billows. The other vagabonds thought it a fine jest to have waited so long before standing, and a wave of laughter passed. Merchant licked a broad, gapped smile, then pulled his hair back, leaving his hands on his head. He was half a true idiot. I pushed past him and the last of the sheep, finally reaching Ridley. The good of my chamomile had faded and my knee wailed quietly. Panting, I stood on my left leg.

"Are there any here with this woman's ear?" Ridley called, smiling. But the smile was like a stone teetering over a path.

"Any man who speaks sense will have my ear, easily enough," I started to say. But someone was calling my name from behind. John Jacobs, again. I was annoyed to see him sidling closer, imagining he would try to help by dragging me from threat of punishment. That was not at all the help I wanted. But I said nothing to dissuade him; I hoped he might surprise me. Things had changed so very much.

Merchant also stumbled to join us. I'd never stood so close to him and for the first time noticed a scar in his beard where no whiskers would grow, a scar in the shape of a *D. D*, for *Deserter.* The mark branded on those who flee from the King's service. I stared at the mark and at his gaping, cruel grin. Probably all English should be grateful that Merchant had fled. Having him under King's arms could only have made it more likely that we'd be conquered by Spain, or Africa, or the Turks.

"Well met, good mistress," Ridley said. He dipped the brim of his hat, at last addressing me properly. Jacobs stood teetering at the edge of what now seemed a little council.

"Well met," I said. "There is plenty of space in the stables, now that the rest of the stock are gone. There's no reason for you to use what's been a good meetinghouse. Nor to show disrespect to those of us who have worshipped in it."

"It's as good a place as any," Ridley said.

"As any," said Merchant.

"Maybe the roof of it is as good as any other," I said. "The floor and the walls might be much the same. But it's not all the same to me where you house the sheep. Don't—"

Ridley interrupted. "Such a great love for a plain frame?"

Surprised, I looked at him sharply. It is true that our congregation never thought the walls especially holy. We had no church, nor ever needed one, believing that any ground where there is proper worship will be worthy in the sight of the Lord. But it was strange that Ridley knew any of that. "You're right that there's nothing special in this house, nothing blessed," I said. "But I'd have you choose another. So would many others you must now call neighbor. For that reason alone you'd best haul these things back to the stables, where they can be managed properly." For emphasis I yanked the wool on a small sheep's back. The motion forced my foot to earth, and pain shot through my knee. I grimaced. Merchant's eyes narrowed; no doubt he had thought my pained face a snarl.

John Jacobs' hands draped on my shoulders. "It's nothing more than a house, now," he said softly. "We have no cause to keep it sacred. It was never more than an easy place for us to gather."

"Did I say different?" I turned, brushing his hands away as I glared. I'd hoped Jacobs would back me. He might at least have respected an older woman's whim. He might have trusted me enough to offer aid, at least until he knew for certain that it was hopeless.

But his lips twitched like waking kittens, beneath eyes that found nowhere to take hold. He only wanted to draw me away from a hazard. There was some honor in that, I guessed, though he owed me more. But then, very likely he didn't know of my churching, nor what it had meant to Frances his wife.

John Stradling, the bald-browed, water-eyed village minister, had refused to baptize Stephen Jacobs. When Frances pressed him, he said what any villager would expect him to—that a man must ask for baptism with his own voice. It had been foolish for the Jacobs to ask, I thought. They knew as well as any that Stradling would never baptize a child before it could speak. They knew that baptism is no birthright for us, but a choice made by each man for himself. They knew well that the souls of babes never reach the Lord, lodging instead in the flesh of bats that feed at night above our river.

But the Jacobs had lost children before, and so did ask. It is a hard, hard thing, watching a child sicken without the balm and hope of holy water. What, in Master Stradling's righteous books, could ease the heart of a mother beneath the crushing ton of a small hand gone still?

When Stephen died, the latest of four, I feared it might break Frances. There are few women among us who lose no children in a life of bearing; it is a loss I know myself. But Frances had the air of other women I have known, who after seeing a child go can find no sweetness in this life. All the years after can be a long wait for one's own death, filled with nothing but a desperate, unslakeable want for reunion with the dear ones. Waiting so leaves living days dry as dusty cider jugs.

Thus I raged at the lack of a churching to give Frances succor. The cleansing ritual of churching had been abandoned, cast aside lightly as a faded garment—but it was a garment stitched by women through their generations, who know better than any what women need after birth. Luke's book tells us that even Blessed Mary was churched. But what the great mother needed for herself did not matter to the leader of our congregation nearly so much as doctrine did. A living woman weighs less than a paper word with John Stradling, a man who would not know how to read the heavens if they turned around his own head. As they do.

So Frances was not churched and cleansed. Along with blood, and pain, and grief, she was left with needless fear and guilt. She had to fear that she'd passed on her own blood and pain to her son, and quickened his slipping away.

Well, John Stradling has his churching. I have mine. I had aided Stephen's birth, and I had fought against his death. I could do nothing about the baptism, but I hoped that I could offer some other help. And so, after the village had emptied like a curled shell, before the vagabonds came scrabbling to fill it, I called on Frances. I bade her to my house.

She came with empty cheeks but in neat clothes, her finest plain fabrics arrayed cleanly on her, her hair bound tightly beneath a coif. I'd raised a good fire and the only smell was its smoke; I had supped on plain bread, that the room would not be filled with the steam of stew.

On the table were four tapered candles. Between them was a chapbook, open to a woodcut print of our Lord Jesus Christ suffering on his cross. His robe had fallen open and he twisted his body, arching his back away from the beams. When you first saw the print, it seemed he was twisting in agony. But then one saw his breast, and how milk showered from it to the crowd below. He was offering his own body, wanting even during his death to give sustenance. The people's mouths opened like sparrows' beaks. They fed from our Lord.

I guided Frances to sit on the bench. She studied the page in silence. I sat on a stool behind, beside the fire, watching as her hands slid back to the wood of the bench. They curled around the seat, then squeezed until her fingers turned white.

I said, softly, that I knew the way of a churching. I had seen them many times in my youth. I'd aided them a dozen times and more. Some lies are not lies.

Frances sat for a time. She asked if it was a plain ritual. I told her there were portions that might bring discomfort to her mind, if not her body. I asked if she would have me go on. She would: she nodded, and turned to face me. I clapped my hands overhead, then, and left the palms together for ten slow beats of my heart.

Then I stood, and unclasped my jacket. I loosed it, and my shirt. To the waist I was bare to her. I knew she would never speak of that. It was something secret between us. A secret that could make all the night a secret, and a precious one. And she could see my body, my flat dried breasts, and know that she yet had reasons for thankfulness and even hope. Mine is a good enough body, but long past the time for bearing. And I've had no better fortune in that than she.

I had readied oils for her. Nothing that I would claim could call down the Lord's goodwill, or affect his judgments. I'm not such a fool as to imagine that I can change the Lord's will. But only a greater fool than I would fail to take up the cleansing stuff the Lord has given us, and to put it to good use. So I had oils, infused with summer mint, and apple-root, and creeping rose. There were balms that shone like bright pebbles, there were emollients like hayfield breeze.

And I had herbs, gathered in late summer. As I gathered them I'd murmured, *Jesus, Jesus, Jesus,* until the word nearly lost meaning yet brought a clear warm simmer to me and, I hoped, to the earthly stems. I used herbs gathered at noontime, that Frances might better take pleasure in the fading half of her day. Some might think it better to use dawn plants, that she could have a bright morning. But I thought that light-minded, a failure to respect Frances' special pestilence, or respect for how a woman can be overcome. When morning is gone one should say so, and turn mind and heart to a better, richer afternoon.

I drew off Frances' coif. Her nightshade hair fell free. I rubbed oil into my fingers. I rubbed them gently on her brow. I blew, softly; her inhale was as soft. I laid a leaf of mullein upon her, and watched the tremble beneath her eyelids. My body was open to the air. I knew she still saw that, whether her eyes were open or no. I laid a curl of youngest, softest fern beside the mullein and I hummed, low and regular, a purr to fill her ears like beaten flax. My mouth opened, my breath spilled—cooling her new oil, spreading that scent. Her lips drew in, a gasp. Then, when my breath formed one word, *blessed*, I saw her start. The tears began to come. If I could not do all for her, I had done what I could.

"Where is your wife?" I asked Jacobs again. This time my question was like a cattle prod.

"Must he consult a wife before he can know his own mind?" Ridley asked. Merchant was solid and silent as a mound but Jacobs shifted, uncertain of my meaning, wondering whether to take offense.

I was in no mood to give him any doubt. "You're a fearful man, John Jacobs," I said quietly.

Ridley shouted with laughter. "Why, that's scarcely different than calling him *coward*. I'll fetch you a pair of gloves, lioness. You'll need them to hang from his beard." He kneed a lamb away, then leaned with lying ease against the cold bake-oven.

Jacobs licked his lips as he pulled his beard into a sharp point. Finally he shrugged. "She's a widow," he said to Ridley. Merchant slid around me to stand beside his master.

"Well, there are many widows. But most among them keep civil tongues," Ridley said calmly. He spoke as though I lacked ears, or a full spirit. The low dry fire in my belly began to smoke.

Merchant had been watching me with growing confusion. "Do your stars move?" he asked.

"No," I said. Then, to Ridley: "I'd loose a shrew in your hall, but I won't harm dumb beasts."

In his pause, so short that none but a probing rival might have noticed it, I could see that the insult confused him. I realized that he did not know that a shrew will kill sheep at night, being hungry for a particular clay found only in their livers. Even I knew that, though I've never owned a ram nor a ewe. Ridley was ill suited to care for a flock.

But if he could not understand my full meaning, he did catch my insulting intent. His retort had two prongs. First he spoke knowingly to Merchant, telling him that any fool could see that my stars were in the likeness of the Steed. Then he turned his attention to me. "You'll do nothing to harm me or mine, Widow," he said.

Once, in our village, there were those who would let a Bible fall open to a chance page, then look to the text for portents of coming days. I always doubted that a message could be found in words found only by luck. But when Ridley spoke, I heard *steed*, I heard *widow*; then I felt for the first time that the most powerful charms might be accidental ones. Ridley's unluckily chosen words were a spell struck to my heart.

The word *steed* was a relic of Northam, the worst place I have known in all my life. Hearing it, my mind flooded with memories of docks bound up with weedy ropes and tired chains. Of moldy frame houses, and forgotten warehouse corners, crammed with split, dry leather, where a wanderer might steal sleep. Of bobbing skiffs, damp with gull dung. My heart felt bound by seawalls as I remembered what was done to me in Northam, and what I did in answer. It was a gray town, a vicious, paupered burg, where people remained out of habit after having the misfortune to be born there. Where they named seagoing constellations *Dagger*, and *Hogshead*, and *Steed*. Where even the joy of finding my husband had been corrupted. Ridley had no right to summon such memories. Though it was an accident, I felt he might as well have spit on my face.

And to name me *Widow*! My husband is dead; there is no shame there. But I do not choose to have men call me widow, as though Widow is my name, containing all that I am. It is true that I have suffered losses. I will not be treated as lessened by them.

Yes, it was an accidental spell. But a spell nonetheless, when spoke with malice by a malicious man. I felt my worst memories mocked, as though I had endured their creation for nothing; and I groped for words that Ridley would find as unforgivable.

"You'd be helpless to stop me," I said. "Cockless man."

Around us talk vanished like stones down a well. There was only the low keen of the shuffling sheep, calming after their run. Even in a rage, my stomach gaped at the sudden quiet. Ridley had more hold over his people than I'd thought. They *should* have mocked him for being challenged by a woman—even if they could not taunt him openly, sudden coughs and wiped mouths might have shown them amused. Instead they turned still and stony. We might have been in far pasture, with nothing around us but ravens seeking seed.

Ridley watched me as he might a cornered mouse, while deciding on a tool to crush it with—so difficult, to choose between his mauls. I knew him then for the worst manner of man, the kind who has neither black humors nor blood, constancy nor mirth. The sort who thinks he can build the world afresh through his very will, who punishes the weak merely to show his readiness to mete out pain. That day he thought me weak.

I leaned towards him, over a sheep, my fists filled with clenched wool. "Cockless!" I said, with a hiss but loudly enough that I could not be mistook. "No manhood between your legs, nothing there but soft hair. I'll buy you a comb of turtle's shell?"

For a moment he wavered between a scowl and a weasel's grin. Then he gestured towards Stradling's old house. A few more sheep had wandered in unbidden; they looked like clouds lost in the shadows inside. "You people have your old ways," Ridley said at last. "No doubt it would be good for us to take some of your customs as our own. After all we hope to have a long, fine life together." He worked his way through the soft confusion of the sheep and towards the door. With a few quiet words he sent Kelly into the hall. The pit in my stomach deepened. I looked about at the vagabonds, and the villagers among them. Save for John Jacobs, the few members of my old congregation had had nothing to say. I'd never have thought that Jacobs would prove my best ally. Nor would I have been glad for it.

I waited for Kelly to drag out the stocks. The heavy frame was stored behind the podium where it could be eyed during sermon, a dreadful promise to those who considered transgressing the law. But when Kelly emerged he carried a gray bag. Though it sagged like drowned skin he bore it as though it were velvet, and held a crown. My heart twitched; my spirit fled. It was a wonder that they'd already found where the bag was hidden. But then, looters have sharp eyes. And these had found the scold's bridle.

The bridle was an iron mask, made of slag left over from other forgings. Of a horrible weight, it was banded with bolted straps, as though mere metal could not restrain a woman's untamed voice. Pinholes for eyes. A broad, triangle nose, like a spade. There was a slit mouth, and a tongue. But this tongue was not meant to mock the watcher; it stuck inward. The tongue was iron. It would probe the wearer's mouth.

The mask looked a goblin. "There's a fancy thing," Ridley said.

It was Merchant that fixed it on me. "I should have sworn they've moved," he said when he came close, looking again at my stars.

I longed to curse at him, and strike the mask to ground. But I would not give the watchers the joy of a fight—the spectacle of an old woman lashing out helplessly. I opened my mouth for the tongue.

The smell and taste of rust was like dried blood; the tongue, a blunt spike, I closed on it in silence. Merchant pressed the mask against my face, then pulled the leather bands tight on my head. Seen through the niggardly pinholes, his eyes were like scrabbling beetles. Metal hugged my skull. Leather lapped me like a bandog. The tapping of my teeth against iron dragged cold nails down my back. Merchant reached behind my head, pulled me forward, and then all was the green of his jerkin. The lock clicked. Then Merchant was gone away and I could see nothing but confused pricks of color.

But I heard the vagabonds—their joy. "So tight," one had said when Merchant pulled the straps. But another answered that as the bridle was the villagers' toy, there was no need to pity them when it was used. When the first answered *aye*, I could hear that he now found the punishment just. He, and all the vagabonds, wanted badly for Ridley to be strong. They needed him to be, so they could see in him a leader, and feel the village their home. For many it would doubtless be the first home they had ever known. They lusted for lands of their own, and houses, and to measure those real lands and houses against old dreams. Surely they had never expected to find a challenge from a forthright, crooked woman in such a well-ordered village, where all should keep their places. What treachery it must have seemed to find defiance where none was expected.

With the mask set upon me, they felt justice had been done. The stars turned as they should. My own loosed with sweat, and slipped down to catch within the bridle.

Inside I screamed silent curses at the vagabonds for their mockery, and at their false and useless rigor in punishment. But most of all I raged because there was not one man or woman who would drive away the sheep. Not one member of my congregation chose to shepherd a passage for me. Not one old villager had courage and charity enough to do that one, simple thing.

I took a careful step that ended against a wooly flank. With my knee I nudged the sheep carefully aside. Foot by foot, inch by inch I went on, sometimes edging around the animals, sometimes prodding them aside. I prayed that my leg would not betray me, that I would not be further humbled before the crowd. But when I stepped in a divot my knee buckled. I dropped among the beasts, into the shadowed mugginess of the flock.

There was no pain, yet, only a sickening looseness at the joint. A wet nose pressed against the mask's eyehole. The smell was like a storehouse of baled wool. Laughter tangled my legs as I pressed myself up and began laboring once more towards the crowd. This time I limped openly. What need was there to hide? What purpose?

Finally I was through. I took three unhindered steps. The crowd parted as though the mask burned red from the forge, and was being borne to the tempering pool. I knew they thought I would continue past them and to my home. If I did so they would follow, throwing clods and fresh sheepshit. So near to me as they were now, they would never strike, but only shout. I would not answer. I closed my eyes. Calls buffeted iron. My ears were naked. Then I thought they would strike.

A malicious turn in the metal crushed my tongue. My mouth flooded, my body trying despite me to eat the thing. I swallowed rusty spittle and gagged as the vagabonds pranced and jeered. I stood, hands at my sides, until they went away. They drifted off in clumps, as brewer's foam dumped amid river-reeds will break under an even eddy. None remained. It has never been permitted to comfort one in the bridle; there was constancy, at least, in that. Alone, I stood in the sun.

All that day I choked on iron. Many women would have fled to their houses, even before their tormentors faded away. But in truth there is no escape. One's own door is no shield. Once it is closed, it joins with thatch and clay and walls as all become the same world, the same cage. Why try to hide what all know? What all have seen?

Though the tongue hurt me, it was meant more to bring shame. But there were none left that I would feel shamed before. These were rabbits, these vagabond cottagers. These were rogue and lonesome hares, who through chance found themselves with the strength of a warren. I had done nothing. I'd no cause for shame. And so, without shame but in raging temper, I went about my business. That day, my business was baking.

I took a handful of yeasty, bubbling proof from the common bucket. On the common table, close by to where road met cowpath at the center of town, I felt my way to knead flour and proofing into loaves. I placed them in the common oven. My face had turned red beneath the mask. I waited for the good crust and crumb to bake, and for the finished loaves to cool on racks.

At last the pinholes of light turned dusky. I waited for the sound of Merchant's step, and for his key in the lock. Then I cupped my hands to catch cut felt.

Later, lying on my bedstead, I felt myself fading, changing into something new. I wondered how often I had betrayed myself, letting my stars say what I would never have spoken aloud. Ridley had seen a constellation I'd believed long forgotten; it seemed an impossible accident. Now my memories of Northam were as a gibbering ape, tormenting my mind's every step.

The sleeping mat I lay on had once borne my weight and Henry's, the two of us together. In memory every stroke of hand on thigh, every kiss, every lusty clinch blurred together into a single, years-long embrace. It seemed impossible that it had been so long since we last lay together, longer than the time that passed between our first meeting and our last, unsuspecting *Good Night.*

It had once been beyond thought that I would not end my days in the house where we'd made our life. But it was no longer any home for me.

I thought, enviously, of my young friend Melode, who I'd thought such a fool for leaving with the rest of the congregation. She'd left among blown oxcart dust, imagining she was leaving this place behind, swinging her hands like oars. I wondered if she had yet come to an American shore—and what plants she might find there, and what good herbs. What flowers would she find cousins to? What buds would twin which stars? Were there new kinds of clay? Of falcon?

When full night had come I rose, and gathered my things. Herbs in one chest. Chapbooks in another, with folded packets of seed laid in over. Loaves bundled in a sack. It took two trips under a slight moon to carry those and other sundries to the stable. There I harnessed my donkey. He could forgive being left so for a single night. Next I went to the dark pasture, limping across the footbridge over the rushing stream, pausing for a word of prayer when I heard the tiny squealing of a bat. I led my cow to stable. Finally I gathered a double armload of hay. At home I dumped it close by to my smoldering hearth.

Again I lay on my bedstead. I thought, *My old village is sunk into its grave.* Then the changes seemed a manner of death. I wept, and listened for the buried waters.

They were deep below me, and overran their gates. They coursed without method.

* * *

My chimney was built for me by Richard Hall and his sons, Richard and Miles. When their household took ill with hacking cough, I had made hot poultices of peony for them against the falling sickness. And I gave them marjoram tea to please the outward senses, for a plunging cough will steal all pleasure. In thanks Richard and his sons built me a chimney. Before that time, smoke from my hearth would rise to a small hole in the thatching. The smoke was a nuisance for cooking when my wood was not perfectly dry, and the sparks were a hazard to my house. The Hall men knocked away a piece of wall, making a three-foot slot from the ground to the roof. They set the new chimney in the slot; soon the only soot on my rafters was that left from long-dead fires. The Halls were conscientious workmen, whose departure for the Americas I much regretted.

Most of the chimney framing was daubed over in clay like dried fish scales. But the Halls left the supporting poles outside the house naked, ready for the blow of an axe. If the chimney ever took fire, they told me, I could rush to chop through the poles. Then the whole chimney would fall away. Perhaps my house would be saved from a blaze. In truth it made not very much sense, Midge's house being so close nearby; there was no place for the chimney to fall. But the Halls built it to show me their consideration and regard. I'd found it pleasant to imagine such an escape, should I ever find my home afire.

Usually the chimney shaft was draped with herbs thick as a waterfall, but I had disrobed it, leaving nothing but a few dried twigs and, in the corner, an empty chest of drawers. I thought of my herbs, sandalwood and madder and bluebell, tucked away in chests in the stable; I watched the corner as though it might again fill from nothing, as frogs are birthed from motion of mud. But of course the corner was empty. It would stay so. I went out to my garden.

Only a bit of dawn showed above the pastures. I put down my candle, and for the last time breathed in my dooryard's sweet spice. As they grow, herbs draw in particular kinds of light, special manners of wind. These bind herbs that grow leagues and oceans distant from each other, as cousins who never meet are yet joined by common blood. I could see that the sprouts had begun drawing their spring force and fragrance.

If one can look at a palm and know the health of the body, I thought, *why not look to a dooryard, and know the household?* Mine own looked healthy enough, each plant budding beside others that might aid its growth, each one far from those that might hinder its strength—the clash between thyme and nep profits neither. It was an orderly place. But the order of this one patch could not stop the loss of the haying festival, or Harvest Home, or cider-pressing, all those joyful celebrations of the year, now that there were too few villagers left to observe them. Nor did it show the ache in my heart. I knew that I would not see my garden again after that morning. It was not likely to long outlive my departure or, even sooner, to survive the heat. I said farewell in silence. I greatly wished for my husband.

Finally I leaned my ladder against the house, and climbed up. My knee felt stronger. Nothing had torn, and whatever had displaced had clicked back into place. Still, it was stiff and tender, and I was careful to set my armpits firmly against the roof's edge as I began pulling the houseleeks. Every winter I planted more in the thatch, for protection. Now, one by one, I let them drop to the ground to dry and die. *Terrible bad luck, to uproot your houseleeks*, I thought. *You're near certain to have the fire they're meant to charm against.* When I thought of that I laughed inside, and pulled out another fistful of white bulbs. They fell to earth like star stones.

Back in the house I set moon and stars on my face in the form of a v. I took up my axe. Then, without a pause, without time for thought, I struck at the chimney, three feet above the hearth. The daub shattered, the woven wattle-framing bowed inward. I struck blow after blow until the cracked, broken stuff fairly blocked the flue. I sighed. The houseleeks could have been replanted, my mule stripped of gear, my cow returned to pasture. But this destruction made me feel that I'd cast off from shore without anchor or sail.

I bent for an armload of hay and tossed it onto the hearth. Soon it began to smolder on the coals. I spread the rest of the hay in a trail from there to the back wall, and on the hay I scattered rags. Then over it all I poured a stoneware jar of sweet almond oil.

Above the hearth the smoke thickened, becoming dense as milk in water. Finally there was a clean, orange, wavering finger of flame.

It gestured towards the blocked flue, blowing out smoke, beginning to murmur. I grinned and ran my tongue across a tooth-hole.

The fire punched upwards, eager to escape. But before it could flee, it had to consume a path through the shattered chimney; the broken wattle began to take. I laughed with the flame. It whispered and hissed, coursing up the chute towards open air. As it whipped upward more bright fingers crept across the hay-covered floor, crawling towards the anointed rags about my feet. Now smoke was everywhere. I began to cough. Soon the cough would become a choke. I took up my axe, bade farewell to the house, and went out.

The sun was near to cresting over the pastures; the world had gone dawn's gray. For a moment I saw it all as though underwater: a cart was a fish-trap, a barrel a buoy pushed under by current. Early robins were fish, mocking an old woman standing bound beneath the waves. I gasped in with cramped, smoky lungs. I looked back at the house. Above me the chimney gave a blast of flame, made a fountain, returned me to the air.

"Fire! All out!" I shouted, and limped around the corner to the chimney struts. My axe was poised, teetering high. I waited for Ridley. "Fire! Fire!"

I'd often exchanged greetings with Midge in morningtime, when we came to our dooryards to greet the sun; after she left, it particularly vexed me that Ridley chose her old house for his own. Now he came from the door wearing only a long shirt and that vexatious crimson cape. He'd pulled a broad hat over his sleep-tangled hair, he winked and blinked. But when he saw me with the axe his face melted like a candle. "No!" he shouted. "Let it burn—we'll fetch buckets from the river!"

So touching, his passion to help save my house. He'd barely said *no* before my axe dropped like a fishing-stork's beak. Crick-crack, the blade bit away the first strut. Crick-crack, and the second was gone. The chimney tilted from the house, as though considering—then tore off, fell away, leaving a gaping, flaming gate. The burning column crashed into Midge's house like a storm-felled oak. Ridley screamed. The chimney buckled, fire bellowing from three ragged breaks in its clay. Flame burst also from my liberated hearth, dancing high as the roofing thatch. A banner of winter water steamed from the thatch and to the sky. *V. Vengeance.*

"Woe! Woe! Woe!" I cried. I danced in circles, hands in the air. I capered and jigged with grief for my loss. Ridley raked madly at the burning heap. I strove to aid him then, but unluckily only jogged his arms, to his great alarm and noisome distress. Doubtless he would have struck me, had he leisure to do so. I left him to his hopeless work.

In my house the oil had taken; rags and hay burst bright. Through the tall chimney-hole I saw my bedstead burning to black. At the sight a root grew in my throat. The roof-thatch steamed as though exhaling a new wind. The clay of the walls cracked, beginning to fall away in scales the size of plates. I stepped back from heat that threatened to sear the coif from my head. I was full of sorrow, but also fierce joy—for Midge's house was quickly becoming a torch.

Ridley flung his rake like a spear at a boar. It rattled against the wall of what had been his home. By then nearly the whole village had come out. The wisest of them set ladders and fetched shepherd's crooks, trying frantically to pull thatch from any roofs that might be threatened by sparks. But most ran for water. Ridley joined the crowd at the river, pausing only for an instant to curse me down to hell.

A gentle hand turned me. Before she'd known the alarm's cause, Frances Jacobs had pulled a blanket over her shoulders. Now she used it as a shield against searing, draping it over her head like a night-rail hood. "Are you well in body?" she said, looking at me with care.

"I am well," I said. Then I turned, that she might not see the scrapes on my face—nor my fierce eye. I stood until I felt the heat blast yet hotter, and knew that Frances had stepped away. She was gone to the river for water, making a useless, kindly show of her desire to save my house. By then I was nearly gone myself, in mind if not yet in body.

Quickly as I could I limped for the stables, knee a-creak but the earth shaking beneath my steps. I slung the last of my gear on the donkey, and tied the cow to follow behind. My house burned bright.

It would blaze to the foundations. The posts were turning to ash, soot spreading across the sky. It would be hours, I thought, before the embers were doused and anyone thought to look for me.

As I led my beasts south through the orchard, past the old apple-tree man that was grandfather to all the rest, ash and petals floated about me, resting on my shoulders and drifting around my feet.

Pitch on my fingers, the smoke of my home billowing behind me, I took to the road. Vagabonded again. A congregation of one.

Two: Bill

*M**urder.*

These thighs are cold, and scratched. These fingernails are full of filth, and cracked from when I climbed. I sit back against one Devil's Point, I press palms against this face. This heart holds worst despair.

The Devil's Points are stones, tall stones, set up straight as fence posts. They are set in a curve, making a half circle as wide as three wagons. Here is where folk come to market, here among the high stones. On a market day there is food here, and feasting, and money and music. But today there is no market. Today I am clouded with tears. For I sit naked, and have twice been tricked.

The stones have plain, bare faces. Once I worked with other stones, headstones marked with names and with winged heads. Those stones, I placed on wealthy graves. Who placed these behind me?

Alms deliver all from sin, and from death,
and will not suffer the soul to go into darkness.
Lay your bread and wine on the grave of a just man.

In this skull the verses pound. Once a man ordered me to mind those words, after I ate the gravest meal I ever put to mouth.

Mind the verses, the man said, *and mind this one: Lay bread and wine on his body, before it goes to ground.*

The bread and wine I'd eaten, the man told me then, had spent a long, black night atop his dead girl's chest. When he told me this, the last crumbs seemed cursed. The last wine went wormy.

That was the first trick. Never did I mean to eat such fare, and so take sin needlessly upon myself. But since that day I have often done so; many such meals I have taken. Yesterday's was one.

And now, what to do? What to do when murder's in your bread?

Below me is a cold, slick mat of weeds. This head droops, like to a wilting daisy. My breathing comes noisy, whistling through this nose. The whistle calls to me a picture of an old, frayed bellows, pumped idly before a hearth.

With these eyes closed there comes a memory. Of coals under the bellows, glowing a welcome then fading farewell. Glowing and fading, until there comes a voice calling out, *Bill, where's the scalding?* Mam's voice, like the warm wet sawdust where Dory would set beans to grow in flats. I dropped the bellows then, and took up the scalding-water boiling in a pot and then dropped that, for I'd forgot to wrap the brown cloth around against burning. The fire was out, the coals hissing their death. Steam fouled these eyes. A streak of red was blistered on this palm. Then I cried for the pain of it and for the shame of it.

But Mam laughed, and tussled me. She said that Mistress Sorley from down the cobbled street had coals she would pleasure to give us. I could go for the coals with a spade. In scarce an hour we could have more fire. Dory and Sally, my sisters, were both smaller than I but together were bigger and could wrestle me to the ground. This they did, while I was still sad. Then they sat upon me as they laughed and Mam laughed and I began to laugh, feeling again some joy.

This head raises with a gasp, these eyes open. Before me is the market ground, and all the ground is rutted and tore. That is where, on market day, bears and dogs will be set on each other in combat, fighting for the sport of it. On one such day I chewed stolen beef, and searched for fallen coins, until a bear was chained to one Devil's

Point and dogs set upon him. The bear then strained against clanking chain-links, his claws nabbling at turf. The stone he was bound to was this one, aside where I now lean. The bear rolled and roared, striking the dogs that would harm him. He crushed one against his chest. The dogs bit and champed. Together all the beasts bled. It was like to what Mam would call battling, when she came and lifted me away from boys who beat me and who I beat back. Behind the battling, the stones were solid as Mam. All those people here, with their turnips and fans and glass and ducks, all those people here wagered and cheered the fighting.

Behind them, behind the battle, the stones were still. Now the ground where the beasts fought is heaved and tore, the turf pushed into waves, mottled like a russet hen. Only by the stones are there sweet, feathered grasses, and clutching weeds.

Never did I know a market could be so empty, with nothing left behind but tamped weeds and ruts, empty cart-ruts crossing. When wagons come to market, many coins change hands, and some may even fall and thus come to these hands. Once I thought to put coins in a bag, and shake until some dust powdered off from each. That dust could be melted, and used to make false coins—a golden covering for copper. So a man once told me. I have never had coins enough to try it. Most silver comes to me with corpse-wine, and must soon be spent on cleaner meat.

Alms deliver all from sin, and from death,
and will not suffer the soul to go into darkness.
Lay your bread and wine on the grave of a just man.
Lay bread and wine on his body, before it goes to ground.

The first trick was in a city, where I lived with Dory and Sally my sisters, in a room to ourselves. We took that room after we lost the other three. Though there had been three rooms, three big rooms, we were happy to leave them. For it was there we'd watched as the plague angel came to lay wings on Mam, on Da, and on Ron my brother half my age. After they were dead and wrapped in sheets, Dory covered them over with more blankets, all three of them lain where Mam and Da had slept. But there was no need to keep them covered by linens, or hid beneath piled woolen blankets. Already I'd begun to labor in the churchyard, digging and burying, whenever Da needed no help with gutters. There was nothing new in bodies for me.

So I told Dory. But she said *Mind yourself, Bill,* with her eyes gone wet and a hand pressed against each of these cheeks. She said we would wait for the bodyman with our windows shut, that the poisoned air might not come again to kill us.

So we waited. We waited for the bodyman, or for the brush of angel's feathers on our own lips.

Mostly I stayed to the little room, where there was the bedstead I had once shared with Sally and with Dory. But that was before I grew, and got me my own mat. Aside the walls were stacks of leaden gutters, brought from the shop where Da did his labor. That month the shop had no place to put the plumbing. Thus these hands were powder gray from carrying and stacking gutters. We lay in the room. The angel's wings flapped against windowglass, like wet blankets shaken. We waited. After a day the bodyman did come.

Then we moved from those rooms, and found a single one to let. It was smaller, and smelled of grain. There the three of us lived. It was over the paperman's shop, where sometimes Sally helped sling out sheets to dry. When they dried they smelled of oats.

Sally worked in the paperman's shop. I worked in the churchyard, carrying the lone coffin. The coffin was proper heavy, for it was lined with gray metal both in and out. When first I went there, the minister tossed me a piece of caning from a broken window. *Lead,* he said. *Could you carry such heavy stuff, were it to cover a box big enough for a body?* I could, I told him, for Da had made me carry lengths of gutters.

There was a small barrow to set one end of the coffin in. The other end I lifted, and pulled the coffin behind me. When hauling it I never quit until I stood hard by a hole, where the body could be dumped. When digging, I never stopped until Master Wolf stopped me, saying *There, Bill, that's proper deep. Should he stand up in his grave, he'll still be buried,* and laughed.

The churchyard was full of headstones with carved skulls. Skulls with wings. The yard seemed full of such stones but not every man had one, nor even every twelfth man. There were no names on any headstone. With a spade I dug, cutting through turf, and skulls, and walnut roots, and ribs and bones of legs. Sometimes a headstone fell from being too close beside the new hole. Then I'd prop it again, that the family might take pleasure from visiting it.

I'd dig one grave. Then one beside it, after the first was filled. Then another, and another, one day after the next, 'till I'd dug and filled graves from the fence to the church's stone wall. Then back to the fence, to begin again with a new row. Months passed before I returned to the first place I'd dug. That was long enough for worms to do what Master Wolf said was their godly task, which was stripping bones ready for the dewy house. Whatever skulls I found I'd stack in the corner of the yard, and later take them up with whatever bones could be easily taken from the piled dirt. I'd take all to the general boneroom. The boneroom was big enough for echoes, but there were no echoes with so many muddy bones stacked there.

Inside the church all was different. In the church there was silk, and sugarwood smoke, and holes in the wall where single men could be laid to rest. For twenty-four years, a man placed in such a hole would have it for himself alone.

Master Ponlet wanted a hole in the wall, for Temperance his daughter.

And so Master Wolf and Master Ponlet argued inside the church, beside the pews. Though I much wanted to know how many holes needed digging that day, I would not enter the church. Instead I squatted in my yard, sorting bones, hand-bones, ribs and knees. The leaves of the walnut tree drooped in the warm day. Quarreling voices broke like pots in my stony yard.

I knew Master Ponlet. He had pretty points on the edging of his clothes, but the points were only copper. His hat held a frayed purple feather. Sometimes he would come to our room, and stay there with Dory. Then Sally would take me out for bread. When we returned, Master Ponlet always was gone.

I moved rib bones into one pile, tiny toes into another. Then Master Ponlet jammed by, in his haste treading upon a fellow's rib. *Well met, Good Master,* I said, but he was going from the yard and down the lane. I hefted a platter of bone, and went into the church.

I asked why Master Ponlet was ailing. Master Wolf still looked angry, but soon he put a hand on this shoulder, and smiled, and said, *He ails because of the death of Temperance his daughter. A hard thing, to lose her after the plague had passed on—for her to die after he thought her safe.* He said I must dig another grave that day.

I was surprised, for I knew that meant a grave for Master Ponlet's daughter. It was strange that he should have a daughter in the churchyard. The yard is where Mam and Da and Ron should have been buried, had they not been ordered burned up in the plague-fires.

I'd grown tired then. But I dug the new grave deep, with clean, square corners, for I knew Master Ponlet. The hole gave up four skulls. I put the four together like a clover, each facing inward to watch the others.

Later Master Ponlet came alone. Temperance was already in the coffin, hemmed by hammered sheets of lead, and there were ropes tucked under her body. I wheeled her through the yard and to the open hole. With the ropes we took her from the coffin, then lowered her in the grave, her shroud draped over like a gown. Inside her there was a child, Master Wolf had said. It made me think of Roslyn, who in her corded gown has sometimes took me to her bed.

When Temperance was in the ground Master Ponlet walked away, though I'd not yet dropped a single spade of earth. Master Wolf told me to finish the work. He went into the church.

At last I tamped down the last shovel. Then Master Ponlet was back. He carried a loaf, and a yeasty bowl of beer. He looked remorseful. *I'd regret not thanking you for your work on my daughter's resting place*, he said. He begged that I would accept a bit of bread, which was life's staff, and beer, which was its substance and joy. The bread was rye and the beer bitter under its foam. I thanked him well.

Digging is hungry work. So champ-chomp, swig-slug, and the happy supper was done. But every bite had been a trespass, every sip a crime—Master Ponlet said so, gently, after all was gone. *Keep these verses to mind*, he said, and spoke them:

Alms deliver all from sin, and from death,

and will not suffer the soul to go into darkness.
Lay your bread and wine on the grave of a just man.
Lay it on his body, before he's gone to ground.

Master Ponlet drew a hand across his eyes. Then he smiled. *Mind those words*, he said. *For your bread and beer spent a full night over my daughter's heart.*

His arm lay over these shoulders heavy as my sledging hammer. *Now you carry her sins*, he said, like a boon companion. *Do not fear. My daughter was a righteous girl. Thank you for this service.* And he gave me a bag of farthings.

Under the mirth and triumph in his eyes was sadness, like pond eels. I shook once, my heart on a jig and captured.

Then I stepped away. Master Ponlet's laugh was bitter as a waiting noose. Bread and beer lodged in me. They turned to blood that leaked into this head, into this voice.

I turned to Master Ponlet. This hand raised to cup his cheek. He drew back. I needed to touch him, for Master Ponlet was a father, one not yet passed from this life. He might have heart to help me. I reached to touch him. *Please*, I said. *Father*, I said.

He caught me up in his arms. I was trapped in his arms, trapped as in a crate. *Sin-eater*, he said, growling. He dropped me. *Sin-eater*, he said, as though both asking and answering. *Sin-eater.* He grabbed at my shirt-collar. He struck me hard, then harder. His last strike broke this lip. His last cry broke itself and he dropped me to the ground. He walked away through tilting gravestones.

There was nothing for me to do then. I lay in sorrow amid carvings of skulls, and winged skulls, and among the skulls, lost.

And so I had me a new profession. But it was never right to force me to it, or to give me any else but clean bread. What manner of man would choose to eat sin soaked stuff? A greater fool than I. Who would choose to make his own body a vessel for another's crimes, not knowing what those crimes might be? A greater fool than I. But I was a great enough fool to be tricked. I would not return to my sisters, so shamed.

Those first sins were the beginning. This belly is uncommonly commodious—so said Sally when she fed me, *Ten men's bellies in yours. Ten bowls to fill you, when one should do.* As I walked the road under snow, and storm, and over the merry dew of morning, I ate what men would give me. For I was sin-eater, seeking out tainted loaves and beleaguered wine. Often I found them. And as I ate, sins leached and lodged all through this body. Thievery came to this hand, vagabondage to this foot. These fingers lumped with robbery. These palms went hard with want.

The more I ate, the less my thefts and wanderings were mine. This body was driven onward by the ghosts of three dozen dead. I watched the theft of a fresh-killed duck as though these fingers were another man's. I walked through slush and snow on another's freezing feet.

There is one blessing. Though this heart is coddled around by malice, the malice is not rooted. It is not live, growing wood. Only a paling of dead boards.

So I wandered until yesterday morning, when I ran naked from a town, across pasture and a rain-drizzled, stump-marked field, and climbed the only oak. Panting I was panting panting, these legs working like a wooden pump. Then I was at the oak and climbing, bark scraping on these limbs. Moss made it hard to grip. It smeared against this skin. I wished greatly for my clothes, which were left behind me, aside the tanner's shop. But the lowest limb was not very high, I could hug my way to it, I hugged my way to it. Some hair tore from this chest, so tightly did I hug and haul my way to that first crook.

Below me men came running. They carried hoes and shovels, and one of them a sword. The sword he bore in one hand, the sheath in another, and he waved the sword overhead as though I knelt before him with neck ready for the blade.

You are a villain, they said.

I am not.

We will show you that you are, they said, *and what we do to villains.*

Among them were the men that came upon me in the barn, where I wrestled from the clothes that marked me as me. I'd found other clothes, and though those were but rags they might make me look a tanner and I took them. I would have worn them had those fellows not come upon me, in the barn.

Will you come down from there, they asked.

By God, I will not, by God.

They asked if I would have them make a fire, and send smoke to drive me down. I answered that I would not have them do that, either. I would piss on any who tried.

Then we must build a fire, they said. This they began, mounding brush and wood about the trunk of my tree. The field it stood in was a new one, with many stumps still there like toads. There were piles of wood from the cut trees. The men dug through sticks drizzled damp, down to wood dry as hair under a cap.

I crouched on the limb, and readied myself to piss. I would aim for the man with the sword, whose hat had fallen off from running. His hair made a right round target, like a flipped bowl. But, trouble! I'd not drunk enough that day. The ladle of wine and murder had not yet passed through me. I choked to think of it doing its polluting work. Below me there was a spark. I saw the spark between men who huddled, guarding it against cold breeze. Then there was flame like a fingersnap. Soon smoke reached this nose from so far below. Each man looked so small.

Then came the tanner, whose cast-off clothes I'd meant to steal. He was on the far side of the pastures, making his hurried way on one leg and a crutch. He planted the leg, then his crutch, and then he jumped. Leg, crutch, jump. He bore a scutching knife. Tanners smell of rotted milk. Leg, crutch, jump. The smoke was coming stronger. When the tanner jumped he swung his left arm wide. Leg, crutch, jump. I held tight to the tree. Every time the tanner swung that arm he waved it, hailing. I felt myself a bee, that keepers smoke to sleep before they steal honey. Leg, crutch, jump. Then the tanner was there, shouting.

Gasping, he told them of the second trick. *Tricked!* he said.

John Wotten came to this man and fed him, and this man never knew the sins of Samuel before he died. This man thought Samuel no worse than a drunkard, and ate fish from off his chest. Then John told him of Samuel's offense. Can you fault him, for striking John to the ground?

For a time they were quiet as the tree. I sat with ear against the trunk.

Physic Potter says John is not to die, the tanner said. *He'll have only a lumped brow.*

Below me some heads nodded.

A lumped skull's a small price for a man as dirty as Samuel Wotten to pay for a cleansing, came one voice.

It is, came another. Then they looked calm. Though all was wet and gray, the men dried like hay in sun.

Killing a man for John's sore head's not my *task.*

Nor mine.

He looks a jaybird, there.

Laughter. But in this body I felt new cruelties coming, lashed aside bones and veins. In the timber aside this heart was a new beam of malice, knotty and iron-hard.

Murder! I cried.

Aye. Samuel did murder.

This fire's to no purpose. That man stomped it out. Others stomped it also. They turned, and floated back towards their town.

Walk with God, called the tanner. He was straight below me, all shoulders and upward-looking face. *Of course you'll know not to come back to town*, he said. *Luck to you, finding clothes.* Then he stumped away with the rest.

He left me in the tree, wishing for solid ground. After I was on it I felt fish and wine soaking into these bones. Then I thought of the Devil's Points, and the market I once saw there, and the ground I could perhaps scavenge from. After a cold blue day of walking, I'd returned to these deep and solid rocks.

As I walked to the Points, sin rose in me like yeasty buns. It made the skin about this face to itching bubbles. Now I despair lest any man or woman look upon me; I should despair even if I had me some clothes. Trespasses have made this neck to welts, and swole up the backs of these hands like mold. I look at red and blistered skin and think of rising buns, as dough pushed up Mam's bowl into a mighty toadstool. Behind my back is the Point's cold stone.

Hands, hands, hands, I say. I wring them into knots. *What were the sins of Samuel Wotten?*

I drop this head between these knees. I shut these eyes, coughing. Sally and Dory are dear, and today they're missed so terrible. Quicker, quicker comes my breath, *a-huh, a-huh, a-huh* against the back of this throat. After a while it calms. But I feel no calmer. Then I look up and she is there, standing on the ground torn by bear-baitings, like she's rose up from waves near shore.

She has a cow, and a donkey. These she ties to the wooden post, where the banded dogs would be tied before they were set on the bear. Then she limps to me. She has stars on her face, and a moon on her face. Her stars are like those in the sky that Dory would call the Anvil. She has a bent stick for a staff. When this woman walks she swings one leg heavily, as though a stubborn pup is tied to her foot. She crosses the stiff cold ground and stands before me. She asks, *Are you hungry?*

I am.

She tosses half a loaf to me. It lands on a tuft of sweetgrass. When I've begun to eat, she says *I'll not trouble to ask if you're cold.* She stands some way away, leaning on her stick as though ready to push herself away if I stand.

I am not terrible cold, I say bravely.

She watches me closely then. I watch her closely. I chew.

You lost your clothes today, or yesterday, she says, looking at my legs. *You did not choose to wander so.*

That thought seems to ease her. She knows I am not such a fool as that. She is not talking to me but to herself and so I ask why she wears the Anvil on her face.

She looks sharp. *Anvil?* And touches her star patches. *That's a name I haven't heard for a long time. You're from Sidley, on the coast. There are few places that call this family of stars the Anvil. Elsewhere they're known as the Gate-ward. Or the Loom.*

I am from here, I say, for though she has fed me I do not mean to tell her all.

Then whoever told you it was the Anvil was from Sidley.

I drop these eyes, and again see on these hands the fresh blistering of sin. I think of the blisters on this face, and lower this head further that she may only see hair. When I peek again she has gone to her donkey. She returns with a bag, and a small iron kettle. She shakes dried plants into the kettle.

Soon we have a fire, that I sit on one side of and she sits on the other side of. When I move a bit, she moves a bit. Each of us has our side. I rub these arms and am full of clean bread. These feet have been so cold that warming hurts them. But it is a pleasant hurt and soon the toes go pink, the blood returning.

Who set these stones? I say, for I know not what else to ask her.

I've never known, she says. *I've heard they were set to mark off a dance. We called such stones near my place of birth the Giant's Dance. They were like these, though smaller. And some had tumbled down.*

When I look at the stones again they seem more lovely, and less set. I can see now that they were meant for a dance, to mark off steps. They are like the marks that Da would set for me in a running game, sending me in a rush from one to the next to the next. Then the water boils.

This is for the redness on your legs and face, she says. When she says that I feel hollow. *Why does that trouble you?* she says, looking close.

I want to cover this face, and the blisters of sin that foul it. I want to wrap a blanket around my legs to hide all there. Instead I look at her straight. *Mind yourself, Bill Palmer*, Dory said, and Sally said, and I often say to myself.

These are markers of another's sins, I say with a shameful plenty of pride. *There's nothing as will clear them away.*

For a while she is quiet. *How did you take them onto yourself?*

In wine, and dried fish.

Hm. She takes a cup and dips it to her potion. She reaches it around the fire, to me. The cup is colored like butter, and has curls on it, like the curls I will idly draw in ash. The curls are colored like pale pears. The potion smells of dust. *Still, drink this*, she says. *It will not hurt you.* She says it kindly, and there is no body here for her to have laid it upon. I drink it down, to please her, until the cup's all dry.

When it is gone, I say: *I can gather wood.* Then I do.

I wake beside coals in darkness. By the glow the woman eats dried cheese. She looks to one side. Still I know she is watching. Even with her eyes turned away her mind is on me in the orange dark. With one arm I push myself to sitting. Then I find cloth beneath this hand. There is a smock, and a shift. A skirt, and another skirt. The second skirt is colored like the night. The woman tells me to dress.

No.

The clothes are warm, she says.

They are for a girl and I will not wear them and I fold these hands before me and cross my legs. I do not care that my yard flops free. I think to myself that I have enough girl inside me already. I have eaten the sins of more than one. Were they to sing, there are enough to make a chorus, though mostly they are quiet.

These are good clothes, of warm cloth, she says. And they are for a girl only if I am a young maid. But she stands and goes, and comes back with two more smocks. *At least wear these*, she says. *A lady's smocks are very much like a man's shirts.*

I think. I think that what she says is true, even if these smocks were once a lady's. I put them on. They fall as low as my knees.

Here, she says, and comes around the fire. She has two woolen blankets, that once were one but that she's cut in twain. *It is cold and these are something*, she says. *Stand.*

I do. She takes one cut blanket and wraps it around this foot, then ties it above this ankle with thongs. I take that foot back and put the other out. Then I see there is no streaking there, on this foot that was crossed by red lines. There is no itching on my face. The blistering is all gone away and I look at her, wonderful woman! And I say that she can take away sin.

I cannot. But there is sin, and then there is a bad bit of fish.

Hugging myself, warm and full, I suddenly smell that it is near to dawn.

I look to her face, so curious patched with black, and I ask her: *Where go we now?*

Three: Sarah

"Northam," I said, though I had not known it until then, nor that the man would come with me. My sole destination had been *away*. I had not had time to consider whether the road ahead would lead me to a hovel or a bishop's tower.

Then my mouth opened, and I said *Northam*. At once it seemed right. With that single word, a picture took hold in my mind. I saw a harbor. I saw a seawall. I saw a beach, that would be bared only at the lowest of tides. Almost I felt myself wading, a cold, sandy wave licking about my calves, a single shell cutting into one bare foot. Almost I could smell the stink of fishing-craft, and hear the begging of gulls. Conjured by Ridley, the name *Northam* had been a curse, setting me on the lonely road. Bill's simple question made the same word a summons.

Curse or summons, I knew I would go there. Ridley had made me feel as though I no longer owned my own past. I needed, badly, to reclaim it. There were few enough years left to take the measure of my life.

The sun was just beginning to rise, dulling the firelight that had glazed the Devil's Points. Dew lay heavy on trampled grass, and on the ragwort and thistles bunched about the base of the stones. A party of grackles began to sing. Though any crusts or bones would have been scavenged by weasels and crows, the ground was scattered with bits of trash from markets past—shards of bottles and broken pots, nails pressed into the dirt, a broken belt buckle by the stained shambles where butchers sold meat. A lone rabbit hopped cautiously from behind a stand of cow parsley perhaps looking for a nibble of primrose.

Bill rolled to his knees and began blowing on the coals. He was not gaunt, as are many road-men, and had some good muscle beneath his clearing skin. His eyes were a dusky green, his hair thick as a thrush's straw nest; he bent with a seagoing goose's gawky grace.

When I thought of all the people who had fed him tainted meat, I had to look away and bite down hard; I did not want Bill to see my face, lest he think that my anger was aimed at him. Sin is not a proper meal, nor sin-eating a proper trade. Those who follow it are often the most desperate of beggars, the least able to refuse any bread. It enraged me to think that this man had been treated like an abandoned ice-cellar, a mere hole where the debris of petty lives could be conveniently flung.

Yes, many of those who fed Bill had acted out of loyalty to their loved ones. But I thought them no better than Ridley, who would drive people from long-loved homes to gain a house himself. *Feeding a man sins—that, I would never do,* I thought. *Never, no matter how hot my desire to cleanse me and mine.* I quivered like a bow to think that others had. They were cruel fools, who imagined they could leave crimes behind as easily as they might drop a cape. I knew I could not leave Bill there waiting for market. Even should he live until the next one, he would find it frigid; all markets are cold for those who have nothing.

A small, bright flame danced over the coals. Satisfied, Bill rocked back to a squat. He held his hands around the fire as though casting a pot. His shoulders shrugged up against the chill. I looked him over, and thought that we would go to Northam together.

There was a pier in Northam, once. If it still stood, I would stand on it again. I would kneel; I would squint between the boards.

I would sniff the wind for sign of storm, and listen to the waves hissing their steady retreat. From the pier, one could see far down shore, to a riven shadow in the seawall. There was a nook of stone there, like the false corner in a grindstone housing that traps more than a miller's fair share of grain. Maybe I would send Bill to lie in it, and call to me; I hoped that I would hear nothing under the play of waves and the hollow tramping of boots and crates along the wharf. Later, standing on the sand below the pier, I would press my hands against the sharp barnacles grown thick on a certain piling.

Memory of pier and nook caught in me like a choke; my hands clenched tight as wet knots.

Bill laid a hand of twigs and grass over the fire. But he had chosen the tinder carelessly; it damped the flame, loosing smoke dense enough for a signal. Bill grunted and stood to search for better fuel. "Where is Northam?"

"On the coast," I said. "It's a long journey. We'd best start walking."

He looked slightly stricken, as at a reproach. It surprised me. I had not spoken sharply, nor meant anything by my words beyond their plain sense. I wondered how gently I would need to treat him. Maybe he needed more kindness than one woman could give.

"It is by the ocean," I said softly. "By the ocean they have fresh fish, which have not been hung to dry for too long in a moldy house. The fish there will never sicken you. At least, I know how to choose those that won't. Finish smothering the fire, and let's be off."

It might seem strange that I would choose to travel with a stranger. And at first I had intended only to feed Bill some good bread, tossing it to him from a distance. But then he asked about my stars, with a respect that moved me.

It's rare for a man to look at the shape of my sky, seeing more than the fact that I wear patches. It seemed beyond belief that two men should do so in as many days. But Bill looked beyond the strangeness, for a shape. He did so without the contempt Ridley showed. That touched me, and would have even if he had decided that the shape had no meaning for him. But what he saw was the Anvil. During my travels, I've found that there is no limit to the number of animals, tools, and men that can be perceived in a chance gathering of stars; thus any country, parish, or even town may have its own names for the constellations. The Anvil was one of my Henry's, one that can best be seen in late summer, in the small of the northern sky. It is made of three pairs of stars; the ones I wear form only the base. Henry named it to me from atop a church roof, where we'd climbed to drink a nabbed bottle of vernage wine. Once, betrayed by a clattering shingle, Henry nearly fell off. The Anvil hung steady in the sky.

That night I asked Henry what led him to wander. "To find the princess who dropped the golden ball," he answered. "To return it to her from the spring."

He spoke so seriously that for a moment I believed him. Then I remembered the tale. "You're not very like a frog," I said. He laughed, and said I should wait before I made such a judgment. The town below us was quiet as the moon, the wine on Henry's lips sweeter than any drunk from glass.

After, he said that our histories were not important. Our future together weighed more than past intentions, more than past deeds.

It had then been months since Northam. Long enough that I could believe him.

My knee ached in the morning chill. But I had been faithful in rubbing it with oils, and soon it seemed to me that the walk was doing it some good, loosening and warming even the muscle nearest the bone. Still I was careful, limping to favor my strong leg even after the ache had faded to an occasional twinge. Bill tramped along beside me, the blanket shoes bagged on his feet, a rope tied around his waist for a belt.

The donkey was too heavily laden to carry a rider, but after two or three hours of walking, Bill thought he might try riding the cow. He claimed his sisters had ridden their own, as a game, when he was young. I told him that his sisters must have been uncommonly small, or their cow uncommonly docile, and that if he tried riding mine his feet would nearly touch the ground. For a while as we walked he watched the clouds blowing overhead, as though he might find a different answer there.

But soon he brightened and asked if we might milk her; in fact she was long overdue for it. When we had tied her to a beech tree, I sat on the ground beneath her with an empty bottle. But being milked without a wooden wall in front of her made her nervous. She stamped thistles flat until Bill sat to hold her rear legs fast, one with each arm. Once the bottle was full we took it in turns to drink down the sweet warm stuff.

While we rested I took the chance to draw up the cloth of Bill's garb between his legs, and fix it there with a stitch or two. He would often run a few quick, unexpected steps, and with his clothes so loose I'd begun to worry that the smocks might flap up to show him as naked as he'd been that morning.

Bill was grateful for both milk and mending, especially after a slip of the needle pricked a drop of blood from my left hand. He said he would repay both gifts.

I was mindful of my leg; Bill was so curious that his path often curved like that of a child's spun top. We moved precious slow. The road unrolled as slowly as a waterwheel in a dry season. Though the land about us was rough, and untended, it was often graced by the wild blooms of spring. Red pimpernel blooms and yellow archangels peeked brightly from below drab yew bushes and dwarf thorn trees.

Gradually the shrubs about us grew higher, yew giving way to chin-high golden gorse that allowed for few flowers. Finally even the gorse was gone and there was only hawthorn, thick and high enough that it might have been planted as a windbreak. The trail before us curved between hillocks, flanked by the hawthorn's thorns and readying buds. *We won't see a man until he's already upon us*, I thought. I'd been keeping a sharper watch than I'd realized. We were not yet far away from my old home.

But we passed only a few folk. There was a tinker with a clinking sack, and hammers tucked tightly into his belt. Later came six children in fellowship, wearing ribbons and suits of tawny cloth, carrying a churn. It seemed a waste of work; even in passing I could smell that cream had been left too long in the churn's barrel, rotting the wood. I asked where they were bound for, but the youngest—a pretty young thing, with hair the color of wheat—only laughed and said I was foolish not to know. Doubtless she was right; there could not be very many destinations among the stands of hawthorn. Bill raised his hands and growled like a bear. The children scurried off, two of them dragging the churn by its piston. As we turned to continue I saw a sprig of marjoram growing wild near the edge of the path, and plucked it, to chew for the scent.

Sometime after noon we came to better ground. The hawthorn ended with shocking suddenness; we emerged above a slope of grass and nodding dandelions as though from a crowded tavern. At the base of the slope was fine, open plowland, at least five carves of it, and then the snug street and homes of a small village. I spat the marjoram aside, and breathed deep to catch the smell of turned earth. *This is a proper spring*, I thought. As we descended to the furrows I almost felt myself back at home.

Here and there in the fields, husbandmen dragged plows and harrows behind braces of oxen. Nearer by, a boy cast a stone from a lean-to and sent a sparse murder of crows to flight. They came to rest in our path, hopping away before our approach.

As we neared the houses, I recalled tales of wanderers being cast out cruelly from villages. If the stories had fairies in them, they might end well, but the true ones rarely did. The most recent of the stories was of Bill himself—and now he looked far stranger than he had in Monkshead. "It may be safer here to claim that we're blood kin," I said to Bill.

"What manner of kin?"

"Great-aunt and nephew, perhaps. Our ages are about right for that, and there need not be a very great resemblance for it to be believed."

"Great-aunt," he said, greatly pleased. "Today is the first day I ever had one of those. Should there be stories for us to tell of my youth and birth? And of my sisters? They would be great-nieces to you. There are many stories I can tell you about them. Then we can both tell the same stories, if asked."

I feared he might play the part too eagerly. "Perhaps it would be best for you to be a mute," I said. He frowned. "A man who cannot talk," I said. "Should any here speak to you, shake your head and point to me. Never say a word." He seemed to think the game pleasant, and practiced as we walked. His mouth gaped like that of a fading, landed fish. Then we were to the houses.

I resolved to walk with all the outward determination I could muster, moving unhurriedly but with purpose. You can avoid many questions by seeming certain of your own business. Though I'd enjoyed passing by the fields, now I wanted only to pass on without being noticed. There was good reason for caution, being still close to Monkshead. There was no reason to give anyone a cause to remember us, or which direction we were going. It would be best to vanish as over a trackless sea.

But then, even as I tried to think only of discretion, I halted—halted sharp. Before us was a church.

Its steeple was proud as a watchtower; a bronzed cross served as sentry. The walls were neatly whitewashed, the stones to the doorway swept clean. It was at least twice as tall as the houses behind, set dead in the center of the village. My congregation would never have built such a looming, prideful, grand place to worship in. Seeing it here was like finding a dagger in a homey gate.

It jolted me to think how the years had smoothed my mind, making me imagine, thoughtlessly, that most men lived as did my old congregation. I felt dropped into a far, foreign land; the sun shone white on the steeple. The people there might be charitable, or they might be cannibal kings—I had no way of judging. I seemed to hear Sam Ridley laughing, tiny and grating as a tin bell, as he mocked my ignorance. *It is fine time I took to walking my own country again*, I thought.

"Sarah?" The voice from beside the road jerked me from my reverie. It was Joseph, a man I knew from market, and had always thought kind. He stood between two washtubs, the kind of fellow you know has gone bald even when he wears a broad workman's hat. Though I'd hoped to pass unnoticed, if someone must see us I could not have asked for a better man. I had often traded herbs for his sieves, for he was both a fine craftsman and given to melancholy when it stormed. Though I thought him kind, with the discretion of a man who hopes you will keep his secrets, I was very much aware of the scrapes on my face.

"Well met, Joseph," I said. A comely young woman in skirts the color of seed-dandelions knelt beside one tub, a girl of perhaps ten at the other. A still younger had been slapping out washed clothes on slats. Now she edged behind the woman as she might behind a dressing-screen.

"Curious that you've never met my wife," Joseph said. "Eliza, I give you Sarah."

"Well met. But you must forgive my rudeness," Eliza said, and raised one sud-covered hand.

"Well met to you and your daughters, who these lovelies must be," I said. The one at the tub smiled shyly. All I could see of the other was a length of hair, pulled from behind her mother's hip between a thumb and first finger. "I'd never thought to meet someone I knew. Though that was foolish enough, now that I think of it. Your village seems a fine place." As I spoke—perhaps too quickly—I decided to say nothing about Bill until they asked. I imagined him behind me, swaddled in women's smocks, blankets bundled on his feet, and thought he was lucky that I was known in town.

To my relief, Joseph made no mention of him. "I hadn't known you stayed. *Down corn, up horn*, as they say—I don't wonder that many of your folk decided to leave after they lost their commons. In fact we'd heard that all had departed."

"Not all," I said. Now that I'd given up on a quick passage, I could better take the measure of their village. Save for the church, it was very much like Monkshead. The houses seemed cousins to those I knew best. But the likeness was like that of a dream, when a man has a different face, and voice, and name, and bearing, and yet you know him. The walls here were of darker clay, and taller, their roofs not so steep. The thatching seemed to have been sewed by a knowl edgeable craftsman rather than stacked in snug but ragged bundles like ours. I thought that, at least, an improvement. There would be less chance of fire. "Do not let me keep you from your washing," I said. "When it's interrupted, washing can seem to take an age, as I know too well. And my sister lives a good number of leagues away. It might be best for me to keep walking."

"No, no. Joseph had just come for his dinner. Join us," Eliza said. "It would give us great pleasure—we've been beholden to you, especially during rain." She took Joseph's elbow in one soapy hand. It warmed me to see them, and how he felt no shame when she spoke of the weather that brought him deepest gloom.

But I was touched with melancholy myself. This place was so like to my old home—and now that was gone, surely as butterflies vanish before the snow. Joseph had spoken easily of the change from grain to landlord's sheep; I did not think he understood how quickly the same thing could happen to him. Let a row of figures, calculated in a distant room, add up in such-and-such a way, and his lands would all be forfeit, seized by his landlord for better profit. *He might not like making sieves so well if that was his only livelihood,* I thought. *If that was his sole means of bread, his daughters' fingers would soon bleed from weaving reeds.* "I thank you," I said. "But I've been well repaid with the best sieves I've ever found."

Joseph was quietly proud. "Will you return before the next market?" he said. "I was hoping to trade with you."

"I'll still be gone. And I cannot trade now, for I won't carry any more than I have. But I'll give you something." When I turned to the donkey, Bill was gone. Making as though stretching my neck, I searched the streets for him, and the dooryards, and the few alleys I could. Then I began rummaging through one of the packs, unsure whether to hurry or delay.

"What calls you to your sister?" Joseph asked.

"She's taken sick. With me is a friend's son, who must retrieve letters from a merchant, who is his cousin's husband. He lives near by to Rachel my sister." I heard myself ramble in the lie, and was relieved to find the small box I'd wanted. "Here is black hellebore, which some name Christmas Rose. Make it into a purgation when the world seems heavy. And here are seeds."

"Seeds?"

"It's a simple cure. There's no need for you to rely on me for it any longer. You should have your own means of growing the plant."

"Seeds are a mighty generous gift," Joseph said uncertainly.

"One we won't refuse," Eliza said. She wiped her hand on her skirts and took the folded paper from me. She held it by her side, firmly, as though it might fly away, and she did not look at her husband. "We're beholden to you still further."

"Here's a thing you might enjoy," Joseph said, suddenly, as though inspired. He stepped aside as though welcoming me into a house, gesturing to an inner corner of the dooryard. At first I thought he was showing me peas, flowering unusually early as they climbed through a small tree for support. Then I realized that the flowers grew from the tree—a tree I had never seen before.

Robust rows of sleek, dark-green leaves; a long string of white flowers that I ran my fingers over. I sorted carefully through the herbary in my mind, but could not think of any tree that might be this one's cousin. "What is this?" I said.

"A locust tree." Joseph sounded delighted that he could puzzle me with a new plant.

"From America," said Eliza. "I've heard it said that when dry the wood is hard enough to make into nails."

"Nails." I wanted to kneel before the tree, pick through its bark, sniff leaves and buds and roots. I wanted to taste it, every part; to boil its bark, and make a poultice from whatever sap it might possess. But I was afraid that if I even began to explore its wonders I would be unable to stop. I might do unforgivable harm to it, this fine rare bit of life. I stepped back, still gorging on the sight. Much was changing across my country, both invisibly and in plain sight. Some of the changes I might be able to love.

"Is that your fellow?"

Even from three houses away I could see that one of Bill's feet was bare. He'd folded the other blanket-shoe into a parcel, that he clutched at the top with both hands. I sighed to myself. "That's him."

"He has business with a merchant?" Joseph asked, and wiped away the beginnings of a smile with one thumb.

"He's trustworthy, and that's enough for this task," I said. "He only needs to retrieve some letters from the merchant. Though perhaps even that will be more of a challenge than his cousin thought, for as you can see he's a ferocious bad gambler. I'll have to watch close to see that he doesn't wager away the letters, as he lately did his shirt." Inwardly I measured Joseph. "But of course it would be better for him to travel fully clothed. Might you have any you'd be willing to sell? Or old shoes?"

Joseph looked at Eliza questioningly.

"My patch box is full enough," she said.

"Not to sell," he said. "But you're welcome to take whatever we have, if ragged or mended stuff will do."

"Anything would."

Bill's folded bundle held two white eggs, and four brown. Though I chided him for the theft, I did not press him to return them. We could not chance trying to explain the robbery, and possibly being seized for it. Doubtless Joseph and Eliza knew that something was amiss. But they also trusted me enough to know that I would not indulge anything worse than petty mischief.

After they saw me limp, Joseph gave me the curved handle of an old sickle. It made a fine walking staff. If the need came, I could pad the top grip to wedge under my shoulder as a crutch. The clothes they gave Bill were better than Joseph had suggested. Though patched in many places, the mending had been done mindfully, Eliza's stitches as neat as the reeds in her husband's sieves. Bill now had trousers, and a jacket, with patches like cornflower, and tabby-cat, and dust. Though in places it seemed more patch than coat, it was immeasurably better than the smocks he'd had. I thanked Joseph and Eliza silently as we walked from their village under a sky that I thought might soon begin to threaten.

Bill sang:

When bawds do honest churches build

And cutpurses their own fields do till
Then are hours rashly broke
And all is pleasantly confused.

For a time I quickened my uneven steps, swinging my sickle-staff before me.

As the afternoon passed the road wended still lower before rising, gradually as a song, up a grassy down covered with dandelions and cowslips. Though the climb was gentle, I had to stop several times. We had gone less than two leagues that day, but most of the work was done by my one good leg; and miles walked nervously are more tiring than those strolled for pleasure. In any case it was clear that my cow could not go much further. She scarcely even glanced at a fine bunch of charlock that she would once have delighted in.

At the top of the down, the road loosely girded a forest. When I turned in a slow circle I could see for miles in every direction except ahead of us. There, trees stood proudly as a halted army. We stopped below them for the night.

Bill went to the edge of the trees to gather wood and brush while I hobbled the beasts. As I examined their condition my heart sank. The donkey looked healthy, if not in great spirits. He was used to work. But the cow was miserable, far worse than I'd realized even while climbing the down. After the unfamiliar walking, her spine seemed almost to sag. Clear fluid ran from her eyes. I laid my palm on her neck; her veins beat hard, and immoderately hot. I did not even have a wisket for her fodder. Though I stroked her, murmuring like a good caretaker, I burned with shame that I had brought her. I knew that I'd done so mostly to keep the vagabonds from having her milk. I took off her hobble so she might search for whatever grass seemed best to her.

Bill returned from the edge of the woods, out of breath. He seemed as spooked as a cat and I looked to see what could have startled him so. But there was nothing there but a border of bracken, and then the trees.

The beasts nosed for charlock and feverfew. Now that we had stopped I felt truly exhausted. While walking I had felt in a ferment, always looking before us and behind. Now I leaned on my crutch and closed my eyes, feeling that I could have slept on whatever patch of hard ground I first stretched on. But I knew we needed food, and warmth, if we were to make any progress the next day. I gathered my strength and began making a fire.

Once it was burning nicely, Bill laid out his half-dozen eggs to be licked by the heat. He sat cross-legged, and leaned in from time to time to turn an egg. Though he turned each with a quick flick of the wrist, afterwards he would blow and suck on the tips of his fingers.

"Those eggs might be needed by their proper owner," I said. I was eating bread, which had already begun to go stale. Bill said nothing. I broke open another loaf and laid it to dry. Better hot-dried than stale, I thought; you might need more water to accompany dried bread, but it's less likely to mold. I tried again: "You can't know how great her need might be."

Finally, quietly, he spoke. "They are Bill Palmer's, to cast away or keep, or give, or share."

I looked up from my toasting loaf. I stared at him. "They weren't yours until you stole them. The theft put Bill Palmer at hazard, and me as well. You're not traveling alone, now. You need to think beyond yourself."

"Bill did not steal them," he said, and flicked a brown egg to turn it.

My frustration grew, becoming something close to scorn. I was in no temper to argue over so basic a thing, tired as I was. "You're an uncommonly lucky fellow, then. It's rare for a goodwife to give a rich clutch of eggs to a stranger as a gift."

He shook his head seriously.

"If you did not steal them, and did not receive them as a gift, how did you come to have them?"

"They came to me through these fingers."

"Then I must call them stolen."

"No."

I glared at him. "You took things that belonged to another. In the end that's between that other and you, and the Lord, and your own hunger. But if you lie to me, and persist in it, then I'd rather you leave before me in the morning. I won't travel with a liar. I've a long road ahead, and I'm too old to spend my time so."

His lips turned up in what I thought a sneer; he looked closely at the eggs. *Stubborn. Willful.* I watched a red spark blacken on the crust of my loaf. When it died I looked back at Bill; I was surprised to see that his eyes looked wet. "None of that," I said. "Simply say you were wrong to lie, and that you won't again. Then all will be right between us."

"It never was a lie."

"You told me the eggs came through your fingers," I said, my voice rising. "Through your fingers. You have the hands of a thief, the heart of a thief, the tongue of a liar." I was nearly shouting, and wholly certain that my travels with the man were through.

"Only the fingers," he said. "It's only stuck in these fingers, and these palms."

Even angry as I was, it seemed strange that he would deny only part of what I'd said. "Stuck. What is stuck?"

"There is thievery all through this hand, these hands. More thievery has been fed me than any other sin. Many, many loaves from thieves have I been given. Often I have drunk their wine." He twisted his neck as though craning to see behind, one way then the other. "At the shoulders the thievery stops."

"It's lodged all through you," I said, slowly realizing.

"It has long been part of this skin, these bones."

I thought of the welts, red as cut strawberries, that had marred his body when I saw him at the market ground. Of course I'd known he saw them as the signs of sin. But I had thought that he'd imagined them as something like clothes, bloody hides that others had draped on him against his will. Now I saw that the sins went far deeper than his skin—deep as his bones, deep as his heart. He believed that they had truly become a part of him. *How can I truly say he is wrong?* I thought. *They guide what he does. Can anything be more real than that?*

Then I wondered about the dead sinners whose ribs had been Bill's trenchers, whose skulls had been his wine-cups. I wondered what he knew of their crimes. I wondered what he feared they might drive him to. Beyond the fire he gently bit through an eggshell to the white.

"Your skin is healing well," I said.

"It was cleansed well," he said. But he did not say, or need to, that I had only cleansed the surface.

It was almost dusk. A wet wind blew from the south, hinting at rain. Behind Bill the cow still grazed, with the stubbornness of an animal who knows what she needs to live. I smelled the donkey's musty sweat.

I thought about sin, and death, and the condition of a man when he goes to die; I thought of the woes he can bring upon himself, and the sorrows another may lay upon him. I knew what I would do.

I waited until Bill again turned his eggs. Then I slid my stars about, turning what had been the base of the Anvil into its pounding face. Bill pushed a whole egg into his mouth, breathing loudly with his mouth open to cool it between chews. He ate without relish; before taking a single swallow he began peeling the next egg. Shells piled before him like storm wrack.

"Here, Bill," I said. "Listen. There are things I can give you, to start the cleansing out of sin." His head snapped up; he swallowed all in his mouth in one gulp. "But some of them are painful," I said softly. "All of them are bitter. And even when used in concert, they will take some time. It will not be easy."

"No cleansing has ever been easy," he said. His voice held a minor note of hope. Though I was glad to hear it, it was not a hope I wanted to see swell unduly. I knew that anything that seemed to be too easily purged could be just as easily planted again. He must not only tell himself he was cleansed. He must believe that he was—he must believe it in his heart.

"Nothing worth having comes simply," I said. "It'll be a hard journey, and a heavy task. But drink what I bid you to drink, and eat what I bid you to eat, and do what I tell you to do. We'll work the foreign stuff out from your body. All that will be left is whatever is between you and the Lord. I'll never claim to affect that."

Bill did not seem to fear the weight of his own transgressions. He bit his lip, and smiled with fettered joy. He rolled an egg to me around the side of the fire, as a bowler might gently pass a ball to his partner. I thanked him, and peeled it. I turned my attention to the road south, thinking that he might want a moment to think in peace.

When I looked back, two eggs were left; the empty shells were gone. Bill sat wearing his floppy, husbandman's work-hat, watching the fire with a determined set to his chin. Under the crown of his hat I could see the thinnest edge of a white shell. I bit the inside of my cheek.

"Where are the eggshells, Bill?"

"In yon bracken, where I tossed them."

"And what do you have under your cap?"

"*I* don't know."

I swallowed my laugh and stirred the coals with a stick. I was the one with patches on my face; I could not in fairness mock a man with shells in his hat. As the sun sank and the clouds came on, our hearth becoming as much a means of light as heat. I tossed the stick on to burn.

Bill sat upright, his back nobly straight, looking past me, I thought to see the beasts. "There's a fellow traveling," he said.

I struggled with my crutch. The air was in a gray turmoil above the wide expanse of fields and the long, northern road that crossed them. But at the very edge of the far horizon the clouds ended, failing at the last to blanket all the sky. From there a sheet of pumpkin-colored light slipped across the fields to our down, making the world feel a warmer place than the chill clouds seemed to permit.

I stared along the road until my eyes ached and the orange light faded. Just as I'd nearly decided that Bill was wrong, I saw a small spot of moving color. Though dulled by the coming night it was perceptibly, absolutely red—like a crimson cock quickly traveling.

"Ready yourself." I crutched for the animals. My face was flushed, my mouth suddenly raw.

"What ails," Bill said, then caught himself short. When he

thought I was not looking, he shook the mess of white and brown shell from his hat.

I unhobbled the donkey and roughly slung on the packs, begging his forgiveness for being asked to travel again. Then I moved to the cow, and hesitated. I did not know how far into the woods we'd need to go. She was already so weak, and weary as I would have been had I not been driven by fear.

In the end I brought her. If the traveler was Ridley, he might execute his sentence on my cattle; if he was a stranger, he might think it a witchy thing to find a milk-cow alone, beside a fire going dead. In either case she would not survive the night. I seized up her tether. Then the bunch of us, man and beast, climbed the last short stretch of down towards the woods.

At the forest's edge there was a small, steep berm, thickly overgrown by a tangle of brambles and dog's mercury. Already I'd handed the donkey's reins to Bill, that he might wrestle him while I coaxed the cow. As I climbed the berm, struggling through underbrush clinging to my skirts, the cow-rope dragged limp. Then it went taut as though I'd snared the leviathan. The cow moaned. I turned to gently brush her nose. She used the moment to back up a step, edging towards clear ground. There was no time for debate or soft reason; I planted my good leg as high as I could advance it, then heaved with all my strength. I gained perhaps four inches. Bill was already over the top.

"Tie the donkey off there. My cow needs goading," I cried. Bill came back as though to haul me from marshy ground. Soon he had the tether. He heaved, I prodded; groaning, the cow thrashed forward. We crossed the berm's rounded top and sank into the forest beyond.

Inside, the woods were cleaner. After tearing past some sharp-bladed, sun-loving hollies, we passed into a high vaulting of oaks that suppressed much of the underbrush. It was a place of ferns, and mosses, and shadows; we would be able to pass through almost as easily as we would have a meadow. Though I'd thought the forest floor would be level, or even climb, it descended softly and undeniably. I imagined the woodland floor was like a shallow goblet, and that we had just passed the lip.

"He is a hateful man," Bill said with certainty. The presence of the traveler behind us was chill and absolute, but Bill's faith warmed me. A small herd of the King's deer bounded away into the precious blue, like a school of perch sinking without a ripple. Though the sun had not fallen completely, the forest had gathered night into its crooks and vastnesses. I glanced back one last time, searching the dim wall of holly and dog's mercury for any hint of dragon-scale red. Even if he were inside, I realized, the cloak would muddy to burgundy in the dim light.

If the traveler was Ridley, it was a horrible sign that he had waited so long to pursue us. If he had started immediately, driven by rage and his own whims, he would have been more likely to return home as the lack of beef and beer began to seem pressing. But a leader sent on the road by his follower's ridicule could never turn back. There could be no end to it then. A leader may allow himself to be seen as a jester—but never as a fool.

Every black tree looked the same. The spaces between them seemed even, the forest made to a labyrinth by night and my fear of getting lost. *How deep must we go?* I thought of staying there, even creeping back to the edging brambles, peeking through to see who passed and when.

But to wait there, wondering if Ridley might come, and find me…I knew I would rather walk a thousand miles through a night-clad forest than wait an hour for a man to bear me my own fate.. The air was full of mulch and the sweat of beasts; I struggled to breathe easy. "What would you?" I asked.

I thought Bill smiled crookedly. "In is in," he said. He was right. Any forest dangers could snare us as easily at the edge as they could at the bottom of the woods. And if we went further, one of our steps would be the first of the way out; I did not think England had any wooded grounds so vast that we could not cross them. Bill made me feel easier. I reached to rub his shoulder in thanks.

Behind us the last light hung in the brush, making it a faded, ruined tapestry. We walked down into the forest.

All was velvet, all purple, all darkening. My eyes widened to rings; our feet shuffled through the leaves of past years. A night-dove whistled her sultry call. There was the smell of damp earth and again, stronger than before, I caught a scent of coming rain.

I pulled three stars from my face. The last one I slid to my brow. It would be my beacon. My northern star. In truth I did not know which way we were walking, or should walk. But soon enough the star's imagined glow was the only light in the woods. When I waved my hand before my face I saw only a scant ruffle. Behind me Bill breathed with a whistle, as though he pursed a reed between his lips.

Then it was true night. I could see nothing except at the very sides of my vision. When I looked straight at the forest floor, it vanished. But when I held my eyes straight before me, as though searching for bats swimming their frantic way, I had a vague sense of the ground. It lay before me like a dull, hammered, stretched gray coin.

Four: Bill

There is a sudden crash in the leaves, and then there is no lady walking before the cow. I stop, and wait. She coughs angrily as she labors to her feet. *We'd better have light*, she says.

Are you hurt, I say.

I'm not. But I do not wish to slip again. Walking along with my chin in the air should ensure it. We're deep enough in, he won't see our light. Talk now. Guide me.

It is dark it is dark it is dark. As I say it, not knowing what else I should say, she comes to my voice as on a rope. Her hands brush me as she feels her way past, to the donkey. Then her hands fumble through a sack.

Donkey and I are in accord. We do not like these woods. As we walk we keep our hearts close to us, so they cannot be stolen by fear or wretched spirits.

She is done with her sack. A cork pops softly from a bottle. Then I smell something that reminds me of stew. *Precious stuff*, she says. *But then, all my oils are. At least this one's more common than the rest.*

I hold to the donkey's neck, and I wait. I hear a clicking, a clacking. A lone spark dances, and takes hold. Then flame blows the darkness back. We are in a room with walls of tree trunks and a roof of arching boughs, and the walls are also made of night. I shout.

Quiet now, she says, though she is grinning. On her face there is only one star, between her brows. She holds a stick. One end is wrapped in a cloth burning with black smoke. *Don't call out if you don't wish to have company*, she said. *Let's find us a place to build up a blaze. Any clear place will do. Let's not make the woods to an oven, and ourselves into roasting fowl.* A wisp of smoke reaches me and it smells like burning herb-cakes.

There is a clear place there, I say. *I have found the good place.*

She looks to where I point, and says I may be right. I think: Good fortune! It is great good luck to have a clear place so near to where she made her torch.

She limps to the clearing, leaving the cow to huff softly behind. I follow behind her with the donkey. I mean to tie him off, and begin making our comforting camp. Here no traveler will come upon us. There will be nothing to make her jump up, and again flee off into black woods.

But here there is not nothing. It is not an empty clearing. Here there is a hutch, crumpled to the ground.

The plank roof has fallen in. The rest of the timber is tilted, nearly flat. It was made with planks only, without strong beams to hold them tall and strong. The planks are studded with nails. The hutch lays as though it fell from out of a tree and broke on the ground. Were I to kick the walls they'd fall the last few inches, soft as feathers, and rest atop each other.

Who would have chosen to live here, I ask her.

That, I don't know. It's nearly too rough even for cottagers, she says. *Poaching huntsmen, maybe? I thought those deer righteous fat for this early spring. Likely there are good things hidden in these woods. Probably it was huntsmen. I don't think it was anyone's lasting home.*

She walks around it, torch held high, oily smoke rising. *They are still here*, she says.

I quail at that, but leave the donkey and walk to her. Thump, thump, thump; I walk on a door. It lies some way from the hutch.

When I look down it seems I might open it, and find a hall leading straight down into the turf.

I step off the door, and away from it, walking backwards to the lady. Though there are no trunks close to the hutch, some trees stretch long arms overhead.

There have not been men here of late, she says.

I think she is mistaken, and yet is not mistaken, for here there are bones. I see them between the fallen, angled walls, and blurry under a frayed mat of leaves. The torch-orange light casts shadows under the hutch planks. Some bones seem laid out neatly. An arm and a leg lay close beside each other, placed neatly as though beside a churchyard hole. Others scatter in disorder. I see backbones, with holes smooth as cut gutters. There is no skull to see. I make for the bones.

What would you do with them, she asks once this hand is on a rotten plank.

Stack them orderly, I say. Though I do not wish to I heave and raise one of the hutch's broken walls. It is different finding bones here than when they come from a hole dug neatly. A tremor shakes this body, like a white dandelion when blown.

Leave them, she says. *We'll need our own shelter before the rain comes. A few more hours open to the sky will not harm them.* She coughs. *And you.* She coughs again. She hunches over, a closed fist to her mouth.

I will wait, I say, and drop the boards. I kick them once, to better hide the bones.

Do you fear to stay here? she asks.

Here is as good a place as any.

But I think, silent and ratty, that these bones need a proper chamber. With them naked under trees, this place has a wrongful jumble of man and beast. Beasts may come for these leavings of men. In the city sometimes dogs would sneak through the gate, and dig until I beat them back with a rake. Here, I think, things will not squeal and flee so readily as dogs.

Five: Sarah

The hutch had once been made of decent timber. But now it was rotten; when Bill lifted a piece it split dustily, thoroughly chewed by termites. It was useless for shelter. In any case, though I would not spend the night burying the bones, neither would I strip away what cover they already had.

But there was still the door. It was made of three boards joined by slats across the top and bottom. The wood seemed thicker and better seasoned than that of the walls and roof. When we lifted the door, round bugs dropped from beneath. To shake off worms still clinging there I tapped it with my crutch, but gently, worried that even thick wood might be rotten after so much time on the forest floor. Under it the leaves were yellow and slick, covered in places with a kind of moss like white hair. Soon it began to rain.

Though I had expected it, the storm came on so hard that it seemed sudden. I'd hoped that the trees would give us some shelter, and that only their topmost boughs would thrash in the wind. But as the storm came on, gusting, howling, the trunks heaved down to their roots. Air flowed as though blown from their bark, the wind spiriting through the woods. I said a brief prayer for the Lord to comfort those who had tried to make a life in that furious place; I prayed also that He would choose to comfort us.

Bill dragged the door to the clearing's edge. I limped along beside, the torch in one hand, a sack taken from the donkey in the other. Raindrops gathered into balls on the upper leaves of the trees, then fell in cold pearls that threatened to damp my flame. Sometimes a gust broke the rain into a fine spray, flinging it from branch and air and leaf, so that water came as much from the side as from above. Then it seemed less like rain than the bubbles driven in a breaking curl. *Will I always see as though under water, as through a drowned man's eyes?* Bill propped the door against a tree. The torch hissed dead.

The shroud of new darkness made me feel anew that I was crushed beneath an ocean, without air or means of reaching it. Even my inner clothes began to danken and drag. I ran my fingers across my brow; my lone, northern star yet adhered faithfully. I cupped hands over my face, and blew into them to feel the warmth. My moist breath was drier than the air.

"Come here, Bill." I felt my way to give him a blanket. His hands trembled, chilled by water and blowing wind. "Come." We snapped the cloth out and lay it over the leaning door, letting the ends drape down on the ground. The donkey stamped, snorted, blowing out rain; the cow was troublingly quiet.

I guided Bill through the blanket and under the door, to lean in the scant lee of the trunk. Then I groped my way after him. When the blanket was again drawn down against the wet I sat gasping, my lungs feeling freed within the enclosure. Bill shivered beside me; behind us the trunk swayed, mighty as a keel.

Six: Bill

M*ore like driven bubbles than rain*, she said. I put hands across this face, guarding it as I would a candle. She guided me beneath boards and blankets, to take shelter sitting beside her.

But now comes the wetness. Though the rain fell on these borrowed clothes while we were outside, it did not truly soak through them until now. Outside it was the wind that was cold, blowing these limbs to blue. Now under the blankets I hug what skin I can, and shiver. I shiver, skin to bone, in pure and potent misery, and fear that my shaking may shake loose old angers.

Rain falls on our blanket and wets it, until it is soggy as these legs are. Though I am glad to have the blanket it is a poor wall. It gives no comfort, as did the blankets I once lay under. At night I would turn as though in sleep, stealing more blankets from my sisters. That was before I had me my own mat.

Outside, the cow moans. The donkey brays—but quietly, as though fearing that his dam might chide him. Cow and donkey both sound sickly, in danger of drowning under the sorrowing sky. When I peer from behind the blanket I find nothing there but black, black, hissing blowing black. My shiver might shake our tree.

The lady reaches to snatch down the blanket. She holds it down. *You're precious cold*, she says. To hold down the blanket, her arm must press down on this leg. Her arm is warm on this thigh. She shifts, and another piece of thigh grows warm. The place where her arm first was is yet warm, like clothes just now taken off. Her clothes are wet but inside them the flesh is warm. And there is her body beside me, solid in the darkness, and all of her body is warm.

Then I think of Roslyn, and of her room above the bakery. Her tawny mat had flour into the weave, white wheat flour and brown oaten flour. At the thought of Roslyn and of her bed, I feel this yard begin to harden—and though the cold is somewhat relieved, a greater shiver shakes me.

Lust was first fed to me from a daughter, and after that from dead men and again from dead women. Now when lust seizes me it is sometimes with pleasure, and often with sorrow, but always without my choosing its direction. When they live, men and women may lust for particular women or men. In death, lust is lust. I wonder whose lust now takes this body—or if it comes from me.

Roslyn's room smelled of jamball rolls, and fatty pasties. I would go with her there and spend all into her, after she gestured to me that her work at the pricking iron was done.

I press elbows between these legs, holding down this yard, hiding this yard. In the blackness the warm lady holds the blanket. *I must play at being your grandmother after all*, she says.

Outside the rain begs. The wind begs. But I think I would gladly go into both. I say, desperate: *I might cover the cow. The donkey.* When she answers her voice is whispering straw.

There's nothing we can do. If they're meant to stay healthy tonight, they will. It was my error to bring them. At least, it was a mistake to bring her. We need the donkey more, and he's more likely to live. We can only hope they both do.

So I think more of life, and less of lust. When lust again rises I think of health for beasts, wishing them well. We sit, and I hope. We sit through all the night, all the storm, until morning breaks through both.

Seven: Sarah

Finally I slept, still gripping the blanket. We badly needed even that poor shelter. Very likely a single person would have sickened in the dank, perhaps dangerously so. But the blanket held our warmth, and the warmth of two together is greater than that of one plus one. Perhaps we would have survived God's rain alone. But we would have been left pale and slick as grubs, unable to take joy in the dawning day.

Once in the night I smiled, realizing that I had not been so close to a man since dallying with Richard Hall eight years before. Richard and I came together after the death of his first wife, I needing any lover, he needing one old enough that he would not feel he was trying already to replace his Ann. But both of us still felt ourselves married, even with our loved ones in the ground; we stopped by silent agreement. For my part the dalliance was less for pleasure than for raw comfort, as the press of my body against Bill had been for mutual life.

I threw back the blanket; though mist hung lightly in the forest, it was soft, like beaten flax. All the deadly murk seemed washed away. A breeze passed, shaking a reminder of the rain from our oak.

I could tell that the sun would soon clear away even the mist, and the thin skimming of cloud between us and the sky. The turning of our luck pleased me greatly until I looked for my cow, and saw that she was near to death.

She lay among ferns, beside a holly at the edge of the clearing, limp and heavy as though she'd tried to fall through the ground. I knelt beside her. Her eyes ran yellow. The veins at her neck beat unevenly, and her nose felt ablaze. I stroked her crest. She moved, but not from pleasure at my touch. It was only her illness jerking her.

"I hoped for them all through the night," Bill said beside me. I wondered if he had slept, for his eyes were almost as bleary as the cow's.

"As did I, whenever I was awake," I said. "But hopes were not enough."

"Might she give milk?"

"No. Not like this. Likely it has gone rank from her illness. But we need not leave her behind entirely. Fetch me the pack. No, the one underneath." And I pointed him to the proper one, which held the square of leather I'd wrapped around my knives. A cow's meat may be sadder stuff than that from an ox, but it can be eaten, and I thought she would thank me for speeding her on her way.

I was never the best of butchers, and my hands were cold. After the first swift, sure stroke at her throat, I was clumsy with the knife. But I carved until we had the chine and haunches. We left the ambles among the leaves, though we took the liver, which Bill said he favored. He dreamed also of steak pies, and of tongues. Once I was done working I joined him in thoughts of roasted collar of beef. I only hoped we could find a place with a proper hearth before night came on again.

I need not have feared. Scarcely after noon we came to the far, edging thicket of thorn bushes, scattered through with hyacinth and deep blue harebells. We edged through the bushes slowly, wearily, the thorns catching on our clothes and Bill's bundle of meat. It seemed ages since I had seen such good, golden light; it steamed the last rain from tall mayweed stems and bugle blossoms. Finally I broke onto clear ground. Then I had a plain view of the sun, gleaming on the roofs of a slated town below us; and beside that town, a lake.

Eight: Edward Keaton

The clock won't work. So he said. The clock won't work, and I must craft a better casing. At least he knows that the casing is the heart of the thing. He knows it is no mere frippery, like clothes. A clock's casing is both shell and spine. It molds the space where the works must click. Made properly, a case holds wheels and wires snug, so the hours will not hurry. But it must not cram the clockwork, lest the seconds slow and laze.

The clock won't work. This most important one won't work. So Limett the clockmaker said through his messenger, the eager Dawker boy, who ran to me from the far side of our town, through the straight-ruled shops, along the cobbled street. The town being so close by lakeshore, its ground is given to going swampy. Thus the cobbles are a profitable thing, letting the water run cleanly away. This morning, before Young Tim Dawker interrupted me at my meal—warm ale, and good cheese—I watched them glisten outside my workshop window. The rain is gone, the pounding night has passed. The cobbles steam themselves dry.

Tim Dawker brought money with him, for the first casing I gave to Limett was properly made. It will serve for another clock. If

Limett had sent a different message, speaking badly of my workmanship, I would never have agreed to work on another case. I do not care that the clock is meant for Lord Renault, as a gift from all our town. I have no need to impress that man. Already Renault knows me as a man of parts; he knows that I am bold while gaming, and skilled at chess.

The Dawker boy brought pleasantly heavy coins, and knotted strings. The distance between the knots shows the dimensions the new case will need. The pillar plates will be so wide. The axle-tree, so tall. The endless screw must divot here. So.

I look up from my planing and out the window, its plank shutter swung open for the sun. The sun shines on a mirror set in the window-frame, sending a clear beam of light to show my work. The air and sun are clear above the lake. This is a fine prospect, with light good for the making of clocks and their cases.

On the lake, cock-boats trim and turn. They pull flapping nets and cone traps. Beyond them, hazed, is the far Dorme shore. I bend to my plane; the clock won't work.

Mary, my wife, does not much aid my work. She is now in the chamber, up-ladder, where there are no windows. Her steps cross above my head. I push the plane, brushing the shavings aside with the heel of my hand. Again Mary's steps bump, lightly as a cobbler's spruce mallet. I lean close to my work. It will be a surprising thing if this casing is not right. The clock will work.

Though Mary does not often help me at my work, I am glad of the game that brought her to me. At night she warms my bed and body. By day she orders my house, straightening and emptying, freeing me to work. I was not so free in the years before she came to me; not, at least, since the death of my last wife, which left my household cavernous. Now Mary comes backwards down the ladder, leaning against the rungs. Though I do not glance from the plane, I know she climbs down in that way. She always does, when burdened.

Her bundle flops down near the corner, where two benches are set beside each other to make a place for folding linens. I finish shaving the housing's first wall; I flick my horsehair whisk, sending curls of planed wood past the copper sundial and out the window.

"Is the sun too bright?" Mary asks.

"It warms me." A blanket slides over my shoulders. On my next stroke the plane slides roughly, my movement constrained. I shake the blanket to the floor. There must be a perfectly flat plane for this front panel. It must be right for etching and inscription.

"There was no need to drop it to the floor," she says.

"The floor is wood. If you swept it, the blanket would not now be dusty," I say. I squint by the mirror's shining light, looking closely at the joints on the casing's front plate. They are small as a babe's knuckles and are the true key to a good clock-case. The best casings need not be knocked together with clumsy brass nails; mine never need to be. Instead they click together at the corners, held as one piece by nearly invisible craft.

But even as my skill has grown, I have found fewer buyers. There is less weight of gold in my life than I would like. "You might sweep it now," I say.

"I will," she says, her voice as pleasant as a chime. The sound of sweeping is like that of brushing long hair. As I work I can feel the dust clear from behind me; she sweeps it into a clay pan, and carries it out to the cobbles. I run the front plate with my thumb, and find no sliver to prick me. When I look at the joints I am satisfied.

Limett is waiting for me down the street. His mind does not have the calmness necessary for my work. While he waits for me he will think of Renault, and grow nervous. He would do better to sit at his own workbench, beneath his clear glass globe of water. The globe is a precious thing, that catches the sun even more brightly than my mirror. It sharpens light on the fine screws he must work. It gleams in his window like money.

But I know he will not be at his bench now. His pincers and wires will be gathering dust. He will do nothing now but wait and worry. This clock and casing must be done before mid-morn tomorrow, when the cartman is off. Limett should tend to his own work.

Mary is a player of the flute. When her sweeping is done, I

hear her case whisper open. She sits on one of the benches, on folded linens that will now be rumpled. For a long moment my mind clunks away from my work. I ready to chastise her, for I expect to hear playful music, playful and distracting, tumbling like children on a hill.

But when her song begins it is regular as a sleeper's heartbeat. It soothes me. My work is less laborious. Mary is a fine player of the flute. And she is an obedient wife.

Her music does not dance; it curves. It fills my house like paper being slowly stacked. Beneath it my work seems to slow, and yet proceeds so easily that I think that nothing has been lost me. Perhaps something has been gained.

"Where will you sup," she asks when done.

"You may go to the tavern, and have them ready a supper there," I say. After a while she is ready. When I hear her at the door, I say "You are a pleasure to me."

"My duty," she says, and is gone.

The light is the color of yeast, then of old time. Still I work far past the hour I'd intended, using a narrow knife to perfect the joining. I could finish tomorrow, but I resolve to continue until done, for even should I work tomorrow there would be no time to engrave the figures of the ancient gods in the detail they deserve. I hold myself to etching their distinctive tools, which after all are at the heart of their character. Jupiter will have no beard, nor robe, face or body—but lightning will flank the casing's open eye. For Mars there will be a spear and shield. For Mercury, winged sandals. A winged helmet.

When I come to Venus I pause, and consider. Her only tool is her body. She is noted for beauty, and the passions she engenders. Finally I etch an apple; the wise will know it golden.

When that is done, I snap the pieces together at the joints. Then I turn it over in the afternoon light. It is solid workmanship, and lighter than it looks. I imagine the clockwork turning within, the weight dropping slowly, the lone hand beginning to rise. I feel inside to see that all is spaced rightly. Then, though I much mislike to do it, I stretch the knotted strings the Dawker boy brought me, making a final check of the proportions. Outside, the lake is turning to melted bronze. I stand, and—walk for my supper.

Beneath the sunset the slates of the town's roofs are angular, crisply defined. After a rain they look particularly clean. Of all the changes I have seen here in my threescore years, I like best the slates that have largely replaced the ancient wooden shingles. The shingles tended to rot. I pull my cloak close. Evening's cool blows through the last warmth of afternoon. The lake has emptied of fishing boats; only two dexterous pleasure-craft still turn and tack. A few anglers have dropped silken lines from the pier, more to enjoy the evening than from any hope of good sport. A lute begins, and then a singer. Both are hesitant, as though hoping that others may join the song. Joining would be a manner of applause.

My wife and ward is not the town's sole musician. There are players of the strings, of tamber-bells and drums. Still, she most often plays alone. Such is her volition; also, my wish.

The tavern is near by to the pier, its footing set hard in the lakeshore's niggardly gravel. It has the best food in Nene, and in the next three towns. Though I think the pork offered by Jason Wilnut without peer, he lives in Scrooby, the fourth town away. Excepting Wilnut's pork, I have eaten nothing better in my life than the fish and fowl here at Tom Boman's tavern. Tonight I can smell, through the lake breeze and evening's wood smoke, that he is roasting beef.

I step into the tavern's close air. The main room is mobbed with fishers brushing off memory of the lake, and brash woodsmen sent by Lord Renault to fulfill his timbering rights in the forest above us. The craftsmen here are quieter, their voices made moderate by life within walls. The fire is built up wastefully hot; skin gleams with sweat, windows are propped open. A haunch roasts before the blaze, blessing the air with the smell of rich juice.

A woman I do not know sits at a table by an open window, resting her arm and a tyg on the sill. There are sores on her face, plain as moss. With her is a man, wearing a hat that droops like a hound's ears. And with the two of them is my wife.

The older woman laughs. Mary laughs with her, holding on to the edge of the table. It disquiets me; my wife seems to know the others well, but I am sure they are not from Nene. Mary has not yet seen me through the heads of woodsmen and fishers. Without greeting her with voice or gesture I work through to the counter where Tom Boman pours ale.

I rest my hands on the worn wood, beside a platter that holds a haunch of beef. It has been carved down to the bone, leaving little but pooled blood. I ask Boman what he thinks the new pair is about.

Before answering me, he yells towards the hearth. "Turn that beef, there—you'll dry the blood in it, motherless whore. Son of whores, I mean." At last I have his attention. "What is who?"

"The pair with Mary. The old woman. The man."

"They came today. This morn. I know nothing abut them, they've stayed shut up in their room." He heaves a keg of small beer to the counter, and with pliers begins working the bung loose. Finding it stuck, he licks his thumbnail, dries it on his shirt, and takes a new grip. The strange gesture seems to help, for the pliers take hold; the plug wiggles, then pops free.

"Do they seem reputable?" I ask.

"Enough so. They were tussled when they came, but not worse than you'd expect, being caught in the storm and all. You'll have it, you'll have it!" Boman calls out to a demanding drunkard behind my shoulder. He reaches for a spout, pounds it into the bung-hole with a bottle's base, and turns the keg on end. "I let them the room beside the chimney, the warm one. There'd been some woodmen there but their coin ran out. A good month, this." He smiles to himself, enjoying the thought of pockets draining into his own.

"But why should they have been out in the storm?" I say, almost to myself.

Boman shrugs. "I see no trouble in her, at least. And he follows her like a pup. I think he's not fully right, though from birth or wound I can't say." The drunkard's cup is brimming. "Will you want a bit?"

"I will." He thuds a black-glazed tyg to the counter. Most tygs have three handles; this one has four. "I should prefer a mug," I say.

"I've only tygs left. A good month is built of good nights like this." He pours my tyg full and foaming.

"They paid for a room all to themselves?" I drop my payment and take the drink.

"Well, I don't know if they could have paid with coin. They offered meat in trade before I'd named the proper price. She said she had slaughtered her bull before beginning her travels, needing the silver for the road. But the buyer took sick, and could not take the meat. I was happy enough to. There hasn't been enough beef of late, and what she gave me was worth the room three times over." As he speaks he pours vessel after vessel to the top. At this pace he will soon need another keg. "Your Mary has a piece waiting for you, I think. A fine, bloody bit, though the rest of it will go dry should that whoreson zed fail at the spit." He barks his last words towards the hearth. Through the laughing crowd I see a small hand, a boy's I think, turning another haunch.

"Thank you, Tom." I maneuver towards the window, losing some drink to careless elbows. Soon I stand over the old woman, and her companion, and my wife.

From so close, I see that what I thought were sores are black felt stars. They stick to the woman's cheeks like numerals. On her forehead a crescent moon makes a bridge between her brows. I stand over the table.

"Edward!" Mary smiles. "I'd started to think I'd need to come fetch you."

"Will you sit," the other woman says. She seems in the kind of fog that may cling to one after a long sleep.

"I would keep my own company, lady. And that of my wife," I say pleasantly.

"Keep your company," the man says. The resemblance to a hound is not only because of his hat-brim; there is something twitching in his manner that makes me unsure of which way he may jump. He watches his own fingers drumming the table. He may only be repeating my words, to learn their sense; Tom did say he was of an unserious mind. But it may be that he is commanding me to go and to take my wife with me. I will not abide a command from any man, not unless he is noble. Were my sons here, they would drag him up to cuff him.

But the woman laughs. "A man of good character can keep his own company even in a crowd," she says. She speaks somewhat indulgently, perhaps trying to calm the man.

"It is a pleasant prospect here," Mary says.

There is a note of hope to Mary's voice. And the woman spoke as though she knew her companion to be in the wrong. Half-willingly, I smile. The window beside my wife is open to the moonlit water. A silvered hull bumps gently against its anchor-lines. When there is a brief pause in the tavern's tumult, the breeze carries in the sound of ripples against moored boats, and the voice of the lute. "That is so," I say. "We will sup here, then. But we must not stay for long. More work waits in the morning."

"I have no doubt of it." Mary edges still closer to the window, making room. The man stands abruptly, then pushes through the crowd like a chisel. I remind myself that he is an idiot.

"My name is Jane Plummer," the woman says. When I look past her stars I see that she is about my age; it is hard to tell, with her face so marked and her hair held tightly coifed. Her fashion is proper enough. But when her eyes catch the light of a candle, they change; at one moment they are oaken brown, then vine green. I like that less than I do the coif.

"Well met to you," I say. "My name is Edward Keaton. My wife will have named herself."

"She has. And she has told us of your uncommon craft."

"Uncommon."

If she hears the distaste in my voice, she does not show it. "Yes, in that it is done well. It must be passing difficult, making casings that will fit clockwork you've never even seen. I do not think many men could succeed at that."

I nod. "Your companion is a man of little courtesy," I say, meaning it for a compliment to her own manners and grace. The anglers on the piers have lit lanterns. Silver and gold ripple and run, calling up fish.

"I am sorry for that. His name is Paul," she says, and drinks. "He is my brother's son, who travels with me for my safety. But he has been simple since birth. Will you drink an ale?"

This Jane knows how to comport herself. "I will, when this ale is gone," I say. It nearly is already; I drain it. The thought that a second drink will be brought to me mollifies a bit for the coldness of the beef, and its gaminess. Boman is a fine cook, but also willing to say what he must to sell another plate.

Jane Plummer proves herself pleasant company, asking after work and life in our small community of Nene. We drink an ale, and another. Then Limett is there.

He leans on our table on arms like fire-tongs, looking at my nearly empty tyg with scorn. For a man of noted success he dresses plainly, without wings on his jerkin. "I wait for your work," he says.

"It waits for you. It is ready, and at my house."

"If it's done, it would be better to have it in my shop."

"True. It will be there come morn. I think it odd that you will send word to me in the morning that a casing is wanted, then complain that it has not been received by that night. You are fortunate I had wood ready to work, or it would not be done this week at all."

"Well, I'd never thought that your first work would be shoddy."

I begin to burn. "I had never thought that you would send the wrong measures. Making cases is delicate work."

He takes up my drink and drains it. "Not many men will tell a clock-maker that their own work is delicate. I'll see you come morn." He wends for the hearth, calling for meat.

"An unpleasant man," Jane says, and calls for her nephew. When he comes she gives him coins, and sends him for more ale. Then she asks about the nature of wardship.

"That question comes from somewhere," I say.

"It does," Jane says, though she seems as innocent as the sun.

"Before you arrived, we did speak of wardship," Mary says. "But not of its meaning, nor its function."

The sound of strings has pecked against the tavern's confused babble. Now the lute-player adds his voice, lower, rougher, and more purposeful than that of his departed companion:

A lusty young smith at his vise stood a-filing,
His hammer laid by but his forge still aglow,
When to him a buxom young damsel came smiling
and asked if to work at her forge he would go.

"If you'll describe wardship, likely I can tell you if we practice it," Jane says. "Sometimes customs will go by different names, in different places."

"True. But it is no custom." I feel generous, willing to relieve her ignorance. "It is law, written in the time of Henry the Eighth. Though it has sometimes lain dormant since, it still is law today. It is meant to keep orphans safe, giving them ready protection."

"How?"

"Through schooling, and diligent management of their ancestral lands." I take another drink of bitter, praiseworthy ale. "As you know, every nobleman owes military service, in thanks for the land and title the King has granted him. What you do not know is what happens to the children of a nobleman who dies before he can tender the service he owes. What is to be done with the children, until they are old enough to inherit their lands responsibly? What is to be done with the lands themselves, which may lie fallow and unprofitable?" I drink. "Wardship solves both problems. The children are named wards of the court, to be schooled by court tutors. The lands are taken under court management, and the profits from it used to satisfy the dead noble's unpaid debt."

"So you are of noble birth?" Jane asks Mary.

"No."

I take Mary's hand. "Some years ago, the crown drove a monkish sect from its land. That land was granted to Mary's father, a prosperous but common merchant. He died not long after. Thus Mary was sent into wardship."

"What of the wives?"

"They may ask that the children be left in their care," I say. "But such requests are seldom granted. I have never heard of one being so. The children are taken until the old debt is held to have been paid."

"So it was with me," Mary says.

"She was given to Lord Burghley for keeping," I say. "He gave her, in turn, to Lord Renault."

"Who lost me to Edward," Mary says.

"Lost," Jane says.

I smile modestly. "At chess. Lord Renault was not husband to my wife, only holder of her deed of ward. He could dispose of it in any manner he liked. The manner he chose was gaming."

"He holds title to much of the woodland near here," Mary says. "We came here so he could watch the boats burn—at midsummer the townsfolk set some old ones afire, to celebrate the destruction of the armada. It's a fine festival. It was then that Edward won me."

But Jane holds a half-smile; it is clear that she has listened only to me. "Gaming," she says. "It has been a long, long time since I've gamed. You must be a fine chess-player."

"I have some practice." In truth I will beat any man who treats it as mere play. Chess is a serious matter, a contest between combating systems placed athwart each other.

"Well, it has always been beyond me. But a tavern always has a board or two. Does the keeper here have a game of goose?"

"He does."

"We call it a game of snakes, here," Mary says.

"Then I claim the honor of a match." Jane sends Paul shambling to fetch the board. "This is much as I remember," she says when he returns. "I don't know why we ever called it a game of goose."

The board is carved with a snake, spiraled, head at one edge, tail at the center. The snake is marked with icons, each one with a hole for a peg. Jane runs her finger from head to tip-of-tail, naming each icon in turn.

"A bird, of uncertain type. The bridge. A swan, *regardant*. Two cards? No, dice, they have no suits. A draw-well. A labyrinth. A castle. Again, an uncertain bird. It's been long years since I've played. But it begins to return to me—wonderful, how one can recall a game! Do we play for coin or pleasure?"

"He likes playing for coin," Mary says.

"If you have enough to wager," I say. I must resist throwing a hard look at Mary, for I wish she had remained silent while I draw this contestant out.

"I have enough for an evening's leisure," Jane says. She shakes out a small bag of pennies, threepennies, and groats onto the table. And there are a pair of crowns. Soon she has arranged them into a solid square, five coins to each side.

Before the night is over I will make that square hollow, or cause it to vanish altogether. As I total the coins, the boatman sings:

Red hot grew his iron, as both did desire
and he was too wise not to strike while 'twas so.
Quoth she, "what I get, I get out of the fire,
Then prithee, strike hard and redouble the blow."

Jane says, "The last time I gamed, drink had a part to play."

The coins are a perfect square. They may be broken down like children's blocks. "Those rules you may teach to me," I say.

"I will do."

Long into the night we play. Bone dice rattle; pegs march at our direction. When playing snakes one must look ahead, artfully dividing movement between one's pieces. You must not leave a peg lodged on the crueler icons. But the dice will have their say: I am a fine player, but even a fine player cannot always move as he knows best.

Indeed, in the early going I often find myself at a disadvantage. Once I land below Death, and once in the labyrinth. Twice I must pay toll on the bridge. My pegs retreat in confusion. But Jane is a kind rival; after the second game, she says she will buy another drink. This time she limps to fetch it herself.

"An injured leg must make for a long journey," I say.

"Maybe she rode," Mary says.

"It would surprise me to learn that she has a horse. The beef did not seem that of a prosperous woman." Mary shakes her head, although in agreement or contradiction I cannot tell. Then Jane is back.

The ale has a dusty edge. "This ale has turned," I say. The crowd has thinned and I can see that Boman has a new barrel out.

Jane tastes her own. "It tastes well enough to me. A different style of brew than he usually makes, perhaps. In truth this is the kind I like best. There's a salty edge to it." She takes a hearty gulp. "That's a proper drink, if you ask my mind."

I say nothing more; I am not one to offend. But the ale seems troubled, as though Boman has used thistles for hops.

Paul joins us for the next game. It is then that my luck turns, for Jane is honorable, and refuses to stop his mistakes. She holds her peace even after Paul's peg bumps me from the well. Being bumped should usually be avoided, but not from the well; it is not so very far from the start. Now Paul is stuck there, fuming. I pass him on the first roll.

Not all falls out my way. But as the night goes on I am more often briefly harried by the swan, *regardant,* than muzzled by the skull. Paul's bridge-tolls add to the common pot, which I capture more often than I might hope.

Mary does not play. Her orange curls peer admirably from beneath her cap as I gather up the coins that are now mine.

By night's end, Jane's square of coins is precious small. And mine has four perfectly even sides, like short, taut strings of pearls. The boatman's song has long since quieted. The windows are closed against the wind. I gather up my coins. "A pleasant night."

"It's been well enough," Mary says. That tempers my satisfaction. Her face has a newly sour cast, as though she would prefer it if I had lost. She would have me buy her fine things, and yet would love to see me lose. Woman is an ugly creature, when envious. Now I think Mary wretched; neither her neck nor her breasts charm me.

We offer Jane our blessings and go out into the dark. Some of the anglers had luck; the night is sweet with the smell of freshly-cleaned fish.

I have had more ale than I intended, more indeed than I have had in months. I did not feel it very strongly until I began to walk. But now the cobblestones waver, as though gauzed beneath a stream.

"You enjoyed the company," I say. She murmurs a reply. I do not like that she will not answer clearly; that has the color of disobedience. Perhaps she thinks I take too much pleasure in my drink. Tomorrow we will speak of this.

Finally we are at my house. I fumble with the latch. Frustrated, I sigh and look back towards the tavern. Quickly as a duck in flight, a shadow vanishes behind a rope-winder's storeroom.

"Paul," I say. "He is out."

"He will do no harm," Mary says. She bends forward, arm around my waist, to help me with the lock.

"Likely true," I say slowly. "He is Jane's companion. If things are found amiss, we have..." I seek for a word; I fail to find it. At last I triumph over the latch.

Mary lights a candle at the hearth. This should be familiar country. But all here is only outlines—my pincers, planes, and awls look hollow, light as air. If I tried to use them they would crumple.

I lie down. Then I find that I am on a great clock hand. The clock is on a tower.

I hear the click of the escapement, and of the sinking weight. Time clicks forward, the hand advances, until I slip.

I wake in late morning. I am bound to the great chair. There is a rope tied hard around the corners of my mouth.

No. I am in the bed. My mouth is free. But my tongue is swollen with the taste of thistles—swollen painfully, as though stinging plants have rooted there. I push myself up. Limett is pounding at the door.

"Mary." My voice sounds soft, formless as a pillow.

"Mary." I will have a proper explanation from her for leaving me sleeping until Limett came to look for me.

But she is not in my house. I wander until I am sure she is not here. I walk to the window through a shattering headache, and lean upon my workbench. Limett might be pounding on my very skull. Light leaks through my closed shutters.

When I look down, I find the coins I won. Someone has arranged them in a circle. And with them is a note:

It may be easier for you to imagine that you sold her, and did not lose her while gaming.

The coins are here. But three things, at least, are gone.

The clock-casing.

The flute.

My wife.

Nine: Sarah

The shore fell away from us, green as glass. A fine day, but I thought it would take a week of sun on my shoulders to make me feel truly dry after our night of rain and chill. Even the tavern bedstead had seemed damp and musty. Bill had insisted on sleeping on the floor, though I told him he could have half the mat. He did not wake until I nearly tripped on him, still confused by my own sleep. But he was not sorry that I had, for by the time I kicked him we could smell the roasting of my poor old cow.

I leaned over the stern. From so far away, the town looked like three stacked tiles: the pebbled beach, then the wood of the walls, and then the roofs, each clean as a slice of granite. I watched until distance dabbled the lines into mush.

"Edward slept powerfully deep," Mary said. She leaned backwards on the rail beside me, one hand gripping a shroud-line. Her hood was the same color as the sail. She'd cast it over her face as she lingered on the dock, loitering behind a fisher's shed with a bag and a clock-casing she held like a favorite pup. She had waited until all lines but one were cast off before scurrying across the pier and on board.

Probably there had been no need for such caution. The ferry's home was on the far, misty shore; Mary knew neither the captain nor his boy. There were no other passengers, only crates of nuts set about the deck. But I could not blame her for being nervous. I knew what it was like to fear capture.

The lake was calm as a blue eye. With the shore further by the moment, her bag and clock-case stowed safely below, the hood seemed to lay lighter on Mary's head, ready to slip off and show her milky skin. "He dropped into sleep so suddenly that I thought you'd killed him," she said. "What plant was it?"

"That, I'll not say. In any case it did not take very much of it. Even without the herb the ale might have put him out. It would have me, had I not sat so close to the window." It had been simple to spill ale from the sill without Keaton seeing. "I don't wonder that he went down so hard. He bore every year of his age like a stone."

She twisted a smile. "You mean to say that he's somewhat older than me."

I hadn't. But now that she said it, the thought of their bodies together sickened me. Keaton could talk about law and custom, and tutors, and responsibility. But in the end, wardship was a girl being given against her will: one more way to squander a life. I'd understood wardship from the moment she explained it to us—from the moment this girl, who could hardly have been twenty, told me that she was both a wife and less than one.

"He is," she went on. "And nothing in his character made me feel the difference in age any less. He loved his games, but only when gambling with men. In truth I could have beaten him or Lord Renault at chess, if they'd have played against a maiden."

"He was quick enough to play me."

"That was snakes, and for money." I nodded, understanding that chess was very different. Snakes could never be exalted enough for court.

The graying ferryman lifted a hand and called out. Soon a boat that could have been sister to our own slid by, crossing our wake, heading for the port we'd left. It glided smoothly as a swan on the gently lapping water.

Bill leaned, gagging, over the gunnel amidships. With a jerk of his head he was mightily, prodigiously sick. I'd been expecting that, though the water was calm, and the boat steady.

"Much more of that and he'll hollow himself," Mary said. "He had plenty to drink as well."

"He did," I said. But I knew that it was a single spoonful—given him in the hold, with murmurs and exhortations—that was making him sick. Bill heaved again, vomiting green into the lake.

"What could he have eaten that was colored so?" Mary asked. On her stomach her fingers were like a crouching spider.

I knew she was wondering if the beef had been bad. But the green was from the ground seeds in the oil I bade him drink. "It will begin your cleansing," I'd told him, and indeed there were things in the oil—woodruff, and angelica—that would help purify and strengthen his body. But the most of it was for the purging; and the purging must be fierce, enough to make him imagine that he might puke up thievery along with his morning bread. I'd hoped he would stay in the hold, and placed a bucket there for his use. *But perhaps it's better that he only fouls the lake,* I thought, seeing how much he was losing. I began to worry that Mary might question me further, and thought it would be best to seem unconcerned. "Did you learn chess at the court of wards?" I asked.

"I improved there. But I used to play with my mother. She had a small red table, by a window overlooking the garden. The top was just big enough for a single board. If we drank wine we'd put the glasses on the floor." She drew the hood from her face as though it was smothering, and looked at me uncertainly. I understood; we hadn't known each other long enough to share dear memories.

Bill spat, turned, and slid to the deck, holding his head with both hands. I had to fight to keep from going to him, and reminded myself that I'd given some men even stronger doses after they ate the wrong mushroom. The infusion left them weak, but alive. "Did the same ailment take both your parents?" I asked.

"My mother's yet alive." I looked at her. "Only my father died," she said. "He was never ill, or not badly—a willful steed threw him. In a way it threw her too, for she loved my father. But her body was sound, once she started eating again."

"Yet you were made a ward."

"She appealed to stop it. But the courts—the courts are the King's. They heard her and denied her."

Though the sun was bright I found myself in shadow. The white planes of the sails were blocked from view by a loosely netted fabric slung overhead. Wind flowed through and drew it taut.

The ferryboy tied off the last corner to the mast. "Now we're a pleasure boat," he said. "Though your friend doesn't seem to think it so." Bill sagged like a sack of iron filings.

"Does hanging a sheet make it a pleasure boat?" I asked.

"A roof does. This is all we have. But if you ladies take pleasure in it, who will say it won't do for a cabin?"

"Well, I do take pleasure in it," I said, and sat on a crate of walnuts. The shade was no improvement over the Lord's bright sun. But I appreciated the regard that hanging the netting showed, even if I knew from the ferryboy's probing eye that it would have stayed folded had Mary not been there. "Will you see to my donkey?" I asked. "My nephew would do it, but…" Bill moaned and wiped his mouth. He was curled up tightly as a mole. I reminded myself that worse was better, for the first cleansing at least. The ferryboy flipped a salute towards me and ducked below.

"Are you truly worried about the donkey?" Mary asked lightly. In truth it seemed unlikely that any trouble beyond water-sickness could strike such a craft on such a day. The lake-waters shimmered, seeming more likely to bear us dry to shore than drown us.

"Somewhat," I said. "Likely it was being below that made Bill so sick. The donkey could sicken too." I wanted to turn the talk back to her, to find out as much of her as I might before we traveled further. "We'll need a healthy beast to carry our gear, though you don't have very much to add to it."

She smiled ruefully, raised both hands to the shroud and hung on it; a careless, almost childlike pose. "Keaton told you my father was prosperous," she said. "He was. But only that. He just enjoyed pretending to be a small noble—wearing silken fashions, eating nutmeg and cloves. He could not refuse the chance of buying the monks' lands. Probably he imagined it to be a great manor, and that his heirs would one day crawl about the flagstones."

"There's a deal of anger in your voice."

"If he'd been content with his born condition, I'd be with my widowed mother. Now I wouldn't know where to begin looking for her. She had no family left. I'd rather be with her than fleeing from a joiner on a cock-boat." She crushed her lips together. Above her the blue netting rippled, went taut. "But I show little courtesy. Just now I cannot think of a better place to be. In faith I am grateful to you, Jane."

"My name is Sarah. His is Bill."

"Sarah." She rested her hands on my shoulders.

I have heard it said that memories come unbidden. But do they ever? More often the world about us calls up old memories, like a pronged holdfast dragging a fox from his den. Let there be the feel of flannel, and the smell of butter. Let a yellowhammer sing as you raise beer to your lips. Let violets bloom amid late snow. Your senses may then join in an unexpected duet, singing of a world you'd thought gone forever.

The water. Mary's steady eyes; her hands on my shoulders. The thought of a woman trapped, and running. Bill lay weak on the deck. And though I stood straight in the morning, I felt no less curled than he.

Cudman was Henry's lord and master. He sent Henry to buy small sugar and he asked to speak with me.

Northam harbor was caked over with geese, the air crammed with cawing, the docks streaked in shit. I walked with Henry's master, down the sandy shore. Men rowed out to take geese with nets and long clubs.

We walked in silence until we came to a niche in the rock, like a cave without a roof. Then Cudman took me, and forced me, and fucked me. His hands were on my neck. The rock dug into my back. I screamed. The geese hooted. The townsmen clubbed the geese.

When Cudman was gone I stayed there. I wanted only to stay there forever—to hide, and waste away. I thought I had nothing worth keeping. But Henry found me.

"What pains, love?"

I said, "Nothing." When he chuckled, I said it was his master. I said I had been forced. After that he was silent. From far down shore came the hum of feasting.

At last Henry slapped the seawall's wet stone. He said that he felt himself breached.

Mary's hands slipped to her side. She peered at me, head tilted. I shook myself back to the boat, the lake, the day.

"I'll take your gratitude, and thank you," I said. "But you're not to feel that you have any duty to me. I can easily spare a pennyworth of herb to help a stranger. We're all cut loose, and will need to find our own ways."

"But you have a destination," she said.

The Nene shore was fading, almost entirely sunk behind the horizon's haze. But in the midst of the nearly vanished town I thought I saw a pinprick flash—a lone, hot, crimson spark. I blinked and it was gone.

A flash off of windowglass, I told myself. *Or from a mirror, that shines red with the reflection from a lady's hat.* Surely Ridley could not have followed our trail through a forest so tossed by storm. But I did feel a sharp, horrid fear, as though the spark had nested below my heart.

"We all do," I said.

We had scarcely begun walking up the street from the boat when I realized that Mary was gone. I'd been too concerned about Bill to notice; his walk was weary and drained, like that of a man who wakes to find himself still drunk.

"It's hard to lose so much at once, I know," I said quietly. "Tonight I'll give something to restore you." Though I'd said nothing that might raise suspicion, I glanced to see if Mary had heard and found nothing by my shoulder but a tailor's shop-post.

She was still close to the boat side of the street, looking about as though she'd lost a prized songbird. She tucked the clock-case firmly beneath one arm, plunged a hand into her bag, and rummaged frantically about; she shook the bag beside her ear. Then she ran the short way to the ferry.

For a long moment I hesitated. I was tempted to continue on. Surely I owed her nothing; and another companion would not make the journey any easier, or safer. Still, the thought of leaving without a word rankled. "Stay here," I told Bill, and limped down the street.

A wagon delayed me, backing across the street so its driver could more easily unload his cages of chickens. When I reached the pier, Mary stood over where the ferryboy squatted, coiling ropes. She held the bag over his head. Both stopped talking when I approached. But of the two, Mary was the angrier—and the one who seemed more to resent my arrival.

"Have you lost something?" I asked her.

"Lost, no," she said.

"We don't lose cargo," said the ferryboy.

"What, then?"

"I found it," he said, so openly that for a moment I thought he was jesting.

"Found it in my bag, he means," Mary said.

"Well, return it, whatever it is," I said. "This place must have some law. You've already confessed. Should I call for a tipstaff?"

"Do as you want," he said. "We'll be gone as soon as we finish loading our cargo for Nene. I've found something I mean to keep, unless the *proper* owner finds me. I think he likely lives on the far shore. Perhaps I should ask there if anyone has lost a precious purse."

"Give it to me," Mary said with a hiss.

"No." He looked up without craft or anger. "There's not need to talk around it. If you call a tipstaff, I'll spread word in Nene of what I found, and what I know. Or my father will, should they bind me here for theft." Mary was almost unable to speak for anger; the ferryboy was lucky she did not have a club. But he knew he had the advantage. "Do you think me so stupid that I can't tell when a woman is running?" he said.

I thought of the traveler I saw before the storm came crashing;

I thought of the pinprick flash, and the taste of iron. I grabbed Mary by the arm and began pulling her away.

When we were well up the street, I asked her what he'd stolen. "It's fortunate that you thought my gratitude payment enough," she said.

Ten: Peter Turnip

He is tall as columns, clad in red, and he is my Mummer's brother. So she said after she opened up the door and melted there, her ice melting all in a moment when she saw him on the threshold. He held a spear with blue and yellow ribbons tied about it. When she stepped to him he swung the spear wide, then behind her as they embraced. He clung to her tight, and swung her 'round and 'round. The spear were behind her back as straight as rooks. When they spun and she faced me, again I drew back behind the cheat-flour barrel.

"Brother! Little brother," my Mummer said. "My little brother Samuel's come home," she said.

Behind her were the hawking of the chestnutter. I heard his prices clear. The nuts were cheap, for nuts sold in the spring are the old ones that fell before wintertime. In spring I may buy them. The chestnutter hawks his wares.

I think our door should always be wide on such bright days. Usually they keep it shut. Now the day passes in like a stranger. It touches on Dad's dour clamps, molds, and tongs, and on other things that may wrench metal or pry out rotting teeth.

There is a hole in the barrel I hide behind. When Mummer jounced the barrel, flour dusted through the hole, down the staves and onto me. Now I see weevils in the dust. They twist, wanting to be back in.

"Ten long years, since you passed through that door," Mummer says. I peek from behind the barrel and find that he has put her down.

"It has been longer than that since I was welcome to," he says joking. She slaps at his arm then. She drops her leather strap and it lies like a dead snake. With both hands she slaps his arms, and again she hugs him. Happy, they look at each other.

"This is Peter," she says. He is a great tall man, and I slink back further. I crept behind the barrel before her brother's knock stopped Mummer from chasing me. She struck the barrel, dusting cheat-flour on my head, then went to the door. Usually she would send *me*, but not when there are tears about my face, and my hair is dusted white with flour and maybe with weevils.

I like to open the door. Then there is air in the house, and light, until the caller is gone. Light turns our pewter to silver, making the gray seem glad and polished. But Dad usually works under a candle's close glow. The door's kept shut against children who might nab his wares. They might snatch the pewter men, and horses, and elephants, and then run.

"You will not be so rude," Mummer says. She picks up her strap of leather. Again it turns lively, swinging from her hand. At the sight of it, the bands it bit across my legs again begin to sting.

Before Samuel came, she said I would not shirk my duty. She told me to come to her, for the blows she'd give me were less than Dad would give, were he to find that I'd not yet gone for water. But I would rather risk a terrible beating than go gladly to the first one offered.

I shrink back. I am smaller then. The barrel shields more of me.

"This *cannot* be Peter," says the man Samuel, his voice filled with wonder. He walks into sight across the room, and puts aside his spear. As he nears the barrel he sweeps open his cloak. His clothing is stitched with fur—strips and patches of fur, fox pelt and gray hides cut to cover old holes. One pelt is like that of the mottled coney-rabbit

I took from Windham Howley's cages. I unhooked the caging door, took the coney up by the scruff and haunches, and took it away with me in a sack. The one I took were a doe. Windham uses his coneys for stewing and for fur. He kills them with a plain rod swung fast as though to strike a ball into a field. The watching coneys scream. But where I took the doe to look at close there were no other coneys, none to see and scream.

Once twisted about her legs, the wires held her still and spread before me. I worked her open with thick scissors. I wanted to see how long she would live, with her insides thus opened to the air.

After a while she only whimpered. But she lived longer than I'd guessed she could. Even after I used the needles she lived a little time. I washed Dad's scissors well and put them back. There were not enough wire for him to miss.

Later, I took the doe to the pile of sawdust behind Windham's house, and I made a hole there. I left her in the hole. Sawdust clumped wherever there were blood, and I piled more sawdust on top. I thought Windham might find her after she'd begun to rot. I liked to think of that. Once he scolded me unjustly—I never did throw stones at his son.

I still have a strip of the coney's soft pelt. I keep it in a box I have, along with an old scutching knife that Dad threw away.

"It *can* be Peter, for there is no ruder child in Christendom, nor a less obedient one. Such a manner," Mummer says. Her hands are strong as the vices that Dad uses to bend metal and they rest on her crossed arms. Her voice is still angry. But now I think that her anger is becoming play. I am glad that her younger brother has come. Though Mummer's hair is gray and spilled about, as always when she's in the house, it no longer seems so wild.

"You did not often speak of Christ when I was last here," says Samuel. He bends before the workbench, bends at the waist as though bowing. He reaches out a hand to me.

"You vanish for ten years, and come back to tell me how I once spoke, and of what, and of who..." Her voice is breadknives. Outside the chestnutter has wheeled his coal-cart close to the door. He sings and hawks. *A dainty, a dainty, a toothsome for your dear one.*

Before me is Samuel's hand, strong, open, held out as though to grip a man's hand. There is regard in his blue eyes. "My name is Samuel Ridley," he says.

"I am Peter Turnip," I say. I am shamed to hear my voice so quiet.

But he takes my hand, and holds it strong in his. "Peter, it is a pleasure of my life to meet my nephew."

When Dad comes home from the peat-cutter, where he has bought blocks of moss to burn beneath his pewter-molds, Mummer has calmed and is happy. She has said that I may stay up late at table, for that would please her brother. She has decided that her anger at him were only play and she has filled the table full with bread, and chestnuts, and butter, and in the center is a roasted chicken trussed about with sausage.

When Dad comes home he heaves a bale of peat before him, and drops it in the corner. He turns to me and then he sees Samuel. He shakes his head. He greets my Mummer's brother with words, but without a bow or an embrace. He takes the great seat at table. Soon the three of us join him there.

Hour after hour Samuel tells us of his life. He has a plenty of tales: he has seen wondrous things. As we listen Mummer clucks with laughter. I listen close. Dad listens silently. Mostly Samuel Ridley speaks to Mummer, and to me. He eats slowly but steady, cracking nuts by the dozen, biting chicken until he's ate twice as much as Dad might.

He has been over seas to mountain countries, where men fought with spears over herds of goats. "That's one of those spears, in the corner," he says.

It leans behind the bale of peat. Its ribbons are sadly still, for with the door closed again there is no draft.

"It was known as Biter," Sam Ridley says. "Because of the ill it did its enemies. The old owner had goats by the thousands. He also had thirty wives."

"Fetch it," he says to me. I go. Without looking at Dad or waiting to hear what he will say I go. A place is stained dark on the haft, at the height of my face, where Sam Ridley must grip it. It were used to battle for mutton, and pastures, and wives. The wood is ash, he tells me. He took it from the broken-toothed owner, who had sought to take Sam's trading-wares and life.

"Have you used it to battle?" I try. I will not look to see Dad's pleasure or lack of it.

Samuel Ridley chuckles. "When last I saw you," he says, "you were only a poppet."

Samuel Ridley has been to war at sea. He has serviced great guns as the deck shattered about him. The enemy's balls struck the mast and filled the air with splinters. The splinters flayed and killed many men. The battle was fought at night, in rain driving purple hard. He and other brave ones packed powder tight around their bellies, to keep it dry and ready. "English bellies make a fine furnace," he says. "The powder we kept close to our skin never failed us."

But one unlucky ball did strike his friend, on the gut, where he'd hid powder. The man turned to fire, screaming until he was ashes. There was blood in the scuppers, and down the flanks of their ship, as they closed with their foe and boarded. Sam leapt into combat in night as black as blindness. Some of his fellows fell between the hulls, and were crushed there, but Samuel caught lines that cut his palm to the bone. Then by the flashing of powder Sam did great and merciless bloodwork.

He holds his hands to throw shadows against the wall. He knots and twists his fingers, making shadows like battling boats.

"When I last saw you, you were only a pup," he says. "Nothing like the man I see before me now," he says to me.

"A *man* is obedient," Dad says, and bites a leg of chicken.

Sam Ridley says that he has heard that said before. "Have you ever seen an ape?" he asks me. I shake my head. Then Sam Ridley speaks of apes. As he does, I see that something slouches in the corner. This is not the shadows, it is his words alone that bring it, and it is more real than the shadows. It has rank, rowled hair, and arms long enough to reach the ground. It eats cut fruit in gulps. It eats a baby. "Your eyes are great as an ape's," Sam Ridley proclaims.

"Have you ever seen a peacock?" he asks. "The Moors keep

them in their courts." Soon where the ape slumped a tail spreads, like a hand of cards—cards tall as soldiers, bright as rainbows.

He asks if I have seen a tusked bear.

"A tusked bear. If you ever saw one yourself, may I be struck down," says Mummer. I want to tell her that she is wrong. She may be struck down. I want to tell her that there are such things, and that Sam Ridley has seen them. For until her words turned it to dust there were a murderous horned thing behind her, and only Sam Ridley could have shown it to me so clear.

But Sam Ridley is not harried by Mummer, his sister. He chews his bread and meat, looking about our home. His eyes catch on cobwebs, and on a pile of dust I were meant to sweep up. When he sees the dirt I am shamed for my neglect. "This is not so prosperous a place as when I left," he says at last.

"Samuel," she says, smiling but also warning. If she had a strap she might wave it at his head, in play that would not be play.

"You didn't stitch your clothes with fur when you were last here, either," says Dad.

"Different countries, different fashions. A shame that those here have stayed so much the same."

"You were English enough when you left," Dad says.

"There's more than one country hidden within England, too. Every man willing to go further than his own workshop knows it," Sam Ridley answers.

"I will not have this," Mummer says.

"I mean nothing by it, Becca," says Samuel. He winks at me. I sit listening, hands knitted before my open mouth. Pulling wire has cut my hands in many places, leaving them scarry. And they are burned from sparks off of peat and coal. Sam Ridley looks at them. When he speaks again his voice is newly sharpened. "But I say it is a shame that there is no longer such profit in pewter doll's-chalices and poppet-goblets for the play castles of lordly boys."

"It was better when they were in fashion," Dad admits.

"Wonderful play, the lordly boys must have had." But Sam Ridley's face says that he did not think their play wonderful. He is angered at the thought of the chalices and goblets, the dolls and poppets, the castles.

"You never had patience to learn the work," Dad says.

But he is wrong. It is plain to me that Sam Ridley is angered that he were once told to make such things. "I never had patience to whore myself to it," he says. Then he stretches, easy as an eagle spreading open his wings. One hand tips his mug. Ale sloshes to the table. The puddle spreads, then begins dripping down through cracks between the boards.

This morning I also left a patch of dirt under the table. Now it will be wet. I will need a cloth to clean it.

Dad has not moved a stitch. Sam begs pardon for dirtying our house. Mummer is again frozen, as she were before she opened the door and saw him there. Samuel pours himself another ale. I hold my breath, and I watch him, and I think it is a good thing that he left pewter-smithing behind. He might have bent his own tools from his very might. It is a wonder that any would cross him. It is a wonder that Dad will.

Dad taps the table. Half a silent minute he fills with his tapping. "Peter. Look at this man, your uncle," he says. "You see an honest enough face." And though my uncle had grown dour, I do. For when Dad says this, Samuel at once looks like a picture of a saint. He makes his eyes go warm and welcoming. His beard seems a hedge, that he keeps trimmed more from courtesy than vanity. His lips are soft and kind.

Mummer laughs and claps her hands. Dad looks less pleased. "You *see* an honest face, but the man beneath it will change whenever he has a mind to."

Maybe that is true. But there is also truth in the change in Sam's face. He is like the players who, during festivals, play at being virtues—Faith and Prudence and Loyalty.

"You were always good at such play," Mummer says. "Let's have one with a voice. Give us Mistress Wentworth."

"*Goodwife* Wentworth," he says. Then his face dwindles like a spider crouching. He stands with great effort, the strength leached from his legs. He needs both hands to push him up from table. With my mouth open I watch him. "A *Mistress* is any woman," he says, his voice thin and old and womanly. "You might offer the name *Mistress* to a whore. I an *Goodwife* Wentworth. You will keep that to mind, for so long as I offer you lessons. Now. Attend. *The Boy who Yearns will come to Grief. The Boy who Gives not Risks a Thief.*"

Mummer laughs and laughs. "Oh, she was a good teacher at least," she says.

"Not so good that you remember much that she taught you," says Dad.

"I remember some," she says. "Any letters Peter has, I've taught him."

"I remember it all," says Samuel. "I remember the room where she would teach us. There was quilt-work draped there. We could smell the tallower across the way. Thinking back on it, it seems strange that there was a tallower's on the second floor."

"It did not seem strange then," Mummer said.

"No. Of course we were children."

"Letters are a fine thing," Dad says. I have not studied as much as he would like.

"Fine in their place?" Sam Ridley asks.

"Give us our old Dad," Mummer says quietly.

Sam Ridley sits. He thinks. Then his mouth firms. His face seems to grow, like a moon becoming full all at once. "To your tasks," he says. His voice is deep, like one booming in a cask. "The food you eat should fuel better work than you've given me," he says. "If you want bread, you'll work the bellows better."

I know this is my grandfather. Though he lived only until I were seven, that was not very many years ago. Sam Ridley has caught the dullness of his eye. The dullness must have been there many years, if Sam Ridley saw it before he left.

"Your father was a wise craftsman," Dad says with certainty.

"He had some skill. Here is one more for you," Sam Ridley says. He looks at Dad and his face goes crinkled. His voice wavers like sparrows. "You'd be helpless to stop me, cockless man," he says. He laughs.

Dad does not. "Who was that," he says.

"A woman I find hard to forget." Sam Ridley looks at me. "Maybe you will meet her one day, also." At that I glow, for I hear the invitation. He has asked me to go with him and I know I will, if I can.

But Dad has heard it too. "And how would he come to meet her," he says. He is swollen up like a toad.

"No offense was meant," Ridley says.

"It was given."

"We do not need this!" says Mummer. But I do not think she looks truly fearful. There may be some hope in her, as there surely is in me. Dad's a window. Today he may be broke open.

"It's true, I don't need any man to say that my son will be taking to the fucking road," he says. "To bed, Peter."

Sam Ridley looks at me. His eyes give me permission. I stay.

"Peter, *to bed*." My Dad's face is red, now blackening.

"He's old, to be spoken to so," Sam Ridley says.

"Will you not shut your mouth!" Mummer cries. But Dad's hand is already in my hair. He smashes my nose to the table and for a time I see nothing but red, and black. When the dark passes there is blood on my hands.

Ridley has his spear. He is standing and Dad is standing. They stand against each other, like cocks before they're loosed. Mummer cries like a cat.

Dad leaps. But Sam Ridley is quicker and he swings the spear down. Rap, and Dad is down.

I do not think him badly hurt. That blow would not have killed even a coney. But Mummer cries out and rushes to Dad. Afore she reaches him, Sam Ridley raises a foot high. He kicks Dad once with his heel. He kicks again, on the ribs. This time I hear a crack. Dad makes no sound for he is out.

Then Mummer is on the floor beside my Dad. But she does not give him care, for she is spitting her hate at us. We might ask her, Sam Ridley and I, what happened to her hopes of seeing a battle. We might ask her why she wanted it.

"I will go," Sam Ridley says. His eyes are aboil. He is asking me.

I nod.

"Sister, I will care for him well."

"Take him, then," she cries. "Take him, and damned to you both." But we are already out to the street. The last words are cut off by the closing door. Her voice is now quiet as the chestnutter's distant hawking.

Our pewter-house is near by to the water. Without a word between us we walk to the river. There are candles on every other house, then on every fourth. Near to the river the breeze is stronger, and house-candles less common. But the moon is strong on the water. My belly glows warmly and we walk on the street beside the river. Sometimes I want to skip, but I do not.

After a time I ask why he kicked twice.

"You are not sorry I did." I shake my head for I am not. Nor am I surprised that he knows it. "You would have done the same yourself." I do not nod. "You would have," he says with certainty, and tussles me. I lower my chin and smile secret. I wipe the blood away from my mouth.

Sam Ridley looks upriver, towards the bridge. Water shoots below it, fast and hard, into our side of the river. It makes crescents I see by torches and lamps all hanging from houses along the bridge's span.

I have never rode a boat under the bridge but I have wanted to. Once I clung to a board and jumped in, and so was carried under, through the arches and echoing. A waterman grabbed me out before I drowned. A boat would be nobler, I think.

"I do not hate your father," Sam Ridley says at last. "But I would not have him follow us. Nor would you. I know it well."

"Better that he not," I say.

"You will not return to him," he says.

Staying away does not seem a horrible fate, and I say so.

"It is not, I can tell you. I left home in much the same manner, after a certain man scorned me, as your father did you."

We walk for the bridge. "You hate the woman you played at being," I say, for I can think of nothing else to say.

"I do, boy." He stops. "I do, Peter. You are old to be called a boy. I will not do so again."

At this I feel a swelling in me. I nod, taking his sorrys.

A moment later I swell still more. For he says, "I have a tale for you, and then a question. If we are to travel in company, I must know your mind." His cloak is open, blowing grandly in the night.

He tells me of a witchy woman, who came to a city she wished to destroy. When I asked why she would want the city dead, he says, "Malice only." She wanted to destroy the city, and the king who ruled there. So she cast curses on the place, hoping the king would grow weak. Then he might be cast down by his own people. "No weak king can truly be called king," he says. "A true king answers insults to his name, or his home."

"How, then," he asks me, "shall the king show his people he is strong? That he deserves to be called lord?"

"He should bring them the witch," I say carefully.

"And why?"

That puzzles me. "That they may see her face, and know she has been caught."

"Her face, yes," he says. He waits. I cannot think of the answer he desires. "But how is he to carry her back, and show them her face?" he says at last. "She cannot be carried very far. She will refuse to walk. The king travels without beasts of burden. How shall he show the witch's face to the people?"

A light breaks for me. "But must they see her whole body?"

He is much pleased. "They do not need to." As we've stood there by the river more people have passed us, perhaps ten. It is odd to have so many by the river, so late. Sam Ridley leans close, his words meant for me only. He whispers. "*I will have her head.*"

I laugh to have gotten the riddle right. "Why should they need to see all of her?"

"Why indeed?"

It is funnier and funnier. "They only need to see that she's been caught."

"They need no more than that."

"You will have her head."

"We will," he says, and his eyes are still and clear. I see down through them, to where his heart beats in water.

"*We* will have her head!"

"We will!"

From far off through the night I hear the beating of drums. Sam Ridley starts and draws me close. He looks about us. The people carry sacks and chests. They are in too much a hurry for people abroad at night.

Sam Ridley draws back from a stooped woman as though her touch might kill him. The distant drums beat, they beat and beat. Aside an alley, one man stumbles and falls. Far away a voice is crying, calling, crying.

Sam Ridley listens. He hears; his face tightens. Then he seizes my arm and runs. He drags me to run beside.

As we near the bridge a longboat shoots under its arches. The river is slurried by torch and lantern, the boat is black and beautiful. The hull sends circles through the crescents on the water. The stroking of the rudder will make more, I know, for I've often watched from the bridge.

Eleven: Bill

All about me straw is billowed. It itches on this neck, sprouts from these ears. There are a thousand itching pricks, everywhere this skin is not clothed. But a mound of straw is a wondrous nest for when I'm taken sick, and this morning's cleansing convulsed me. All the beef I puked into the lake, before it could make me strong. And after that I could not sup, or drink anything but a sip of weakest beer. Even that beer needs warming before I can drink it. I warm it in a jug, nestled beside the donkey in his paddock.

When we came to the barn it was still day. Birds flew startled about the rafters when we pulled the wagon in. Then the wagonman left us, going through a yard of chickens to his house. I made to stroke the donkey, rubbing him down after a long day on a boat and walking. I leaned on his flank, thinking I might rest there.

But Sarah took the cloth from me. She would not let me work.

Soon the wagonman brought back the jug of beer. He talked with Sarah and laughed with Mary. I put the jug beside the donkey. Then I went to another stall and lay back on hay. The wagonman stood near to Mary, on his toes. He talked painful loud. *It will not be very far to the barges, tomorrow*, he said.

When he was gone again I dug down into the fodder. The barn has half a score of stalls. Two are used by horses and one now holds our donkey. Two more are empty. The rest are heaped with stored hay. I made a trench in one of those. The trench was deep where these feet would go, shallow for this head.

You'll smother if you dig much deeper, Sarah said.

So I finished digging. I lay in the trench, and pulled in straw after me, until I was a grub. The straw is thick over these legs, this body—but on this face is only scattered lightly, for concealment.

I knew the straw was fresh before I ever lay down. Barns have often been nests for me. No one need invite you to sleep in a barn. I know to smell straw before digging, so even at night I may know which is fresh, and which has been bedding for stock. Though this itches, it is sweet. Around me it grows warm.

I need thank you, Mary said today, after we'd left the lake. She put her arms about me. I pushed her back, these hands on her hips. *You've turned rose-red*, she said laughing. *I never knew I had such thorns.*

Hush that, Sarah said then. Mary smiled and loosed me. Never did I touch her, all the rest of the day, except when helping her into the wagon. Her cloak smelled of flowerbuds.

Now the time for sleep has come. But I lay quiet, weak from cleansing, listening to Mary, and to Sarah healing friend. Though this body wants sleep, their talk keeps me wakeful. I watch them through a fistworth of straw, no thicker than hair fallen over my face. One can hide behind straw, but it must not be too much.

Sarah and Mary talk of food. While they do I will not sleep. The potion Sarah gave me did not go straight to sin. Along the way it took roasted cow and even toasted eggs. It spilled all to the lake. It left me weak, and this body hollow.

But Sarah and Mary have force left to them after the long journey. They have appetite. *Pork-pie*, comes one longing voice.

Apple-pies, comes the other. *I'd have sweet not savory.*

Pears.

Aged cheese. Cheshire cheese.

Brawn.

Oh! Simmered brawn, and cloves.

Plain bread and butter should be enough.

Both hum in agreement. These eyes squeeze shut, as though that might also close these ears. But through eyelids comes a pink flashing. The wagonman comes from the house, walking through the yard with a lantern. The lantern shines through gaps in the barn's slats, and onto my thin straw. Flash, flash. Flash.

Hinges whine, and then the glow is steady. I shift, and I peek. The wagonman is there. Under the lantern his face is strong. *Here's a loaf for you, and butter,* he says.

They laugh to startle him. *Are you in league with spirits? You seem to have heard us from afar,* Sarah says.

Or do you know a person's wishes? Mary asks.

Neither thing, I think, the wagonman says uncertainly.

He has a basket. He rests the lantern on the edge of the wagon's bed and he opens the basket on the ground. *I thought you'd be hungry*, he says. *I was myself, after the day's travels.*

I'm grateful, Sarah says. *I did not mean for my jest to prick you. But we were just speaking of bread, and how happy a loaf would make us.*

The wagonman has one. Also a crock, that I think will hold white butter.

Just what we had wanted.

Shall we try another? Another wish, I mean, Mary says. *Our first was answered so quickly.*

No harm, Sarah says, *unless we ask expecting the wish to be answered. But I do wish that this man's hospitality might be repaid.*

For myself, Mary says, *I wish that he will get his deserved rewards for carrying us so far.*

I wish sleep might come, I say. I speak quietly, but I do so when all have fallen quiet, and so they hear me. All laugh.

I had nearly forgotten that there were three of you, the wagonman says.

Has he been awake this whole while? Mary asks.

As like as not, Sarah says. *Are you hungry yet, Bill?*

I've a crust and butter here, says the wagonman.

I moan. These knees draw up closer. *He's been sick*, Sarah says.

Sick as I've ever seen, says Mary. *It's a wonder he has any flesh left on him.*

She knows little of me. I have more flesh than I did this morning. Some fingers have become mine. At dawn they belonged to the dead.

I wiggle one finger. I wiggle two.

Well, I'll to the house. The wife will want me. Here I am, with two fine ladies and only one other man.

Stay, Mary says. *You haven't been here so long that she'll miss you yet.*

Maybe not, he says, and sits down close to her, out of my sight. *Where are you bound for?*

A fine question, Mary says.

And the answer?

London, Sarah says.

Have you family there?

I lived there, before the plague.

And wish to return, after such horror? Your early memories of the place must be fine ones.

They are, she says. *Do you often carry passengers?*

When people ask me to. There's far more money in carrying freight from the ferries. Still, I don't often let passengers ride for nothing.

They are quiet. Then Sarah says: *Listen. I thought I heard a voice calling. Are there any about, except for your wife?*

No.

It's her, then.

Well, I'll go to her, he says. He stands, stretches, and takes his lantern.

Our thanks for supper.

Welcome to it, he says. The door closes. Again the light flashes. Then it is dark. In the dark the straw seems cooler.

You might have shown him more courtesy than that, Mary says.

When did you hear me be rude?

Come.

All right, Sarah says. *There was more rudeness in your kind words than my blunt ones. Showing such kindness to a man shows little to his wife.*

I wanted only to offer my thanks.

Well, there are many ways to do so.

So Roslyn said, when for the first time she reached for me. *There are many ways to do this.* When I think of that first time, and the times after, my burrow warms.

No woman had even taken me as Roslyn did. No woman has since. In these hands her hair was black, black as the dark room where I lay with her. She opened over me. She was on me and around me and over me.

At that memory, this yard lengthens between these thighs. This flesh is coming hot.

I will not be called whore, Mary says.

The only one who has spoken that word is you.

I think of Roslyn, who was soft and sometimes hot. These hands creep. But there are voices, voices coming through the straw in quick dispute.

This yard heats more, begins to slick. When she was on me Roslyn was a wave in tall grass

But Sarah's voice is brash. It fills my ears more fully than does the straw. Her voice is shaped like her. Roslyn's hair is hers. These hands stroke this yard, and there is Sarah before me. This is a hateful thing. I cannot stop seeing her. She is nearly a relation, this is sin. But these palms will move when they will move. It does not matter that three fingers have been cleansed.

There is thievery and there is lust. I am near crying and Sarah and Mary quarrel and Sarah is on me when I spend, and cry out.

Bill?

Away there, I say. This head pushes down. I want straw to blind these eyes.

Are you ill? Sarah's weight shifts the straw on one side of me.

Better to leave me be.

But her hands are above me. They are above my face, stroking gently, as though the straw was this skin. *Not cleansed*, I say.

I did not say you would be, yet.

Sin full, still.

No. Not cleansed. But not that.

Less full of something *than he was a moment ago*, Mary says. At my side the straw that holds Sarah shifts, and lightens. It grows heavy again. She is back.

I do not believe that you've sinned, she says.

But she does not know these thoughts, that swirl and mob and take.

Twelve: Sarah

Bill was sorrowful; so shamed. It was the deepest shame I'd seen in a man since Robert Leach's crimes were discovered. And Robert had much more reason to feel disgraced. He'd loosed his seed on a cow, rubbing himself against her warm flank until he spent. That was a great crime, though not a deadly one, as swiving an animal would have been. Any man who did that would be hung, then thrown into a pit with the bodies of the beasts he'd loved.

Robert was only stocked, then exiled. The shame he showed, as he walked from town for the last time, was very much like to what I heard in Bill, felt in Bill.

Though I could feel Bill beside me, the straw made his features blank. There was something familiar in that. It came to me with a snap—sometimes a babe will be born with a caul, a plane of pale skin that covers most of the head and all of the face. Leaning over Bill reminded me of the village left behind, and of cauls taken to bury under cribs in earthen jars.

For an instant I seemed to see the cauled babes before me: the healthy ones that might be seers, the weak that grew up strong, and the ones who went to the Lord within weeks of dropping from their mother's sea. Most of the infants I caught were strong enough. But it was the third sort I best remembered.

"I do not believe you have sinned," I said. Bill seemed to choke. He had told me of some other sins, other woes. But this one he would keep to himself.

"I know you for a trustworthy man," I tried. He stayed still. But this time his stillness was not to conceal himself; he was listening. Though I knew it would only make things worse, I wished I could touch his skin. "I know you for a brave companion," I said. "And a trusty one. I've felt safer on the road since we met than I ever did before."

"Does he need comforting? Perhaps he only wants to sleep," Mary said. I tensed. I wanted to tell her that he was no babe; we did not need to imagine what he might want, as though he was too young to speak.

But I had seen the straw as a caul. I had had a flashing vision of babes. I'd offered Bill words as I might have milk, had I been his wet-nurse. I wondered at myself.

There would be time later to think over the right or wrong of it, I decided. Just then, he needed solace. "There are those who would take my gear, if they found me alone," I said. "Your being with me means I need not fear that."

He listened. But I felt no further loosening.

"There are those who would seek advantage over an old woman, traveling alone," I said. I could not seem to find the right words; I could not tell him that I'd told more than one girl how to cure herself of greensickness. I saw nothing wrong with that in woman or in man. "You would never…"

He shuddered, as though laid in ice.

I'd been about to say that he would never allow such a thing. "You should never do that," I said, confused.

"Never," he said.

"No. Never." Through the straw, I felt his hands move to his trunk. He wrapped himself in a light embrace. Soon he breathed evenly; I knew that he slept.

* * *

Often, after fleeing from Northam, Henry and I had hid in a loft or stable. The barn, and the things in it—the rustle of the resting team, the smell of feed and bedding, the draft that no stable is without, the flap of an owl stretching before beginning the hunt—seemed familiar, even after almost twoscore years.

On my last night in Monkshead, I had thought of Henry. Now, as I drifted between sleep and waking, his hands might have been on me again; gentle but leathered, with that one hard place between thumb and first finger where he held his walking staff. I turned with longing. I raised my chin to meet him.

The owl beat out through a hole in the roof and settled into silent flight. I rolled, seeking a soft place where I might fall away into sleep. But Henry was there, as much a living presence as ever since his death. I thought of what lay ahead; I talked with Henry about what I should do.

His voice was weak, and wavering—not from uncertainty, but from unbridgeable distance. *What is it that so dismays you?*

Bill's sorrow.

He can bear that.

He can, if it is his own sorrow. I do not know that it is. Someone might have burdened him with it. He seems so terribly heavy.

But he could bear his own sins.

He could, I think.

Henry said: *Let me bear my own burdens.*

Though the night was warm, I shivered as though snowbound. *When ever have I not?*

Who have you told about Northam?

Melode. Melode, my friend in Monkshead. I told Melode.

What did you tell her?

That we went to Cudman's room, the two of us together, at night when all the town seemed empty. You brought a fishing knife. You pressed it to Cudman's throat, until there was a prick of blood and he woke. I bound his hands and feet. I crammed his mouth with a ratty old shirt-sleeve. You carried him across the street, down the wooden steps to the beach, then under the pier. Together we lifted him by the feet and pressed his legs against a piling. His hair swept on the sand. I tied his feet as you held him. I cut away his clothes and left him naked. Then we left him there. The water was rising and we left him there. We stood on the pier until we knew it was done.

Did we.

We did. We did.

Did we?

Stop this. I am going to Northam. Stop your questions.

What did you do there?

Stop. Leave me alone. Go. Go from here. Go.

At last he was silent. Then I lay alone. I waited for dawn.

Thirteen: Peter Turnip

The folk passing us are as busy and fearful as coneys. They walk with white lips; when not shouting at their children, their dogs, they hold their breath. Only Sam Ridley is firm of heart, there where he watches from the bank rising beside the river. They are rabbits, he the falcon.

We sit upon a bank of grass and clover. On one side of the bank is the river, slipping through the sun. On the other is the road. It is chock of folk and fear. It has been so since the cries came, crying *Plague. Plague. To your homes. Plague.*

We sit. We watch.

"I have chased her over roads and through the forest, and across a wave-swept lake—a lake deep enough for beasties, blue enough for nymphs," Sam Ridley says idly. Though he said we would only take a moment's rest upon the bank, it has been hours since we sat down here amid white and yellow flowers.

Further up the road the people are all stopped, suddenly, as though there is a wall to stop them. But there is no wall—there are soldiers. Some have muskets, and coils of smoking match. Others have horses. The people stop and quaver there.

Once I saw a man with a looking-glass catching starlings. He shone the light cleverly, to confuse the birds. The starlings loved the light—they flew crying before the glass as the man's companion threw nets. I see the people here and think of starlings.

Some of the soldiers afoot wear glinting helmets. Some have bound back their rusty hair with tied cloths. All stand in a line behind the guns. Each gun's barrel rests upon a pole. Thus the barrels are as high as the people's chests.

"And I've chased her downriver—that same river that flowed by your old house, and that we see before us now," he says. He talks as though telling stories. He did not call my old house *home*, though his voice tripped as he chose the word. He chose right. That house were never more than a house to me. "Already I have chased her league on league. I am sure she is near, whether hiding or still in flight."

I place pewter soldiers on the grass before me. These are different from those on the road, these are clad head to toe in armor, and they carry sword and shield. When Sam Ridley saw those down road he gestured me to the high bank. "We will stay here until a good chance comes," he says. Then he gave me the four pewter soldiers. I set them on the grass and make them fight. I do not know when Sam Ridley nabbed them from Dad's stores. Were there not living soldiers on the road to watch, I would never look up from the metal ones.

Amid the shouting crowd one man howls to split his throat. Others throw clods at the soldiers. But they are excited, and too far away, and they miss.

The soldiers shine like a looking glass. The people cannot leave. Behind them their town has turned deadly. Here, a net may drop on them. But this net will be made of leaden balls, screaming from long iron barrels. It may happen soon. I move my toys about but I watch close. Sam Ridley watches close.

Moments after we began running we heard the town's alarm bell, like axes crashing. "A horrid chance for us," Sam Ridley said. He hoped the alarm was for fire, and not disease. But he feared it was for plague. That would bring panic, and useless greed and looting mobs. Then soldiers might come to stop the mobs, but that would only make things bloodier. Even a rumor of plague could do that much. Thus we ran ahead of the few families we'd seen. We ran silently, along the river, on streets like black glass.

The soldiers' banners dance in the river breeze. "You will see a massacre if those fools try to force passage," Sam Ridley says. "Soldiers are ashamed to betray their own people. So when they do, they are vicious as judges.

"She will come to me," he says. "Her crimes bind us together. The river will bring her to me, as surely as it would carry a twig, or bit of mossy bark. We will come to each other, she and I, and also you. If somehow she has outpaced us, then we will follow the river as we hunt. In the end our eyes will gaff her. And there will be no escaping from that."

Perhaps fivescore folk have come here and become starlings. Sometimes they move for the muskets, so close that I cannot see the soldiers' still faces—only the banners, and the mobbing folk. "The soldiers won't step aside for commoners," Sam Ridley says lazily. "Only nobles could command that." He chews a bit of hairy grass until the stem is flat, then twists the stem to pick at his teeth. He has none of the angry humors of those that pass us. He chews his grass and blows it to the air. He leaves his face in the sun. He is a man with an eye for the good chance.

"There is no greater crime than setting a fire," he says after a while. "It gorges on anything that men can build. It makes men's labors into dust, and their dreams into nonsense. Fire is a treason to all—those scorched, but also those spared."

A girl in a blue cape passes. She carries a cage of ringed pigeons. Then there is an old man, sitting limply in a barrow, pushed by a boy who is perhaps his grandson. There are people in flatshoes and cloppers, people with naked feet a-hurrying.

Last night we walked quick as beetles. "There is no reason to stay in a plagued city," Sam Ridley said. "Often, only a few will be touched. Or it may not be the plague at all. There is another sickness that looks much the same, though it does not kill. It is only the plague's eunuch twin. But we will not chance that. When the plague does strike, it can come on as hard as a flood."

That were all he said, about the plague. Since then he has

spoken more of fire. He's told me of how it makes skin to noxious crumbs, how it makes human flesh to ham. It turns cities to hot dead pollen.

"In an hour, even the staunchest housepost can burn frail and white," he says now. "Men's greatest hopes turn cinder-black. Their faith chars."

In the crowd a fellow falls. He struggles to his feet and strikes about as though blindfolded. Another man strikes him from behind. In the middle of the crowd they fight. Other men fight too, crushing fists into each other.

Beside the crowd there is a field, open as a door. "Why don't they try to run around?" I ask.

Sam Ridley tosses pebbles like jack-stones. "Look there and you will see," he says. And I do, for two families have begun to steal away from the mob and across the open land. They walk quickly and with purpose. But before they have gone two spans, there is a thundering from behind the gunners. More soldiers ride on horses, galloping for the families, one mounted soldier for every man and woman and babe. Their manes flame, their hooves crash in dirt.

I hold my breath and wait for the killing. But before the horses reach them, the fathers turn as though to gather up their families. They run from the mounted soldiers, back the way they came. They run to the road.

Since we sat we have shared a heel of bread, and a knob of cheese, and half an onion cut up with his knife. Sam Ridley takes a bite of onion and watches the horses, as he might watch combat between poppets. "Stay here if things go badly," he says. "Wait until I call you."

A man like a bulldog passes, with a brace of sons like bull pups. They carry blades meant for butchering and they walk past us towards the mob. Sam Ridley sits up, to better see what will come of this. But before the men have gone very far, I hear the sound of horses.

They come from the town we left— three men, with two horses. The one on foot runs to keep abreast of the mounts. The two who ride hold themselves as stiff as churches. One is surely a lord, wealthy as gold, for there is gold trimming on his coat, and a feather in his cap. Were the feather made of metal, surely it would also be gold. This lord would think silver beneath him. Probably he has never touched pewter—maybe even his servants have not. His brows are creased. His lips are tense but fat, like a frog's.

"Good sire, my lord, a word," Sam Ridley says. Somehow he is in the road, though I did not see him stand or go there. He bows deeply, holding the spear-haft crosswise on his chest, taking off his hat to loose his yellow hair. He stands athwart the road, the spear's shaft crossing it from edge to edge as he bows. If the horses are to pass they must go around, or else he must give way, or else they must ride over him.

"Stand aside," the man on foot says. He has red boots, badly scuffed from trotting.

The shouts of the crowd rise—the bulldog man has joined them. He is not a man who will easily be turned back. He moves for the soldiers. Many follow behind him.

"I ask only a word, if your lordship will condescend to hear me," Sam Ridley says. The lord shifts nervously atop his mount. Sam Ridley speaks only to him.

"Stand aside, Japers. Or else risk a broken head," the man on foot says. There are red wolves sewn into the cloths that drape down the flanks of the lord's horse and the man on foot is thinner than the wolves. I think that he will let Sam Ridley speak, if he is wise.

"There are few men so great that they have no need of more servants," Sam Ridley says.

"This is one of those few, fool."

When I hear that insult, I expect Sam Ridley to strike the man down. I wait to see him bleed. It will take only one blow, so strong is Sam Ridley. I want to see the insult to him undone.

But they do not fight. For behind us is a bang, and another bang. Then a string of bangs, loud as though I'm struck by lightning. The battle is come.

A few people run forward. Most fall back like blown feathers. The shots hit a woman, an old woman I think—bent like a half-fist before the balls jerked her, jerked her as though she hung on a rope. The crowd's howling turns to a general scream. The soldiers reload, fast as though building dikes.

I know how they feel—I know the fear of seeing the people come on. For some of the mob is running towards us. Some of them have seen the lord and his mounts. They course towards where Sam Ridley stands, their eyes gone wild and blazing.

"My Lord, we must go," the man on foot screeches. The lord's horse forges forth, his companions follow; Sam Ridley sweeps his spear aside, letting them pass. They are past him but they do not go towards the running mob or towards the soldiers. They ride up the grassy bank, towards me.

I snatch up my toys and crawl down the bank's other side, over yellow flowers and towards the flowing water. When I know the horses are not coming, I rise to a crouch. I climb the bank carefully, and I peer over the top. The mobbers have swarmed about the horses. Though one horse paws and bucks it cannot move forward. The lord's horse has been seized by the bridle. He gives a squealing whinny, held in place by the bit. The lord tries to draw his sword but the people have his arm. They have the sword's pommel.

His companion has his sword out. He strikes here and there, helpless to aim as his mount rears. I see one man hit across the face. When he turns to me I see that one eye is gone, his nose half slashed away.

The man on foot tries to drag a man away. But another swings a chunk of wood to crash on his head. Once he falls I cannot see him. I wish to join the mobbers, and beat him for the insults he offered to Sam Ridley. Then Sam is there himself.

He is through them like a hawk, raising his spear. But he does not stab the man who wronged him. He stabs it into the back of a man clinging to the lord's thigh. The lord is croaking fear. His companion crows with panic.

Sam Ridley leans until his target is speared through. Pain sounds different than fear. It sounds less doubtful.

Sam Ridley pulls the point free and swings the haft like a

sickle. A flight of ringed pigeons flaps and flutters overhead, making for brake and dale.

Now finally come soldiers with halberds. Perhaps they are heartened to see Sam Ridley's great courage. The mobbers fall back. They run. My heart thumps, it cries the victory. Only one man here truly has a nose for blood, a want and willingness for it, and that is my lovey uncle and dear friend.

I stay in my crouch and wait to be called, as he bade me do. I think from this moment he will be the lord's companion, and I with him. When the soldiers stand aside for the lord, they will for us as well. For this has been the good chance, and Sam Ridley has seized it.

Fourteen: Bill

Again I have me my own bed. When we came here the bed was only a frame, that had been left forgotten in what Sarah called an alcove. At dawn the window glowed dimly under thick, gathered dust. Now we've wiped the dust off of glass and furnishings. The bedstead is stacked with blankets, enough to make a firm mat.

The woman who lives here, and works in the kitchen, gave us the blankets. *No one lives in the dorm house*, she said. *None have for year on year. Now it's where we toss our broken stuff.*

That is true, for half of the great dorm room is piled high with rubbish. There are musty clothes, and chipped, green-glass bottles with square sides. There are spindles, and enough broken spinning wheels to make a hill. There is wood for chairs and tables. There are pieces of clay pots. It rises near to the roof, all the rubbish the woman has tossed here in the years she has served. I am glad she throws bones from the kitchen window, or the room would stink, and be home to packs of rats.

Alcoves line both walls. Each alcove is arched, each has its own window. There were broken dressing-screens among the rubbish. We propped them in front of the open alcoves, and so made rooms.

By the ceiling more windows glimmer, letting in light. The light here would be grand, if not for the dust that sticks and dims the higher panes.

I pick about the rubbish, scavenging for string. Sarah is on a high ladder. She has a wet rag on a stick. Working there she is beautiful. She is sure and graceful. When she is done with a pane it shines clearer, though still dirty on the outside. Then she comes down the ladder, climbing jaggedly. She slides the ladder along the wall. But the floor there is uneven. The ladder wobbles.

Come, Bill, and aid me, she says. When I hold the ladder firm she raises her good leg, sets it, and brings the wounded one to set beside. Then she holds tight and raises her good leg to the next rung, before her bad one can betray her. *Hold fast*, she says without looking, and climbs to the top.

When she is there she looks down. *After this we should eat*, she says. *It's almost noon, and tonight you should take more cleansing. I believe you are near to shaking some ill-will loose.*

I lean to help hold the ladder down firmly. I lean also because I am still weary. This belly is still tender, and I still weak from loss of food. I have eaten in the past two days. But only bread, and not much.

Still I am glad for the cleansing. I have not thought of lust since the haystack. When I see Sarah, I think only that she is a woman of beauty and determination, though very much older than I.

The window she cleans is high as the black banners by the river, that told us of the plague.

The banners draped from poles set beside the water. I knew them for a dread warning. They were twins to the black angles, cut from cloth, that hung from the steepled church where I dug graves. After the plague came, I could not work at the church for there were to be no burials there. Banners on the steeple warned strangers not to seek entrance to our town.

Black banners, black sores. The sores came quickly, in a single night. They swelled and filled until they burst, their juice running out over skin. In their room Mam and Da cried out. Beside them Ron my brother cried out also. He mewled from his place on the floor, where he lay on buffing-cloth. The room was no longer a place for Mam and Da alone, but for any taken ill.

Sally never let me in to see them. But before the church stopped taking bodies, I saw a plenty of people killed by plague. I saw their gray and blasted skin.

The three of them cried out spikes, they cried out harsh as hedgehogs, until the plague angel bumped wings on the windows of their room. He called out their ghosts. One by one he left them dead. *It was quick*, Sally said.

Please to God that it is so quick for us, Dory said after some small time.

Sally shushed her then, *shhhh*. I sat leaning on a stack of forms for molding gutters, crying for the pain in this heart. Sally and Dory cried no less, nor felt the losses less. No longer would Mam and Da and Ron greet us, or make ale warm and spicy, or joke, or play at Hare and Hound, or even tell me to haul gutters. But I thought it was wrong to say that it had been quick. Their first pains came on a Sunday. It was four days later before the plague angel called them—called their ghosts out over embers and through the chimney, with all the other smoke.

Those four days were a year. They were chains and boulders.

The night Da died, he being the last of them to die, the three of us yet living lay together on the floor. I had my own sleeping mat of linen, stuffed with grass. When I turned it rustled, like breeze blowing. But I would not use it. I lay on the wood with my sisters, so we could better mourn. None of us had much slept since plague came to our house. We had feared losing Mam, and Da, and Ron—losing so much of our blood at once. Now I feared the angel might still tap me, or either of the other two. Those he had already touched lay in their room, hard and cold and dead.

I cried. Sally and Dory spoke in soft voices. They were tired and they spoke as though I was not there.

We should make for the country, Dory said.

We should have, said Sally.

We should now, Dory said. *There must be a way out. The city cannot be wholly sealed.*

Silently I said *Yes* to that. I wanted to walk, and fly from that horrid place. When these eyes closed I saw pictures of Da's dying, and Mam's, and Ron's, as they swole up and twisted and their skin bubbled and filled.

Coal, Dory said later. She was looking from the gray window and she laughed, cooing.

When their skin opened it was full of flaked coal, she said. She scratched at her own arm. Sally bade her hush.

I saw Mam only in the first hours. She looked trapped, a cat in a crate. When she told me Good Night it was good-bye. After that I never saw her breathe.

Da was quiet after she died. Sally said he had sunk into the plague's sleep. Later he woke, and moaned. Sally'd pulled Mam off onto the floor, onto a sheet, and wrapped her there. I thought of Da and his empty bed.

Then all was silent, and stayed so. There would be no more moans, gentle but needy, when Mam and Da were in their room alone. There'd be no screams, as when brother Ron was birthed. When the three were dead and wrapped I helped put them back on the bed, and under covers.

Sally said, *It's too late to think of leaving. There will be soldiers on all the roads, sealing the city. Da used to talk about it.*

He'd never seen it happen, Dory said. *He'd never seen a plague.*

But he'd heard about them, and how many men have died trying to flee the illness. If we were going to leave, we should have done so days ago.

Well I wish we had, Dory said.

Hush that, said Sally, and she had begun to cry. *Hush that. That we should have left them. That we should leave them now, now that they are dead.*

Do you imagine that they'd wish for us to join them in death, just so we could first care for their bodies? Dory said. *They'll go to the fire or the pit, whether or not we're here to see it done.*

Hearing her, so grievous and weary, I thought that she might have chosen to join them herself, if she could have done so without pain. If it was easy, she might add her own body to those waiting for the bodyman.

Both my sisters cried, and I cried quiet. Finally both of them slept. Then I rose, and crept from the room. I crept to the ladder in the hallway, that led to the hatch to the roof. The roof was shingled, and sloped sharply down. Should I slip and slide, there was nothing to catch me save for the chimneys, and the flats of sawdust set above the chimneys where Dory would grow beans. I sat atop the roof's peak. Below me were the flats of sprouting beans and then the city. Sally often told me tales of oceans that killed mariners, and held monsters. The city was like that.

The moon was bright and full. It glowed down on my roof and all the roofs about. Lit so, the roofs were like the rafts I once made from bark, when rains sent rivulets through town. But these rafts held still. If they drifted, they did so slower than these eyes could see. This sea was frozen.

Past the tilted houses was the red glow of the fire where sentinels burned whatever cats they could catch, and the bodies of folk found dead in the street. Smoke rose into the moonlight like a long cloud. There was the stiff, slow clank of the bodyman's bell. This body was heavy, these limbs like fisher's weights.

But I felt me most alive. The plague angel was fickle, choosing three to take from a house of six. Maybe he would still beat his wings above me. Maybe this mouth would be crammed with his feathers, and these ears hear his summoning call. But the moon was bright on the rafting roofs. The air in this throat was clear save for a whisper of smoke. Five streets distant, black banners hung from the church.

When plague stabbed the city, Master Wolf told me I had best stay home. If the sickness took hold, there would be no time nor place to bury all those it killed. There would be no graves but the general one, at the city's edge, where all might be dropped like kindling.

The banners hung slack. But there was no need for banners, so long as soldiers sealed the place.

After a time the clank of the bodyman's bell crept close. His cartwheels jolted on the street. Soon a fellow answered his soft call.

I slid then to the chimney, laying flat for safety. I held to the chimney and looked down. Below me there were heads, moving to and fro, and a cart, and there was a body. The body was wrapped in a sheet. I could not see the face but it was Roslyn. It had her form. It sagged between two men.

Then breath froze in this throat. I had thought to cry for the bodyman but I did not. Though their deaths were grievous, it seemed worse still that Mam and Da and brother Ron should go in the same wagon with Roslyn. There was the family and there was her. Those were two different things. I could not lose both together. I could not lose them all at once.

All that night I stayed on the rooftop. And all the month after we stayed in those rooms, Sally and Dory and I, until the plague angel had departed. I heard many men on the street calling our city blessed. It had been lightly brushed by the winged man. Not so very many had died. But though Sally was yet living, and Dory, and I, I did not think any of us passed over.

Then one day ago we came to the banners by the river, and all of the banners were black. This stomach dropped away. But I said to myself that I did not need to fear. Banners are often hung for joy in the way they flip so lightly in the wind. I should hold steady. All would likely be safe.

But the bargeman shouted orders to his boy. For long miles the barge had drifted beside us, held close to shore with a rope guided by the boy and his horse. The bargeman shouted and the boy guided the horse away from the river, drawing the barge to the riverbank. There were reeds there, and flowers, and grass. There was no place for the barge to dock.

I heard the bargeman's fear and I felt his fear. I moved to the donkey and I hugged his neck. I needed to touch flesh.

What are we to do? Mary asked.

We could dry some toad, Sarah said. The answer was biting. I thought she was naming a charm she had no faith in, to silence Mary.

The banners hung in sunlight. Trees do not know when they

are garbed. When hung with banners they seem more naked than before.

We need to seek sanctuary, said the lady—my Sarah.

Mary said yes to that. They talked about where we might go. But I could not take comfort in hopes of sanctuary. Should the plague angel choose you, he is certain to bear you away, and bruise your soul when he does. Hiding is a jest. Even as the ladies parlayed he might have beat above us, his wings clear as glass, his body hid by glare of noonday sun.

From far downriver came sounds of a storm. But it was a small storm, and all in one place, and the sky was purest blue.

The ladies stopped and listened. Now the crashing sounded like a hunt.

I know a place, Mary said.

Well, then, said Sarah.

But for a time Mary said nothing. *I will not trust a woman who will not trust me*, she said at last. Sarah looked at me then, her mouth tight. She took Mary by the elbow. She drew her away from the donkey, and from me.

The sky was clear but felt clouded. I hugged to the donkey for comfort. It was something. Flesh is flesh. Finally Sarah came to me and said *We are decided. There is a place we may go to hide. We may even find some comfort there. Mary knows where there is an old monastery. Such places are spacious, and the one Mary knows of has been made into a lord's country house. We can go there for as long as is needed.*

Come, Bill, she told me. She guided me from the donkey. But as she stepped, one of the boy's dogs danced about her feet, leaping with joy to see his master work so desperately as he made the barge fast. The dog danced and I felt Sarah slip. I felt it as though it was this knee that wrenched.

She fell to earth, and in fury lashed at the dog with her crutch. She struck only the weedy dirt. When the cur ran Sarah threw the crutch after. I went and tried to lift her. I wanted her to stand again. She should stride proudly.

But there was no more walking for her then. We helped her to the donkey, and set off on the path the same way we had come.

As we started, Sarah said—quiet as razors, her words not meant for these ears—that Mary need not have spoken so innocently of our destination.

Thus we walked to this place, with its garden and kitchen and dorm-house and church. In the garden there is a lane for playing bowls. Sarah says I must cut it clean of weeds so we can have a tourney. I have often played at bowls, in alleys or town squares, but never on a path so thin and straight as the one here. The thistles overgrowing it stung these hands.

Sarah looked at the gardens. *It's been a great long while since the potherbs here were tended*, she said. *Since they were shown the sun.*

Now she stands atop the ladder, cleaning windows with her rag.

The brambled trail that led us here was as overgrown as the bowls-lane. Mary led us to where it split from the barge-path, passing unseen under thorn and vine. Mary leaned into briars and pushed them aside. Then the trail was plain as a well.

Before we plunged into it Mary stopped. She chewed her lip. *Anybody might have hung black banners. Even boys at play.*

Sarah bent far forward on her donkey's neck, so branches would not tear her from her seat. *That would be an earnest game*, she said. *Men may be killed for hanging such warnings in jest.*

You cannot know, Mary said. *Perhaps there's no need for sanctuary.*

That was not thunder we heard, said Sarah. *Nor a dozen men gone fowling. The city has been sealed. Try to walk back to it yourself, if you're so sure of safety. You'll be turned back by soldiers, but by that time you'll have drawn near to the ill. Who can know how close is too close? You know nothing of plague.*

But I thought that I am no babe, and should not be spoken to as she does to Mary. I know about plague.

Mary made no answer, but she had a deal to say. Her face looked like this tongue feels, when I bite it to keep from talking. I did not care what she would do, wanting only to go far from plague, and to take Sarah with me, away through this tunnel of thorns.

At last Mary nodded. One by one we moved on. The door of hedging closed behind us. These feet flighted, as though they had become moths. Each was drawn towards hidden fire.

The woman here, our host, is kind. Her skin makes me think of sweet, waiting dough. She saw Mary and fell towards her. She took her in embrace.

And so you are welcomed, Sarah said, and smiled.

She always will be. She always will, said the woman our host. Then she took Mary away with her, to her own sleeping chamber, away from all eyes and all ears.

I went to the yard, that Sarah called the cloister garth. I watched chickens scratch and strut. The yard is a square. Three of the square's sides are the walls of buildings, the church and two other houses. The fourth is made of the low trees we came from. Along the walls is a stone walk, with columns broken and crumbling. The yard is grown high with weeds.

Deep in the trees, beside a brook, is the kitchen. Mary's mother lives there. Close to the kitchen is the reredorter latrine. It overhangs the brook, to wash away filth. Here and there in the trees are more houses. Some of their roofs are gone. I do not know what those houses are for.

There is strength here. Though walls and doorways crumble, there is a firm notion of where things should be. There are runty trees, and vines. But strong minds thought of this place.

When we came there were workmen about the cloister garth, come for their dinner from the fields. One of them was sketching. Dory would sketch, drawing birds on the hearth with a burned stick, and I watched the workman sketch.

To speed the time, he said when he saw me watching. *I have already drawn the garth, and the buildings that form it.*

Close by, another fellow sat lazily. He did not watch the man drawing but they were together. The first drew with a sharp black stick and the second stayed near, like a red dog minding her pup. On the ground before the sketching man was a paper, drawn over with trees and a bridged river. It was a wonder to see.

This was not a very great monastery, he said. *Only a daughter-house, not nearly as large as a priory. Probably it held eight monks, or maybe twelve.*

His coal-stick sped. *Might I see*, I asked him.

When it's done, he said. His companion looked at me and was amused. I was not and I went to watch the chickens. I hoped to follow the birds, and come upon their treasured eggs.

Sarah had been sitting, rubbing her leg, and waiting. After a while she crutched her way behind the sketching-man. I watched a hen, brown as cloaks. She pecked and scratched. Two turtle-doves flew beside her, and pecked about her feet.

Then Sarah came. She was angry and she led me to the dorm. *Where monks once slept*, she said. But when monks were here the place was surely kept more orderly. Then there was no rubbish, no buttons of greening metal cast about the floor.

Sarah reaches high. She cleans the window's highest curve. When I look back the trash seems lessened, the mound shrunk down under force of sun.

The door opens. The sketching man comes to us, carrying a cloth. *Apples*, he says. *One barrel from last season is still good, and there's a fine roaster in the kitchen. It's like six anchors stacked upon each other. You stick an apple on each point. There's one for each of us here.*

Heat has wrinkled the apples' skins, and softened their flesh. They steam in his cloth packet.

Sarah has finished her scrubbing. Still she stays there, looking out at whatever prospect she can see. I think she may see beyond the cloister garth. She may see past the stone houses, and the trees that hem them. She may see pastured sheep and then distant hills.

The man offers me an apple. But I wait until Sarah climbs down before loosing these hands, and taking it.

Though this stomach is raw I gird, and taste his gift. The apple is touched with honey. That makes it sweet as any I have ate.

Fifteen: Sarah

The steam of roasted apples rose to where I wiped a window, clouding what I'd already cleaned, fogging from view the courtyard of hemlock, and nettles, and cats. I ran my thumb along a pane. But of course the fruit could not send steam so high; only my mind made the glass seem clouded. For a long moment I rested my forehead against the window, making a circle with my breath.

Outside, the courtyard was like a sickly heart, throbbing softly in the afternoon. What better place could there be to recall old things? What worse place to be burdened by them? Ancient walls crumbling, yet thick with vines; antique gardens, their herbs snared by darnel. Had the garth been properly tended it would have been like a map, carefully plotting a monk's ideas about what the world had once been and could be again. But by the time I came there with Bill and Mary, the garden had long lain hidden under creeper and thorn. Now the monk's house was nothing but a rich man's occasional home—a place for leisure, and maybe forgetfulness.

Seeing the condition of the gardens, I knew the master of the place must be a man of slight contemplation. He also lacked kindness, and grace, if Mary could be believed. For the monastery's master was

Lord Renault, who she had been placed in wardship with before he gambled her away to Edward Keaton. *Perhaps*, I thought, *it is not so strange that he enjoys this place as it is. A man who would so toy with a young woman would see only profit in a monks' home gone to ruin, and in the sheep-meadows beyond.*

Beside the nave wall a pair of tabby kittens wrestled, like a restless dream amid the courtyard's slumber. Nearby a sleek gray cat skulked, unnoticed, under naked rose-branches. He crouched, then sprang into the contest, knocking the kittens about like pins before again scuttling for his sanctuary. The tabbies seemed not to know what had broken them apart. They soon returned to their mock combat, a-teeter on their hind legs, batting at each other's paws as cornflower butterflies drifted aimlessly above.

I wiped the moisture of my breath from the window, knowing that the boy standing below me had brought the apples as an apology. But though he was ignorant of how he'd wounded me, that did not mean that I felt the wound any less, or found it easier to forgive him.

It can be cruel to see oneself through another's eyes. I felt myself weighed, measured, branded with strange signs. It was not just for me to blame him; surely he did not realize how he had offended me, or why that pain might burn more brightly even than the smoldering ache of my knee. And it spoke well of him that he would offer an apology not because he understood precisely what he had done, but simply because I was hurt. I could ease his mind with a glance.

But I did feel that the fellow had struck me. I did not look down.

On the morning before, we had walked along a barge-path, talking lightly to ease the awkwardness of our night in the barn. We talked of ballads we once knew; we sang them badly. We recalled our earliest memories. Mary's was the taste of a peach, cut up by her father, fed to her with his gentle fingers. Bill's was of reaching for his door-latch and having his hand snatched quickly away. Mine was the time that Helen, my good sister, showed me how to make cowslip-tossies. She taught me how to cut a slit into a stem and draw another stem through, weaving until the yellow blossoms made a hollow sphere. We spun the golden circles against an April sky.

Warm spring sunlight flooded the barge-path. The green of far hills was leavened by the whiteness of what I knew must be a wealth of daisies. On the river a barge of flax-bales drifted, slow as a meditative man. A boy walked the path before us, passing under the regular shadows of elms, paced by the tread of a stout horse drawing the barge's tow-rope. Horse and boy were flanked by a brace of dogs; they panted, licking at nothing, often going to lap at the river. The bank was covered in clover, and cowslip—I smiled—and in daffodils. There were dandelions thick enough to seem mats. Sometimes there was a stump among the flowers, always cut low enough to let the tow-rope pass over. Though the river was sluggish as a sated idler on a feast-day, the horse merely paced the barge, letting the tow-rope sag behind.

But always there was Ridley. Even as I laughed and sang I knew that he would not have forgotten me. I had often told myself that I could not know whether the man on the road had been him, and the flash of crimson at the lakeshore could have been a glazier showing off fancy wares. Nonetheless I was sure. I might sing lustily, I might tell old tales. But always there was Ridley's tread, soft and sultry and horrible. I might act careless, but could not leave my dread behind.

I tried to think of something else—of Helen's face, so clear to me even after scores of years: her eyes, set wide as a cat's below the hair she let fall free when at leisure. But as I thought of her, and of the tossy, its blooms turning slowly in old sunlight, I realized that on the day we first wove flowers I would not have been more than four or five. She was only two years older than me; but the girl I remembered was perhaps sixteen. My memory of the tossies had stolen the face of an older Helen, from years later. Surely, had she been only six, she could not have leapt so lightly over cowslip and clover; surely she could not so easily have swept me up, that I might fling the tossy further, and watch it spin in air. Surely it was only my love for her that made it seem that she could have, and did.

Love, yes. But it seemed a betrayal. I wanted to recall Helen as she had been in truth; and now that I knew how young she must have been, trying to remember her only cut up her face like puzzle-pieces. As her lips lost age and fullness, becoming more innocent and less alluring, they also skewed—going tilted, off balance. Her nose turned as though broken. Trying to make her hair the white-blonde of childhood only left it bleached and colorless. The very edges of her face blurred, leaving it without form.

I retreated, trying to retrieve the face I'd first pictured. I would take what my memory offered, whether it was truth or lie. But at that moment, at least, even Helen's grown likeness was lost to me, and my heart was left in shadow. I took up a cowslip blossom and handed it to Mary. "Here's one of those we'd make to tossies," I said.

She placed a sprig behind her ear. "And one I'll make to a crown," she said.

"A coronet, at the least." As we walked I craned my neck, as though to crack out the kinks left by the night in the straw. But the truth is that I was trying to pull myself back into the day. *To lose a loved one's face for a short time is a common thing*, I told myself. *It means nothing.*

From time to time the boy bent for a pebble, then held it on his palm and flicked it with a finger, sending his dogs scratching and tumbling in their haste to reach it. We cried out mock-plaintively to the bargeman. We prayed that he might allow us to rest on his bales of flax, and so ride to the city in ease and comfort. Bill danced playfully, frighting a flight of pigeons from the brush.

For a moment the bargeman turned from his rail, looking at us as he might at buzzing, crimson bastard-flies. When he turned back down river he started as though struck by a snake. He howled for the boy to make the barge fast. It was then that I saw the brace of black pendants hanging from the elms.

We needed a place to take shelter; we needed it then. And Mary said she knew of such a place. But during all her laughter that day, she had held on to her resentment of the night before. For she refused to tell me where the place was, unless I named my own destination. "I will not trust a woman who will not trust me," she said.

I drew her from Bill then, as though the name must remain

secret even from him. For a moment I thought of lying to her. But then I heard myself telling her the truth, quickly and easily, naming Northam as though flinging her a tossy or other trifle. I wanted, maybe, for it to seem a pitiful detail, something that she might do with what she wished. More than that, I wanted to feel myself that it was a mere pittance, that could be taken or given or cast aside without consequence. Still, I felt as soon as I had said it that it had been a mistake.

But it was done. Later I would wonder if I had needed to name any place at all. Maybe the fear in my face would have been enough to convince Mary to abandon her lie, and to confess that she knew where to find her mother. For in truth she may have needed little convincing to seek the monastery. She had wanted only an excuse.

In the courtyard, a parcel of workmen lay complacent as badgers among waist-high weeds, and broken tiles, and shards of glass. Only a few courageous stands of rosemary allowed me to recognize the yard as an herbary. The workmen chewed dinners of bread, and plain cheese. When Mary's mother rushed from the kitchens, holding her skirts as she ran to take her daughter in a half-willing embrace, the workers watched with as little wonder as they did the chickens pecking through the garth.

"You find yourself welcome," I said.

"Aye she always will. She always will," Mary's mother said. She held Mary with one hand on the back of her head, pressing their foreheads together to touch. Mary tugged against the embrace, lightly as a fish testing a line. But when her mother took her by the hands, and made to lead her towards the kitchen, she seemed to go gladly. They disappeared into the small, stone cookhouse, through one of the few doors that was not nearly overgrown behind a hedge. I smiled to myself.

Most of the workmen seemed dull as gray stones. But one fellow was drawing on a board propped across his knees. He sat on a broken footwagon, long since overturned and covered by creepers.

I sat heavily behind him in the piers of a ruined window. I

had not yet seen his face, he being too intent on his work. But the cloth of his jacket was a faded purple, a richer shade than field labor would permit one to buy. I watched him curiously.

Bill followed a chicken, imitating its gait, far too close to it if he meant to find its nest. When his quarry twitched to look at him he turned his face to the sky, as though he only wanted to know the weather.

I leaned against the stone window frame, watching the fellow draw. His subject was a single figure, sketched in charcoal; thin, almost gaunt, at first seeming stiff and mannered as though posed. But as I looked closer I began to see, within the frozen posture, a sad, tottering quality. A mournfulness, and even a hint of pride. It was both awkward and convincing; I recognized Bill.

I waited until he had finished, meaning to offer my compliments. Making a likeness of any part of the world is difficult; this fellow knew precisely what traits to exaggerate and what to diminish, helping an observer to see the truth of a man or a thing. But before I could praise him he paused, and wrote along the base of the drawing: *A Man, Careless of Himself.*

A chill passed over me. For a moment I was in my haystack, sleepless, hearing Henry's whisper: *Let me bear my own burdens.*

"He is not so," I said.

The boy turned, seeming surprised at my sharpness. "Surely anyone might recognize him from this," he said. One workman, who had seemed asleep, tilted his head back slightly. Under the brim of his hat, I could make out his eyes among reddish whiskers—lazy, curious, amused.

"I mean the label," I said.

He looked back to he paper. "Well, I did not mean that he is dangerous. At least not to others. I was only trying to mark a certain quality of mind."

"Why must you add a note to the drawing at all?" I asked. But I began to feel ridiculous, confronting him over such a thing. He was only an idly sketching boy. One by one, the workmen were standing. No doubt it was to head to the sheep-meadow, but I imagined it was for a better look at me. Without another word to the boy I walked for Bill, as steadily as I could. Then I took him by the elbow and led him to the dormitory, that he might no longer serve as a callous fellow's model.

A Man Careless of Himself. The words returned to me as I worked, cleaning dust from the windows to show the overgrown courtyard and then the sheep-meadow beyond. For a time I saw nothing, not even the clearing glass; I was so angry that sometimes I had to stop myself from punching through the pane and into open air.

I hated to see a man ill-prepared to defend himself so insulted. And I hated to think of that same squinting gaze turned on me, where it might see nothing but a limping, failing widow. But I had to confess that neither of those things had enraged me. All the world need not love my friend before I could, and I was, I hoped, beyond caring what a flighty boy thought of me. No, what fed my rage was fear—fear that the boy might be right.

I could not know what Bill would do. Oh, I could trust him. I could love him. But I could never know. And if I could never know, how could I presume to offer him cleansing?

No, I told myself. *I offer him no cleansing. I am not so presumptuous as that. I offer only freedom from pollution, a pollution that exists only because he believes in it. I only try to undo the crimes of the people who have fed him.*

I tried to concentrate on the windows. Every pane was warped, and streaked with bubbles inside; any grandeur came from the sheer amount of glass rather than its quality. *The glass,* I thought. *Watch the glass. Mind your work.*

Again the window clouded before my breath. Then it seemed, for an instant, that I saw Henry in the garth—watching, waiting, smiling with one hand on his hip. When I wiped all clean there was nothing but the kittens, dozing after their play. But now I could hear him, soft, insistent, as clear as when I was in the barn. *Let me bear my own burdens.*

Since I'd lost him I sometimes felt that seeing was the only sense I had left; touch had no delight, scent no savor. What reason was there to feel or smell if I would never stroke his hair, or breathe in the air of him above me? Measured against his memory, the living world sometimes seemed a vacant, sagged snakeskin. Sometimes I felt that God made the world like a field of flowers as a jest, simply so we'd have a ready place to drop our corpses.

Let me have my own deeds, Henry said.

I do.

Do you dream?

I do.

And of what do you dream?

I dream of Cudman, after we killed him. I dream of him screaming, gnashing at minnows and at picking crabs, howling for vengeance. I dream of his drowned shouts sending bubbles to break the surface.

A lovely dream. Perhaps it is a comfort. Now tell me what is true.

I took a deep breath; I closed my eyes. For the first time in years, waking or in slumber, I let myself think of what I'd truly done that night. *The truth. Very well. The truth is that I waited on the dark street, beside a naked shore and a sea that seemed a pit, for you to return from Cudman's chamber. When you did you were hunched as though over a small, heavy chest; but you carried nothing. You told me you had slashed Cudman's throat, then driven your knife through his heart. You showed me the blood on your hands and sleeves. I embraced you and could see, over your shoulder, the first soft burn of sunrise on the harbor. Then you were leading me from the sea and from the geese's daybreak cries, leading me along the road that led through Northam and away from it. I walked through the city as though for the first time, weeping, holding you, through dismal, slowly brightening streets. At night, I could believe that all of it—the rape, the killing, our flight—was nothing but a poison dream; that the nightmare had coated her claws with venom before she stabbed me. But at dawn, all was real. Dawn made walls gray and shapeless as the night's last candles guttered and went out. We stumbled past fallen timbers, and cats dragging salmon guts. A baker, sweaty from his oven, leaned and took a moment of ease in the clammy morn; he leered at what he imagined had caused my tears. I thought everyone in the city a stranger; lovers were strangers to those they laid with, murderers strangers to those they killed. As we passed through the city, I wept—*

I wept for you, and I wept in gratitude for what you had done. I wept in horror at how the act bound us. I wept that I had not done it myself. Finally we passed from the crouching streets, and into the blind plains beyond. That is what happened.

That truth was not so fine as my dreams of murder; my part was not so satisfying. In the truth there was nothing like the smell of the ocean splashing at our feet. Or the look of fear in Cudman's eyes. Or the feel of rough rope and justice in my hand. There was only a slaughter behind closed doors; a killing I was ashamed to have allowed another to perform. When I opened my eyes Henry was gone, body and voice.

When I thought of the crime I had let Henry commit, I would have given my life to have killed Cudman myself. And I would have given it to have Henry truly back, for one small, precious moment, so I could tell him I was sorry.

I was sorry for allowing him to kill for me, yes, of course for that. It was a burden he should never have carried on his own shoulders. But I was sorry also because, though I always loved him as best I could, there was one thing that made that love uncertain. If I had been given the choice of giving up that night in Northam, all of it—both Henry's arms and Cudman's hands—if I could have freed myself of my worst memories, and in doing so lose all the years with the dearest man I ever knew, what would I choose? I had no ready answer.

Below me Bill stood watching, his mouth opened like a sparrow's, with more care for my aged and worthless body than I felt myself. He would not loose the ladder to take an apple, though I knew how badly he must want one after so much purging. A swell of love for him smoothed the frantic whitecaps in my heart.

Beside him was the boy. To him my silence had probably seemed only a discourteous moment. *A gift*, I thought, *is a gift. An apology is an apology.* I took one last look out beyond the garth walls, at the sheep-meadows and hills that the plague would keep us from for weeks. Then I climbed down to the boy, and to the man who suddenly seemed my lone reason for breathing.

Sixteen: Bill

The boy I saw drawing is Randall. His friend with the red and ragged beard is Thomas. They bring me with them to their beehives beside the wooded stream. The stream runs rapidly, dancing over rocks and pebbles that waver clearly under the water. Beside the stream are purple flowers blooming, blooming high as these shoulders, the blossoms clumping like spearheads. Above those tall flowers is a smooth bank covered with what the boys say is wild thyme. *There's no better honey than that from thyme*, Thomas said, and Randall squeezed his arm.

The trees here are tall, with smooth dark leaves. Their yellow flowers droop as though longing for the damp ground. But where the wild thyme grows there are few trees, so that at noon as it is now the sun can find the bank of herbs. Above the thyme, bees fly—here humming, there touching petals lightly, flying through sunlight and the shadows of the high dark leaves.

I see all this because there is nothing else for me to do. Randall asked me if I wished to come with them, and I said *Yes*. Then I followed them across the small footbridge. Randall had a pail, Thomas a smudgepot that trailed smoke. *We think the monks once kept bees, here*, Randall said as we crossed the water. *But we found this swarm in a hollow tree. It took a good deal of smoke to make them docile enough to take to the new hive. But now I think they're happy enough with it.* That was when Thomas said the best honey was from wild thyme, making me think of honey, and how I should be happy with a taste.

But now that I am here there is nothing for me to do but watch. So I do, as the boys climb the bank towards their hive. It is a simple, square box, with legs to hold it two feet off the ground against the damp. Only the blurred air about it shows that it is a home for bees, that feed from this forest's flowers.

The boys kneel beside the hive with their pail and the smudgepot filled with coals and damping straw. The smudgepot smokes under the hive. I wish I had brought thick clothes, or a blanket, to drape over me. This may anger the swarm, making them an army. But Thomas has no thick clothes. Nor does Randall. They seem to trust in the smoke, and in their own gentle movements.

Slowly, slowly Thomas removes the top from the box-hive. Slowly, slowly, Randall leans beside him. Together they lift a dripping slat from the hive. Most of it is pale and golden, but even from so far away I can see clumps that must be drowsing bees. The boys tap the clumps gently, dropping them back into the hive. Then they angle the slat of honeycomb over their wide pail. Randall takes a blade from his belt. Slowly, slowly he scrapes. At last the honey runs.

It gladdens me to think of eating honey. In the past few days some strength has returned to me. Sarah says I am near ready for another purging, and I think the honey will make me entirely so. I sit on the bank then lay back, gently so the bees have time to fly away. Lying there I smell crushed thyme, and also some smoke. Far overhead sunlight plays in branches.

After a while I stretch my neck to look up the bank, for I think they will soon be done. Thomas is feeding Randall honey. He dips his fingers in the pail, and brings his fingers that now drip raw and golden to the other's mouth. Randall holds Thomas by the wrist until the honey has surely melted all away. I close my eyes, and for a while listen to the water, and the wind, and the bees.

Seventeen: Sarah

Dirt caked beneath my nails. The earth went proud about my fingers. There was still some good hidden in the gardens; fruits and herbs planted many years before still struggled to find the day. But they were tangled, constrained, chained by other plants—even by their own growth. Balm battled hemlock; rue strove against thistle; parsley lay faded under crowflower. An occasional stand of rosemary made its stubborn way. Under mayweed and charlock, stunted savory could still be had. And beside the potherbs, which are more often grown for their usefulness than beauty, there were other things planted only for their signal delights. There were forgotten carnations, enough to make a crown. There was oxlip. Honeysuckle and eglantine crept about the crumbling rock.

The garden was once tended by men who loved growing things for their own sake. Even the bowling lane, where a plain hedge or even fence would have sufficed, had once been rimmed with roses. Seeing that, I'd known that life would still beat below the weeds' pestilent teem. Both herbs and flowers had long been left bereft. But all things that can live, will. It heartened me.

I shifted on the pad of folded blankets where I sat with legs to one side. Already my hands were tender. It had been far too long since I did such work; I had fled from my village just when my garden was beginning to grow in earnest. Now I savored the crumble of earth between my fingers. It was calming, a kind of healing; any weed I pulled might disrobe a sprout of yellowed musk-rose, or the remnants of a patch of climbing beans. Life returned to me, slow and rich as silt.

Bill hoed, clearing the bowling-lane. In most of the garden I wanted to work carefully, without anything so gross and clumsy as a hoe, but thought there would not be anything good planted so close to the precious roses. Bill seemed to like the work; but soon he stopped and rested, his arms a circle atop the hoe-handle.

The cleansing had taken its toll. Some of the muscle I'd seen at the Devil's Points had shrunk, giving him a looser look. His skin had paled like milk after the cream is skimmed. He rested a good long while, as chickens pecked at the heap of gnarled stalks he'd raked, and I wondered again if I had been wrong to purge him. Maybe it was only vanity, or pride. Bill's shock of hair draped over his face like a mask.

No. I remembered well how purely miserable he was when we met. My reasons for trying to help did not matter. I only knew that I had to try.

My knee throbbed. I breathed the garden deep. The smell was earthy as loveplay; it was joyous as dancing, and lace, and colored silk. I forgot the pain in my joint. For a little time I felt peaceful, more peaceful than I had since the smoke of my old house burning had crowded the clouds. Amid that garth and garden the world seemed still as a sunlit pond, or winter's crystal sky.

The quiet broke under the clap of hooves on cloister stones. I looked up to find Mary riding bareback on my donkey. He was led by Thomas, Randall's scruffy and hatless friend. They passed through the cloister towards the sheep-meadows. Mary sat on the donkey's back comfortably as on a litter, looking as peaceful as I had felt. For a moment she raised one hand to me—half a wave, half a salute. Then she and the donkey and Thomas were gone, vanished through the tumbled stones of the far courtyard wall.

My knee's ache prodded me like a child. There were gardens to comfort me, yes; but there were also the walls that bound them, reminding me of the looming plague. I had not yet talked to Mary's mother about how long we would remain, and which road we should take when we left. I rubbed my leg, girding myself, then struggled to my feet using the sickle-handle as a lever.

I crutched for the kitchen. It was a stone cottage, set above the brook, a bit upstream from the reredorter latrines that would pollute the water further down. The kitchen was squat, but also capped with a curious sort of high, wood-shingled dome. The dome had three windows, which would have made it a watchtower had it not been so hemmed by high alder.

The lower windows were mostly overwoven with ivy. But through one that had been cleared I could see Mary's mother, determinedly slicing meat on a rough table. The table was strewn with flour, and handfuls of spice. There was far more spice than I would have imagined the household possessed. I saw cloves, and four nutmegs, and sticks of cinnamon like an elf's firewood.

When I entered, Mary's mother started as though splashed with water. But she was quick to smile. "You've caught me at a hurried moment," she said. "I built my fire too early, and I need to finish making the pie before the oven cools."

She pushed aside a small heap of cloves to make space for the meat, which I now saw was a pile of boiled lambs' tongues. I felt a surge of hunger; I had once loved lambs' tongues. I hated what sheep did to a village's commons, but there might, I admitted inwardly, be some advantages to keeping a few. "Put me to work, if that will help," I said.

"You can cut onions, and with my thanks." After I had settled on a stool, my broad blade working, onion-skins beginning to pile crumpled beside me, I confessed that I did not even know her proper name. "Heather," she said. "Though in truth it's been a long time since I've heard it used. Mostly the fellows here call me Mistress. Or else Goodwife."

"Which displeases you?"

"Ah, it makes me feel older," she said, and chuckled. I could understand why she'd object to that. Though there were some lines hatching in the skin near her brows, her eyes were yet a robin's, and her cheeks were full and humorous. She must have been quite young when she had Mary. In any case she wore the years lightly, in spite of the misfortunes she'd suffered—the loss of her husband and lands, the placing of her child into wardship. She pushed bits of tongue to the side, once popping a piece into her mouth with an impish smile.

"At least they show you respect," I said.

"They're good enough fellows." She swept the tongues into a neat pile, and began one more chopping pass, rocking the knife she held down with the heel of one hand.

"I fear I've treated one of them less kindly than I might," I said as I wiped my eyes against the sting of the onions. "Randall."

"Ah, he's the pick of them. Our young prince!" she said with a laugh. "He came here about two months ago, and spends as much time sketching as he does in the fields. When he first came he would scour through the heaps of junk in the dormitory, searching for any odd candlestick or bit of old ceremonial gear. The others indulge it, as long as he lets them divide his pay for the time he spends drawing. Also they dearly love having their likenesses put down on paper."

I had thought, when we arrived, that the workers were lazy to the point of dullness. Now I realized that they had been posing. "He's not like them."

"He says he is a tanner's son," she said. "But he also says that he's dedicated to drawing the whole world. I don't think he knows much about tanning, or any other hard labor. The way he talks—I think he's probably high-born, traveling for a conceit."

"Like a storybook."

"Like a storybook," she agreed. She cut a hard-cooked egg in half, then lay the halves beside each other to slice with quick sure strokes. "If it amuses him to think he's deceiving us, and that we believe him to be a commoner, well then let him be amused. I like the boy. Not so much his companion—the fellow Thomas."

"The one who went a-riding with Mary." I regretted the words as soon as I spoke them. It was not for me to fan Heather's dislike;

she would think even less kindly of him after my news. Mary's taking up with the boy might have been an intentional stab at her mother, for all I knew. Doubtless she had wanted some companionship other than that of Bill and I; but her choice of Thomas could have been prodded by old anger as much as want. Probably she still blamed her mother for the past few years.

And a chill did seem to come over Heather, as though the windows were suddenly full of a blowing storm. "Aye, did they so," she said. It was only half a question. She went to the hearth, where a small, hot frying pan waited.

"They did," I said, trying to speak lightly, for she seemed even more upset than I would have guessed.

Heather knelt. She dropped butter and onions into the pan, along with some dried bread-crumbs and a single stick of cinnamon. Soon all was sizzling. Heather stirred with a wooden spoon, roughly, as though to scrape the pan. Then, head held stubbornly down, she spoke in a burst: "I've always done as well as my strength would let me."

Her humor seemed much darker than a pleasure-ride should have brought on, even one against her bidding. But I sensed something real under the sadness. Something solid, more so than the wet weather that would sink Joseph into his glooms. I felt the urge to leave her; I felt myself a spy.

I opened my mouth to make my excuses. But before I could speak, Heather's clenched silence spoke to me; there seemed only one thing that could so steal her grace, turning her smooth way with knife and pan into short and silent jerks over the hearth.

She knows her daughter, I thought. *She knows their privy language.* Mothers and daughters speak to each other without words, using a tongue made up of history, and wrongs done, and favors owed, and wounds well known. Surely as though it was written on Heather's back, it came to me that Mary had struck the most tender place of all; she'd shown herself to her mother only so she could leave without a word.

I shook my head. I dearly hoped that Thomas did not intend

to stay with her for long—that he would return with the donkey. If he did not, we were mired at the monastery. We could not leave until I could walk.

I crutched to the ivy-draped window and leaned on my elbows. Behind me was the sizzling of the tongue-pie filling; from outside came the clicking of ninepins. Bill had been so eager to play that he had not even waited for an opponent. But then I felt myself struck, as though with a club. My eyes wavered. *Impossible*, I thought. *Not this. Not so soon after our means of flight has vanished.*

Through the wild trees, a trio of men played at bowls. I could not make out their features nor their forms through the screen of vine and leaf. But however thick the creepers and boughs might grow, they could not fully obscure the flash of Sam Ridley's crimson cloak.

Eighteen: Bill

Near to noon she gives me the clock-casing, and she says that Mary is gone. The casing is etched with lightning, and winged sandals, and a spear, and a shield. On the back is something like a hearth in a forest—a circle, with a thin trail of smoke. Though the casing is a crafty thing, Mary left it. Now it is mine. *She did take the flute*, Sarah says.

We must hide in the dormitory, where I went to rest after I was done clearing away the bowling-lane roses. It would be better to run, as soon as it is dark. But without the donkey and with Sarah's knee gone painful we no longer have any means to run. We hide in the dormitory, hoping that no one will come upon us.

At first I wondered why Sarah was so afraid. Then I remembered the red cloak, that we saw on a man walking far behind us. I remembered how Sarah looked when she saw that—then the need for fear seemed plain. When we first saw the man, we went running to the forest. This time we stay in our alcoves. We wait. I do not know for what.

When night has gone black as capes, she comes to me. With rasping voice she drags me softly from the sleep I have nearly fallen into. She says the time for cleansing has come again. The air is cold, and full of dust.

I blink then, and blink, and struggle to throw off blankets. I come wobbling to these feet. The windows we already cleaned glow, as green as bottles. Sarah is a shadow.

Tonight is the proper time, she says. *We'll perform the last cleansing. There could be no better stars for it than those I read this eve.*

Her own stars form as much of a circle as they can with only four of them, and one moon. Her nose makes a maypole that her stars and moon may dance around. She embraces me, quick and fierce. Then she goes away.

At the embrace, fear burrows into this head. But this heart mounts eagerly.

She has begun to prepare. Her shadow squats beside the muddle of monks' stuff. I go to her.

She has brought a pail of coals from the kitchen. Now she pours it out onto the stone floor. Her face glows dull red. The pail is charred and smoking and the smell of dust fades before the smoke. I hug these arms to this body. I wait to hear what is right to do.

Sarah sets a kettle amid the coals. Then she takes out a packet made of folded paper. She opens it, and holds it beneath this nose. *Here's our means of healing*, she says. It smells of otters' pelts, and roses. It sprinkles to the water like snow.

What is in it? I say.

Wind. Rose-petals. The will of a cloud. The heart of a dolphin that saved a seaman from drowning. Other things that I'll not speak of.

She places both hands atop this head, as though to draw me close. But she does not draw me close. Instead she folds her hands before her solemnly, as though they rest on a reading-stand. *It will need to steep for a time*, she says.

We sit quietly. As we do, the green windows lighten. At last the edge of the moon shines bright in one. It slides slowly into view. Then the windows shine like torchlit parades. Ghosty branches scrape on the panes. The kettle steams, and smells bitter.

In the brighter light I see that she has taken curtains from the monks' trash, and curled them on the floor. Probably they were once fine, but under the moon's light I cannot see any color. They only look gray.

They once draped the altar, she says when she sees me looking. She has made a nest with them. Sparks pop from the coals. One rests on the draping. Dying, it scorches a dimple. Sarah bids me lie on the nest. I crawl to it, and smell the tang of must and mold. When I lie down I think I can hear an old echo, of a song or dour chant.

Alms deliver all from sin, and from death
and will not suffer the soul to go into darkness.
Lay your bread and your wine on the grave of a just man;
Lay it on his body, before he's gone to ground.

No fear, she says. *For anything.*

But there is much fear in this body. It tries to smother the eagerness in this heart. I think that all the purging she's given me—twisting me sick, keeping me from food, wrenching me and wrenching me—has only shaken loose a pittance of all the sin I hold. I think this last cleansing must be much greater, and more pitiless. I try to lay still in the nest. But I shift like a rat.

After cleansing, I say quietly. *What will we do then?*

Hush. There is only the moment, she says.

She sits beside me, and lays her hand upon this head.

Thinking of the future can only harm the now, she says. *Think only of the cleansing. Of how it will feel to have your body pure, and wholly yours. Think of the grandeur of that. Never wonder for the future. That will bring what it will bring.*

Then comes the thought that she has no answer. She tries to talk so that she need not offer one. But I fight that thought. These eyes close. This heart murmurs, trembling.

What the Lord wills, will come, she says. *What he has brought you now is a chance of healing.*

Around me there are herbs: crushed, sharp, bitter, boiled. I smell them in the steam of what I am to drink. Sarah's hand is heavy as was Ros's smooth trunk above me. It is warm and welcoming as Roslyn's cooney.

Alms deliver all from sin, and from death
and will not suffer the soul to go into darkness.

Lay your bread and your wine on the grave of a just man;
Lay it on his body, before he's gone to ground.

Lay quiet, she says. *Quiet. Lay soft…*

My breathing slows. It is slow. It is smooth. The night could fill with bats; even that would not make my breath rumble.

Step back from your thoughts. Loose your passions. They'll govern you no more. Step out from your body. Leave it behind. It is no more you *than are your old clothes.*

I start to sweat. I sweat under her hot hand.

Release all that you have, and so make all yours. No longer will you be your body's slave, or its fool.

She pauses, stroking me. Not as she would a cat, or house-dog. She strokes as she would an udder, to draw forth milk.

Loose, she says.

Tide, she whispers. The word floods me. I have never seen a tide. But when she speaks I know a tide would cleanse me, would cleanse this body so flush with sin.

Alms deliver all from sin, and from death…

Such a brilliance, she says. *Such grandeur.*

Were these eyes to open I think they would see nothing. This head is a twin to the night. It is as black, as empty, as waiting.

And will not suffer the soul to go into darkness…

The cup touches these lips. It sears these lips. It is searing spilling about these cheeks, this neck. I gag, I stutter without words. But as I do I drink. For Sarah I will drink.

Soft, she says. *There. Take all.*

Lay your bread and wine on the grave of a just man…

I have took all I can take, this tongue is surely blistering, this throat howls. But still there is more and I spit, coughing, spilling, trying still to drink but coughing and spilling more. It goes on and on until the will to try is dust.

Lay it on his body, before he's gone to ground.

Finally it is done, mouth and throat and even gut made raw from the gush of burning water. I squint these eyes tight, so I will see nothing. Most of all I will not see her. For my fury is come bubbling, bubbling like her potion.

Then I know for the first time what rage drove Samuel Wotten to murder. This body boils with hatred for her treachery.

A strong man, she says. *A fine man.*

To stop from snapping at her I must bite against these teeth, hard enough to hurt this jaw. Her potion has me. It is not meant to shake sin loose, as I thought. Shaking would only feel like sickness. This is meant to sear, it will scour sins away.

Her hands fix on this hand and on this head. They fix like iron. Men have thrown sins down me like coins down a well. Farthings and groats, angels and sovereigns. Pennies and half-pennies, the common coin of crime. About me men sing, and women sing, and babes—desperate and dead, chanting of their sin-hoard.

I clutch and claw at this chest. I would howl but then her hand is on this mouth. She holds a bunched curtain and I howl against it. I gnaw on cloth that tastes like a cellar. Thievery bubbles from these thumbs: theft of a loom, of cattle, of a child, of trust. Gluttony leaks from this tongue, vagabondage from these feet. Lust gurgles fearsomely from these legs, this yard. Lust has come to me with pleasure, and with sorrow. Whether with pleasure or sorrow, it always comes without choice, or direction. Lust is first and last of all sins. Without lust, what crimes could come?

The potion scours sins loose. They scrabble through these limbs like spiders and beetles. There is thievery, there is menace. There is fear given and there is pain. There is hate to make me shudder. Maybe Sarah will see these things, and know the hold they have had on me. Maybe she will see lust, and know that she was its target. Maybe it will surround me, a red cloud as I choke it out.

Still she sits there. She holds this hand. She is also a thief. She steals these things from me, and will know what she has stole.

Then, on this face, I feel a light soft brush, as though she has begun to paint. I smell a forest fern. The tip slips from this chin to the crown of this head; it lingers there. It grows fat and heavy. It swells with ills. Then it is gone.

I will let it fall in the river, she says. *It will float between rocks, and under roots. And so at last it will pass away.*

Then hands pull on this head, as though to draw me into clean and fearsome air. And through the pain that bursts and blossoms, that will steal this mind and all this body, comes whispering. Whispering like springs of water.

I cling to the hand of Sarah, who whispers. I pray to her. She prays to me. She says all will end soon. I will sleep. Waking, I will know myself a whole man. And now the scorching and the healing feel much the same. Though I still sweat from the pain, it is now only a remembered pain. It is no longer a fanged, flabby thing.

I lay quiet as she coaxes me. Over me she drapes a ring of blossoms.

Carnations, she says. *For you are the lord of all your body. Few men can say that.*

I breathe deep. I breathe in the sweetness of blossoms, and her love. And when I do, I know the coin of sin was counterfeit. At last I can fall back where I already lay. Back, and back; into the nest, into the night that now seems welcoming.

When I open my eyes, the sun comes streaming. It courses through green boughs. It shines on clean windows, and through them. It strikes my eyes; it drives off dreams. And when morn has come, this heart is mine, my heart…

Nineteen: Sarah

Always I have thought the wide world to be the Lord's best cathedral, the sky His finest vault. The church was not my first choice of a place for salving prayers. I would rather have gone to the brook, and knelt beside a stone on a mossy bank. I might have heard the song of blackbirds, there, and smelled the dew of morning as I opened my mind and heart.

But the slope to the running water was steep. And when Bill woke he might make for the brook, which I knew he found calming. I needed a place where he would never think to go. So instead I stole to the church, the loneliest house in all the monastery. From there, if I chose, I could crutch slowly around the cloister walls, and then across the sheep-meadows. Heather had told me that Lord Renault broke his fast an hour after dawn; there was no need to fear encountering his servants before that.

Trying to leave the monastery on foot was a desperate thing. But I knew that I had no choice. When I returned to the dormitory after seeing Ridley, the clock-casing awaited me on my bed. That, I knew, was a farewell from Mary—the only payment for my donkey I would ever receive. It did not matter whether Thomas returned or not. If I left, it would have to be on my own legs. I had only to decide if I would go alone.

The nave door fell inward off of rotted hinges; I smelled the ancient, dormant air of the church. I picked my way through the pews by the light of my single candle. Before the ambulatory I pulled aside a fallen pew-back with my sickle handle. Beneath it, a fist's-worth of baby rats mewled in a nest of chewed paper—the remains of old books, I realized, seeing that a lone letter had here and there survived in the gnawed slurry. Probably the covers had been torn away for the value of their gilding. It was a common thing, when a monastery came to ruin. Sometimes the pages were used for butcher's wrappings.

The thought of verses soaking with the blood of chickens and wild boars sank me low. I felt my life passing on towards its end; it made no difference whether my death would come with the Lord's quiet summons or through murder at the hands of a vicious man. The nest made me feel that all the world's knowledge was turning to dust, like rotted mortar.

The nave should have been full of the monk's brotherhood. It should have been filled with men—flawed men, yes, and often weak, as all men are. But men who sought knowledge, and to open themselves vigorously to God. Maybe the best of them had found as many questions in their books as they did answers. Maybe their studies had given them reason for compassion; maybe they were not the kind who read only to hear answers they thought they already knew.

I left the rats there. Before the choir, where the altar once stood, I shifted a timber to make a clear place. Then I knelt on stone. It did not matter that the pain made me clench my teeth, or that kneeling might worsen my wound. However much it pained me, I needed to kneel before the Lord.

In my old village we would never have prayed for help. *Who are we*, the congregation's leaders would say, *to turn to Him for aid? To imagine that He might answer? How can any man presume to think that his words might affect the unknowable intentions of God?* At times, these questions have seemed just to me. But at others, they have seemed prideful themselves, offering an excuse to those who fear asking for any help.

As I knelt on the stone, I was weary of life, yet fearful of losing it. *There are many perils in the world,* I thought. *Asking for aid is not one of them.*

I murmured, quietly. *Let my choices be good. Let them harm no man. Let them lead us to safe harbor. Let my choices prove good.* Every choice I had made since meeting Bill had weighed upon another's life. And now there came the hardest, weightiest choice of all.

It had taken a vastly unlikely chance to bring Sam Ridley to the monastery. It seemed the workings of the Fates, the Norn sisters, who haggle maliciously over our winding life-threads. Seeing Ridley had made me feel like inevitable prey, as though the Fates had guided me through the forest and over the lake and to a brambled ruin only so they could watch me be killed. I had no more chance of escape than did a goose on feast-day. I was weary, so that light seemed to have fled from the world; I wished only that my murder would come with impossible swiftness. And in that moment, I determined to leave the monastery alone. I could not bear the thought that Ridley might harm Bill simply for being my companion.

But I could not pretend that it was only the need to complete Bill's cleansing that had kept me from leaving yet. I thought of the smell of perch stew, and of the donkey as we walked along the sunlit river. I thought of the taste of water, and of a stem of chewed clover. I thought of firelight flickering on thatch when I was in love's embrace. I did not fear death—but oh, how I feared to lose my life.

And so part of me still clung, ashamedly, to what little protection Bill might offer. Though my heart said that death was nearing, there was still a tiny, torturous whisper of hope that I might have more years. It made me falter, when I needed to be fiercely resolved.

After casting a ball down the garden lane, Sam Ridley had handed his cloak to a boy nipping loyally at his steps. They stood with their backs to me, watching another man bowl. I could have run then. I could have snuck away, past the cloister, across the sheep-meadows and the questioning looks of the herders there. I could have hobbled over grazed grasses, and through my bitter rage at Mary for stealing my mount. I stayed for Bill: to help him, and maybe to get his help in return.

My mind was like a bucking beast, fighting its reins in fear and pain. I begged the Lord. *Give me the strength to walk away. To leave him. I must do so in the end. I know it. If I did not know it, surely I would already have gone, and taken him with me. Give me strength.*

There was a scrabbling behind me. One of the rats, I thought vaguely, seeking to wriggle from its nest. I prayed and prayed, stroking and taming my mind. And slowly, slowly I did feel strength begin to return to me, like the vigor that a lick of honey will bring after a long fast. I told myself that Bill could not offer me a shield. I thought of the life he might have if I left him here, gathering eggs and catching fish for Heather. And I thought of what it would do to me if he were hurt for my sake.

Finally the trickle of strength became a flow. *When I leave*, I thought, *I will leave alone.*

Resolved, I pushed to my feet. It was still early; early enough that I could steal to the dormitory, silently gather a few things, and make for the meadows. If Bill woke I would tell him that I was going to gather plants, and that I would see him that eve. I would kiss him on the forehead, knowing it for a farewell.

My mind was taken with the thought of that final leave-taking; I crutched carefully, imagining what I would say, and wondering whether I should risk kissing Bill if he was asleep. Thus I was halfway across the church before I saw Sam Ridley sitting on the last pew.

He balanced easily on the pew's back, boots on the seat below, as he might sit on a bounding stone appointed as a meeting place. The church was still dark; I could see little of his expression. But in his stillness, his silence, he could have been the ghost of a monk calmly refusing to yield holy ground.

At last he straightened. I thought perhaps he had winked. He stretched lazily; as he did so I saw the spear leaning beside him on the pew-back. The haft was black, and ribboned.

"You left the door wide," he said. I glanced towards the open frame; I heard a lone thrush begin to sing. I thought, pointlessly, that if the door was left open the rats' chewed nest would soon be pillaged by the courtyard's cats.

"That was my error," I said. My voice was curdled as though

the mere sight of Ridley was enough to hamper my tongue. Memory can be a mighty curse.

"No," he said, almost kindly. "I was coming here even before I saw it open. I'd have found you in any case." As though I'd questioned him, he went on: "A man must have his morning prayers, if he's to walk peacefully through the day."

I saw that he was serious. It should not have surprised me; I had no reason to think that he was not devout. And a man who intends to do bloodwork will often seek a blessing first.

"And so we find ourselves in company," he said when he saw I would not answer.

I felt aware of every crack in the stone walls, every seam between the roofing shingles, as though I might turn to mist and escape through them. The doorway seemed a great distance away. Probably I could have covered it in ten steps. For the good it would do me, it might have been imagined, or dreamed. "A curious chance," I said.

"You need not play," Sam said abruptly. He rocked slightly on the pew's back and took up the spear. He leaned forward on the haft, absently grinding its butt against the floor-tiles. "I have hunted you a pretty while," he said.

The spear looked sharp as lightning. Where head joined shaft it was beribboned, tied with strips and bright rags. If he threw it, it would rend the air like thunder. As clearly as though it was already done, I saw it protrude from me; I saw strips and rags soaking with blood against my breast. I saw him watching me die.

I took a breath. "Do it," I said, and cursed my shaking voice. Quavering would only make him my master.

But he shook his head. "In such a blessed place? Oh, Sarah. The contempt you show me! I should never think of it. If I wished to kill you here, I might have done so the moment I found you."

"From behind," I said. "But I think you would want me to know who did it."

"You would have," he said seriously. "There would have been time to turn and see my eyes. There are many place to strike. The kidneys. The base of the back. Many places that kill, but not quickly..."

He tapped the floor with the spear haft, as though marking a diagram.

It burned and chilled me. He could not have spoken with such precision if he had not considered doing just those things, mapping my body for a torturing, slowly lethal stroke. It might have taken him half of an hour to cross the nave with the necessary silence; but I had no doubt that he was patient enough, evil enough, to do it. I might have been wrenched from prayer by my own death.

I imagined him coming at me. I would raise my crutch in defense as my knee buckled beneath. I would fall among the rats and chewed paper; I'd wait for death as helpless as a worm.

He tapped his spear on the floor, naming liver and lights, offering a merciless lesson in my own body's frailties. My stomach flamed as though his weapon already pierced it. He raised the spear from the floor, letting the haft swing like a pendulum. I wanted to ask him more, redeeming myself with a firm voice—but before I could think of what to ask, the pew cracked out from under him.

He flailed like a fisher falling from a pier with his pole, rearing the spear overhead, trying to spike it against the ground and stop his skull from cracking on the tiles. I heard the iron point grate against stone an instant before he thudded to the floor.

For a long moment I stared at the empty air where he had sat. Though my heart howled for me to run, my feet held fast as though clamped and locked. Flight would draw him; I knew, for certain, that if I acknowledged his tumble by running then his humiliation would goad him to a quick kill. He would run me down, and thrust his spear. He would nail me to the floor, no longer caring that it had once been thought holy.

Then, nearly as swiftly as he'd fallen, he stood. We watched each other blankly. There had been an odd quality to the entire encounter; something ceremonial, like playacting. The fall was like a joke inserted clumsily into a drama's careful last act. It was unseemly and neither of us, I think, knew exactly what to do.

Finally he settled on a rueful, almost shy grin, and on honesty. "I wish you'd not seen that, but I'm thankful that only you and I did," he said. "I'll take it as a sign to take my leave, for a time. Good morning to you."

His haughtiness had returned by the time he reached the door, the swing of his spear blowing the ribbons back. His feet tramped on the fallen wood and he was gone. It was later that morning that I gained my shadow, the boy Peter Turnip.

Twenty: Peter Turnip

When I was at home with Mummer often I would slink—shirking, she said—and so dodge the tasks she wanted me to do. I was a traitor to their house, she would say. Then she would slap and rap at me. Later she might go for her leather strap.

But slinking were never a waste of time. It takes skill, as much skill as did making the pictures Dad etched on pewter.

Now I slink behind the old woman that Sam Ridley has tracked and trapped. I creep behind a cracked stone column. I crawl to a rain-barrel that leaks green and slimy water between its staves. I squat in a clump of grasses, where brown hoppers jump. Often the old woman sees me. Sometime she does not. She wears stars about her face. I think her mad.

When she first saw me she nodded, as though I were expected. Then she spoke to her companion, who walks with flapping feet. He cast a rock at me. It clapped and clopped along a walkway of tilted stones. The old woman spoke again, her voice screechy as wagon brakes. The man fell still, and sullen. After that he threw nothing for a while. But when she was inside he broke off rocks from the courtyard wall, and cast them at me. He threw a piece of red glass he'd found. I laughed inside to see his anger. My slinking torments the old woman and the man, far more than would my following them outright. The workers laugh to see it.

Sam Ridley is as wise and clever a man as I have ever known. Who else would think of becoming a servant to escape the plague? It is a wonder and a blessing that the plan should lead him to his prey. Doubtless it is God's reward for Sam Ridley, and shows His approval of our righteous cause.

Wherever flagstones do not damp the stalks, the court is overgrown by weed and thorn. Also the old woman has cleared away some weeds. When she walks the garden trails she tries to stand tall, as though we are all companions who happily share this place. But I see how she and the man walk too closely together, closely as a pair of rabbits huddling. As I follow from one stone column to the next, I imagine that the court is a cage. That makes me smile, and think of Windham Howley's coneys.

When the workers have broke their fast they go to the pastures, long hooks tilting on their shoulders. They laughed to see my stalking, they thought it play. The floppy man is wiser than they are. He was right to throw things. The workers do not know that Sam Ridley told me to do this. I will do it until he looses his rage upon the woman.

Only the man who draws knows what I am about. I see him watching me. I know he understands, and so I smile at him.

When the woman goes to the latrines I hide in a tree, hanging by my knees from the limb of an elm. I watch the latrines like a bat. I pay no mind to the floppy man's glaring. He is mad if he thinks I would want to look at such an old woman while she's about her business at the latrines. I do not try to see inside—but I will not look away from the door, I will not loose her from my watching even when she's at something distasteful.

When she works in the garden, picking at her flowers, plucking this petal and that bud for her belt-bag, I watch from behind a fallen door. Once it were fixed to the church. Now I've leaned it against a wall, to make a place where I may hide, like a fort for play. It will not be long before I'm too big for such. Soon I'll need to stand tall and proud as Sam Ridley.

When the old woman is in the kitchen, helping the other woman with her cooking, I peer in at them. There is the chimney they use, and then there is a second chimney, that is always cold and with cracks in it big enough to see through. Maybe one day I will climb to the roof and clamber down the cold shaft, down far enough so that they see my dangling hair, and cry out.

"Does he ever leave you?" the cooking woman asks.

"No, he never does," the old woman answers.

She spits a buttered chicken and trusses it about with sausage. Then she puts it on the hot hearth. When I see the chicken I feel a slap, like my mother's leather band. But this slap is in my head. It is not generous to hunt a woman that feeds you, and this chicken I'll likely taste tonight, after the lord has eaten. Often he gives us what is left, that we loyal fellows might share it. But whether or not it is generous to hunt the old woman, hunt her I will. At night I sleep on the dormitory threshold. Then I am not a hunter, but a guard. When I feel sleep coming, I stand a row of square green bottles before the door. If the door is opened the bottles will fall. Their clinking will wake me.

Every morning I am the first to wake. I wake earlier even than the drawing man, who watches me watching and looks at me as he should. By the time he or any of the others have woken, I have already set the bottles aside. I do not want them seen, and known for an alarm. I will not fail Sam Ridley. Neither sloth nor slumber will make me fail this task, or him.

Sam Ridley himself is busy with tending to Lord Renault. He follows him as faithfully as I do the old woman and the floppy man. His devotion is only right. Lord Renault is a grand man, with tassels and purple and with a sword. When he serves Lord Renault, Sam Ridley's face is peaceful and just—it is his own true face, nothing like the faces he wears for play. There is no doubt or sorrow in him when he serves the lord, bringing him roasted meats from the kitchens or wine from the hidden cellars.

Once, I wished that Sam Ridley would look at me with such care. Then I was ashamed. There is no reason for me to doubt his love.

Though Lord Renault owns this house, it seems to bring him little pleasure. Samuel says he calls it shabby, and poor, and a ruin. Lord Renault is often bored. He prays for the end of the plague. There is nothing here as amusing as city theatres, not even the woman that at dusk comes to him from the village across the bridge and through the trees.

Last night the lord called for two workmen. He made them wrestle until one's nose was broke, bleeding down his chin and chest. After that Lord Renault looked at me with a flushed face. If one of the workmen has a son, I think I'll battle him soon. If so I'll triumph quick. I'll fight hard, for my uncle's pride.

Though the lord called this place shabby I think it is grand, though he is right that it is crumbling. When I sleep outside the dormitory, sometimes a tile comes crashing to the ground from the church roof. I start awake then, leaping to my feet before I see that the bottles still stand stiff as sentinels. When that happens I nevertheless listen for a while, to be sure that I can hear only crickets, and not the soft thumps of the old woman crutching.

Even if she tries to run, she will have a long way to go. "Most of the worth of the place is in the pastures," Ridley said. "Should she flee, she'll have to cross those bare acres, or else keep to the road. In any case we'll catch her. But the sooner we chase, the easier it will be."

The pastures are covered with sheep. Mutton is a fine meat, and once I said to Sam Ridley that I hope we will serve here for a good long time, that we can eat a plenty of it. Sam laughed at that, and told me that in Lord Renault's city halls we could have as much mutton as ever we could stomach. Also there will be fried pike, and roasted capon. But if we are to live so richly, we must not spill blood before Lord Renault's eyes. He must not even suspect what we intend to do to the old woman. Surely the lord has no affection for Sarah, Sam Ridley told me. But he imagines that she is in her dotage, and would think that killing her might bring a curse down on his house.

So we must wait until she flees, running for shores she will never reach. Once she has left this place we can have our vengeance. Then we can return to serve the good lord. Our future will shine green and triumphant, whether we feast in Lord Renault's halls or rule over our own village. All things will be ours, unless I should fail at stalking. I will never fail.

I watch them at their cooking, as they peel stewed chicken from bones. The stew they make is not meant for us; come the chance, I will sprinkle sand in the pot.

I watch them at their work among the growing flowers. When I hear snores, I'll trample potherbs beneath the moon.

I watch them when they sleep. I climb a tree, and through high windows see them slumbering.

There is no way for them to escape my watching, save for fleeing from this place. And then they can be slain.

Twenty-one: Bill

Clear water runs over my fingers. It runs, and ripples, and is clearer than any glass. It runs around my ankles. I splash it on my face and leave my hands in my beard. Then for a while I squat in the shallow part of the stream, at the edge of the pool where I like to fish, listening to blackbirds sing.

Again I splash my face, then rub it with my palms. When I open my eyes there is a frog at the far side of the pool. That is strange, for though the water pools here, still it is running water and not a good place for a frog. But the frog is there, yellow eyes blinking above the surface. I watch until he ducks below, perhaps kicking away from fear of an unseen fish.

I kneel in the cold brook. I bend to let the water run over me, my elbows, wrists, and hands. Between my hands are weeds waving gently, happy to grow in the slower water. And there is a rusted ring, that I think was once part of a gate's lock. Maybe after it was broken a monk tossed the useless thing into the stream.

Your body is yours, Sarah said. The cleansing was swift, strangely swift. I had thought it would take months more. I was full, full to the top with crimes and the need to be rid of them. Without them I am empty. That is the joy of it and the fear of it.

You are your own master, Sarah said, and I will never leave her.

For a long time I hid from my sisters, ashamed of what I'd eaten, and what was in me. Now maybe I can return to them. Maybe I can. Maybe I can find them, and hold them in my arms.

But the thought is not so joyous as I'd thought it would be. I do not want to leave Sarah. There are people who wish her harm, and that I will not allow. I will not let the man put his hands on her, or even speak to her unkindly. If Sarah did not forbid me, I would chase off the boy who follows her; if he did not run, I would thrash him.

But even if she were safe I would stay with her. Sarah is my still place. I will follow her, and do what she tells me to do.

Plants trail around my ankles. I pluck them, and rub them in my palms. They smell of mint. I chew a stem. It is sharp on my tongue. And there is cold water, and there is sweet birdsong. I am here.

Twenty-two: Sarah

A garden plot has often offered me a harbor; I love a garden's gentle tides, so different from humanity's usual blast and blow. I have often sought comfort in the prick of thorns on my fingers, and the smell of crushed mints, and the sight of spiders crouching on glimmering webs. But that morning I had another purpose in the monks' plots. Amid the carnations, wilting marigolds, and rue—amid the honeysuckle, and creeping eglantine—I hoped to find a means of escape.

In the two weeks since Sam Ridley found us Peter had trailed me, steadily as though he was Sam's second pair of eyes. Peter was there when I tended shoots, and when I roasted meat. He was there when I tarried on the bank above the brook. I could feel him when I slept. He was a shadow that even noon could not erase. It was strange to feel something more than annoyance towards a boy so young. It was awful to feel afraid of him.

Before coming to the garden that day, I'd sorted through my bags for seeds to plant. At last I chose a peach-stone, that I found nestled among specks of carrot seeds like a duck's egg tucked into down. I planted it carefully, in soil made rich by straw mucked out from beneath one of the chickens' many roosts; I hoped the stone was hard to survive Peter's trampling. He'd already stamped down the borage.

It eased my mind to think of a tree bearing fruit years after I was gone. But in the end, planting the peach was just a ruse. I only needed a reason to search the gardens without raising suspicion. And there was a great deal of garden to search. I'd found a birdbath under a tangle of sweet-briar; a ragged crown of darnel hid a sundial, its copper needle long since gone green. Nearby was a young yew tree, so small that I thought it must have been planted in the monks' last days. There were some crab-apples, that might be roasted for a holiday treat. There were potherbs, and healing simples by the score. But there was none of the plant I wanted.

Oh, there was poison enough. There were roots that could nearly behead a fellow with pain, hemlock to bring quick doom, buds that would kill a man's mind and leave him drooling and staring and mute. But I would not use them. I'd sought vengeance enough in my life; I'd even allowed my beloved to pollute himself with a killing he knew I wanted. I would not seek revenge in anticipation of a harm that might be done me. *When I leave this world*, I thought, *I'll leave calm, if I can.*

But what I would have given for a single stem of the plant I'd used to put Edward Keaton to sleep! I had needed only a few petals of it to ensure he would not wake until late morning. With the juice from an entire plant, I could put a single man to sleep for a month. Or I could make everyone in the monastery slumber for hours. But there was no more to be found; and I'd used up all I'd had helping Mary.

Again I cursed the girl for leaving with my donkey. A small voice told me to forgive her—she might, after all, have learned that Renault would return soon. She might have been forced to become a thief, fearing that she would otherwise have to return to his bed. But I did not believe it. She had left on a selfish whim, stealing the one thing that might have saved Bill and I in the first hours after Sam Ridley arrived. I could not forgive her so easily.

The thought of Ridley haunted me as I weeded along the garth's sunny northern wall. I cut and yanked, freeing crab-apple shrubs to take light and air. I tried to think of festival drinking bowls, filled with apples floating merrily. But I was always aware of Peter's eyes marking and measuring me, and of Ridley's spear.

In midmorning, I looked up to find Randall picking his way past roses. He held a cylinder of glossy green felt, the kind that might have been used for a gown or a rich curtain. But when he unrolled it a few feet from me I saw that it held only brushes and coal-sticks. He began filling a sheet as I returned to tearing out thorny spires.

I'd become accustomed to his constant drawing. I even liked to see his work when he was done, for he'd often show a plant in a way I'd never considered before. I had to confess that his vivid, precise exaggerations had let me see the wistfulness in carnations, and the pride in columbine, and so deepened my love for both plants. And since our first dispute, Randall had treated me with cautious respect. I was glad of it, for Heather had been distant and edgy since her daughter fled. Probably she would always blame me for the pain of losing her girl a second time. I'd not urged Mary to leave—far from it—but I had brought her back. I'd made it possible for her to leave so cruelly. Also I had carried the news; I'd seen how it grieved Heather. Though it might be unjust, all of that made me a convenient target for blame. So it was good to feel Randall's shy, friendly presence—good to feel that every person there did not hate us.

From time to time I glanced at Randall's work. His coal-stick swept and looped; black herbs grew on the paper. Just then he was sketching rue. He began at the woody base, but the shrubby stems seemed to grow a season's worth in a few moments. In fact I thought it grew too much; he tended towards the grandiose, with curling blades and branches more profligate than there actually were on the humble plant. But he was a spendthrift with paper, drawing the rue again and again, each time paring away at the frippery until he had reached something like its heart. When he finished, I thought he had captured everything but the sickly, bitter scent. I thought of grace, and weeping, and the clear vision that rue may bring.

Watching Randall sitting there against an old barrow, hair falling forward past his ears, completely intent upon his craft, it was easy to forget that he was noble-born. Perhaps it was that dedication that kept me from ever seeing a hint of entitlement in his manner. Surely I never had to duck my head before him, nor touch a knuckle to my mouth in deference as I did when I encountered Lord Renault.

"Where's your companion?" he asked after a while. Drawing the gentle inclination of a stem of nep had proved a challenge, and he drummed his fingers absently on the page.

"Fishing, by the stream," I said. Bill loved to sit with a slender rod beside a small pool in the flow. In recent days, watching the change in him had been my one real pleasure. He wandered through his days in a kind of disbelief. Not the disbelief of a man who suspects a cheat, but of one who simply cannot believe his great luck in a dice-game.

But even my happiness about the change was not pure. I could not know for certain how long his joy would last—or how long he would be alive to enjoy it.

"Yes, I saw him there—but I didn't mean Bill. The other one."

"The boy," I said. He nodded. "Peter, his name is. He's in one of the elms by the kitchen. From there he can watch Bill and me at once."

"Such devotion," he said. "If he had a gentler soul, he might be devout. Even holy."

Though he had continued drawing, I saw that his movements were slower, less concentrated. "But you know he is not," I said.

"He has the singleness of mind to be. I think that true worship demands concentration, which is what keeps most of us from ever performing it—it's not easy to be fully absorbed in anything. Usually our minds call us away to other places, other tasks. Peter seems to think of nothing at all beyond what he is doing. But there is an anger in him…a mockery." Randall tapped the tip of his coal-stick on the page, marring his work with a cluster of dots. "Once I saw a red ape named King Phillip," he said suddenly. "He was kept in a wagon that had been built up into a cage. The keepers had nailed some wooden pots to the outside of the wagon's bed, so that vines could clamber up the bars. If you squinted it seemed that there was no metal there at all, only forest creepers in strangely even rows. And when Phillip watched you, it was as though you were the one imprisoned, trapped by the branches of his old jungle home. You felt he could part the vines as easily as a curtain, and seize your neck...you could see that he believed he could. It was as though he was only indulging us—that the cage was only so we could imagine ourselves to be safe. Peter makes me think of Phillip. He only needs a red pelt."

"Some might think it cruel, to compare a boy with an ape," I said after a moment.

"It's not a hasty judgment. I've seen how he watches you. If I'm being cruel, it's towards the ape. Phillip had no malice. He had no choice in what he was. The boy does."

As surely as his drawings had altered the way I saw columbine, Randall's words began changing the way I thought of Peter. He capered in my mind's eye like a vicious goblin. I struggled against the new vision. This was only a boy. But I had already confessed to myself that I feared him; Randall touched on something real. "And his master. What do you make of him?" I asked. It would amaze me if he could judge people as truly as he did herbs.

Randall stopped even pretending to draw, and looked me full in the face. "He's a salamander of a man, breathing neither air nor water. I don't know where he would really belong. And there's something about him that makes me think of the other sort of salamander—the kind that lives in fire."

"A pretty picture you make of him," I said. *And a true one*, I thought. Ridley had been a vagabond, then a leader, then a hunter, and now a servant. None of the roles fit him well; he forced himself into them as he wanted, as brutally as was necessary.

"I don't mean it to be," Randall said, seeming unaware of my bitter jest. "I don't see much beauty in him. There's little room for it when he looks at you as he does."

"It's true that mercy is not one of his virtues."

Randall looked at me curiously. I expected him to ask what I had done to so offend the man. "If you and Bill were to part, and flee along separate roads, which of you would Ridley chase?" he asked instead.

"Well, we will not part." There would be no point after that morning in the church. Now that he knew that Bill was my friend, Ridley might pursue him before chasing me down. He might want to show me the blood dried black on the head of his spear.

"You are faithful companions," Randall said.

"Chance brought us together. But yes. We are faithful now." I pulled a root, shook dirt and a white worm.

"But if you left Bill, I think Ridley might follow you," Randall said decisively. I did not argue. For a while we worked in silence as the sun slid towards noon. A pile of torn, wilting weeds grew beside me. The roots went gray as they dried.

Steady as a ship, Lord Renault passed between the birdbath and the bowling-lane. Ridley followed as though on a tow-line. Neither looked at us. Lord Renault, I imagined, was thinking of the stables, and his customary mid-day ride, and Ridley knew that Peter watched us.

"Now *there* is fine faith and loyalty," I said. "Good Master Ridley scarcely leaves his new lord's side."

As I spoke, the pair reached the edge of the gardens. Before passing from them, Ridley half-turned to wave cheerily towards the kitchen. An elm branch, covered in spring leaves, shook in answer. "What did you do to anger him so?" Randall asked.

"We both have reasons for anger," I said. My skin remembered Ridley's bridle; my mouth recalled his iron tongue. I swallowed. "But we must end our talk," I said, as teasingly as I could. "Surely you'll be needed in the sheep-meadows after dinner." Earlier in the day, Ridley had chased a few tardy workmen from the courtyard with a switch. I wanted to see how Randall would try to explain his indulgence of his own sloth.

"It was fortunate that he didn't notice me here before," he said awkwardly.

"Heather told me that he might be choosing not to notice you," I said.

He smiled shyly. "I thought you might ask me about that."

Peculiar, that he was so ready to talk about his high station. He must have been even lonelier than I'd imagined since his friend Thomas left. "Who are you, in truth?" I asked.

"Randall Holme. In truth."

"But you're not a laborer."

"No. I was born to a high house." He brushed at his nose with his thumb, as though a fly had alighted.

"Drawing's an uncommon skill for nobility." I'd wanted to say something that would lead him to tell his story; I succeeded far more than I'd expected, for the tale came in a rush, without further prodding.

"I learned because of my father," he said. "He loved the Holme name, and the Holme coat-of-arms, but in truth he feared that neither was so old or so worthy as he claimed. He used to spend long hours staring at the coat-of-arms, which was an odd beast, with one head like a fish and another like a bird. My father wanted badly to discover its source. He'd look through books of similar devices for anything with wings or fins—a sparrow, a phoenix, a humble fork-fish, a toothed whale. When he found something his face would splotch with excitement, and he'd have me copy it over. Making those copies are my first memories.

"But drawing noble blazon soon bored me. The coats and crests were monotonous—all were different, but always in the same way, with a claw standing in for a hoof, or a lion for a bear. And whatever my father thought, coats-of-arms don't have much meaning. They're like signposts pointing to themselves. So I took to drawing common tools and devices, the small things that actually fill our world.

"I began with a needler's shop. The fellow was as thin as his own pins, and bemused by my interest. But he let me draw the marking shears he used to score wire, the stock shears he used to cut it, the tongs and guttering knife he used to groove the needles' heads before making the eyes. There was a punch for that. There was a rotary washing-tub, to scour the needles. There was a curious anvil, like a pyramid set on one point. Even he didn't know why it was made like that—it was just an old custom, perhaps nothing more than a needler's crest. At last I drew the needler himself. By then I was fascinated by the man, who used so much to make so simple a thing. After that, I determined to draw as much of the common world as I could."

"And so you'd choose to draw Arthur's pageboy instead of Arthur himself?" I asked. "It's an unusual choice."

"But not a bad one. Wouldn't we be richer, if we had a single statue of the pageboy along with all the hundreds of sculptures of his king? Wouldn't Arthur's glory be even greater if we knew what kind of commoner chose to follow him?" He was growing more animated, leaning towards me as he gestured with his coal-stick. "Come with me," he said, and with one hand helped me to my feet. Soon we were in his small, windowless chamber. Beside his bed was a small table, stacked high with paper. Precious paper—seeing so much of it, in such a plain room, was like finding emeralds amid a stable's straw. Randall gestured towards it. "Crafts. Tastes. Smells," he said. "Everything I can think of or discover."

I turned page after page. There must have been hundreds of them—and these were only the finished ones, clean and labeled, each done over what must have been many drafts. There were drawings of millers and soldiers and coopers, beekeepers and beggars and dukes. There were drawings of equipment, and of dress: a surgeon's spatha, lenticular, and trepan, a musician's French oboe and trumpet marine. There were hats for Russians and China-women and Jews. There were badgers and silk-worms, elephants and unicorns; there was a Moor astride a mighty camel. Page after page: *Hair. Sounds Made By Men (When Tortured, He HOWLS). In January, Set the Kernels of Apples and Pears, and Muck Hop-Yards with Pigeon-Dung. This is the Form of Noah's Ark.*

Suddenly I felt sorry for the boy. He was trying to collect all the world, as though writing things down would allow him to keep them. But we can hold nothing in this life; we can only try to keep our spirits whole and steady, as we tumble helplessly on. "It's a great endeavor," I said.

He answered with pride. "It has not always been easy. The fellows here nearly beat me after I fed onions to the milk-goat—I'd only wanted to hear whether they'd call the bad milk rancid, or rotten, or a cheat, but they saw me do it. In the end they only tied my clothes in knots and threw them into the brook. Thomas and I worked for hours to loosen them."

"Were you friends from childhood?" I asked, suddenly hoping that Randall might know where he and Mary had gone. There might yet be some way of retrieving my donkey.

"I met him here."

"That surprises me. How long have you been here? I thought the two of you seemed close." *But not so close that he thought to tell you he was leaving,* I thought.

"A few months. If I *must* go out on the road, my father at least wanted me heading towards a safe place. He and Lord Renault have been friends for a long time. I came here just to soothe him, thinking that I'd leave after a fortnight. But I found it far more interesting than I'd imagined. You'd scarcely believe how much you can find to draw among the ruins—and much of it can't be found anywhere else." He sat down on the edge of his sleeping mat; I took a small stool. "Now it seems hollow to me," he said. Then he went on, hesitantly: "It's hard, watching someone you love vanish."

He's more foolish than I'd imagined, I thought. *He's so young! To speak about loving a woman he knew only a day or two...surely Mary never did anything to earn his deep affection.*

But the misery in his voice cut at me; the incision let in light. For an instant I saw Randall, and Thomas behind him—Thomas, watching, quietly present. And I knew that it was not Mary that Randall loved.

I cannot know, in honesty, how I would have felt had Thomas still been there. Maybe I would have disliked seeing the particulars of their affection. But as it was, all I saw on the sleeping mat before me was a portrait of dejection—of love lost.

"You loved him," I said gently. It was extraordinary, that he should trust me so. To speak of such love was to risk drowning, or the gibbet; it was to risk turning workmen into a mob. I had an urge to stroke his cheek. I would have, had I been certain that he would know I meant to comfort him, and not to pull him by his sparse beard.

"One cannot choose love's target," he said. He seemed heartened, relieved that I had not recoiled as from a snake.

"True," I said. "But there are some loves that most would try to hide. If not because of shame, then at least from the need for safety."

"I don't think you'll tell anyone. If I'm wrong, it's on my head."

"You're not wrong," I said, and waited.

Before going on he stood, and went to the small table. He bent over it, leaning on one hand, and began drawing as though he hoped to inscribe a summoning charm. "He won me with a story about poachers and thieves," he said. "Thomas had gone into the woods, not having the money even for a tavern's common bed. Anyway he was used to sleeping outdoors, and preferred a bed of heather and thatch to being kicked through the night by a carter. So he stumbled through the woods until he came to a glade—there was no warning, he said, not even the thickening of brush one sometimes sees on the outskirts of a forest clearing. He was in the woods and then the glade, suddenly as falling down a well.

"More unexpected still, beside a lone, small bush at the clearing's center was a loaf of bread. It was not much bigger than a roll, but in that wild place, on that bare earth, it stood out plain as a glimmering coin. He ate it down. It tasted of honey and rosewater.

"He had scarcely lain down when he heard a crashing in the brush, so clumsy that it could only be a party of men. Thomas knew the wilds were full of thieves, and he quickly climbed a tree, fearing that the sound of him fleeing through the bracken might call them to chase.

"A clump of men staggered into the glade, slowed under the weight of three dead deer they carried upside-down with poles. They had draped themselves with bells and silver bangles, ribbons and kerchiefs. And each wore a white mask.

"Thomas sat in the crook of an elder tree as the poachers made their plans. The leader spread his arms wide as wings; bangles drooped from his sleeves. *I am Oberon Lord of Faerie*, he proclaimed. *And holder of this wood!* The poachers laughed, and drank his health, and took up bows. Then they sunk into the wild woods, seeking more harts. They left their earlier kill in the clearing.

"Thomas waited until the sound of thrashing had vanished in the distance. Then he stretched one leg for the bough below him. But before his foot reached it, he heard a noise like ice breaking. He stared at the moonbeams stabbing the glade; they seemed solid, as though angels might use them for ladders. Then one of them stirred. It was no moonbeam, he realized, but a pike, that seemed made of crystal. And it was held by a man only then visible to Thomas—a man made of the moon's coursing light. He moved slowly, but with the grace of a waterfall. And when he began to sing, the sound was like birdcalls; a score of birdcalls at once.

"You would think there could be only one man like that in all the world. But another eased into the glade, as much like the first as two icicles. Then another, and another—a dozen of them, a goodly troop. Each face was fair as a lily. Each was dismal as forts and marsh. So beautiful, so stern and dire! They ringed themselves for a conference. Thomas was shocked to find that he could understand every whistle, every gentle hoot; then he remembered the rosewater loaf.

"The faerie were in a fury. But it was a quiet, almost sorrowful fury; they knew what they had to do, and seemed nearly as angered by being forced to it as they were by the poachers' crimes. They did not care so much about the deer—but to do it while playing at being faeries, in the faeries' own woods, left them no choice. They shivered their spears.

"Fast as a blink, they melted into the woods. Thomas saw his chance and clambered to the ground. He ran and ran, his face being whipped bloody by branches he had no time to duck under. When at last he broke from the forest he saw that the moon was only a sliver. In the glade it had been ripe and full. Perhaps in those woods it always was.

"He never knew for certain what happened to the poachers. But the next day he came to a goat standing beside the road. It looked at him intently, and with quiet terror. Thomas imagined what it would be like to be trapped inside the wrong body. Then he cut the goat through the neck."

Randall's drawing showed Thomas in profile, looking down at the ringed faerie troop. "At night he fills my dreams," he said. "I do not mean that I see him. I don't. I never see his face. But his spirit fills every dream; there is not a moment that he is not there. He changes the flavor like salt in water." He looked at me desperately. He said he trusted me; but some part of him may have longed for lashing. It is not uncommon, after a terrible loss.

"That may pass. Or it may not," I said. "Last night I dreamed of a man who has been dead some ten years. His fingers have gone to dust, but I can still feel his touch. I smell his sweat, though his skin has turned to ash."

He smiled sadly. "And so we are their prisoners. How to escape from them? Maybe I should not have spoken so harshly about Peter. He might not have any choice in what he is. I don't have as much as I'd like to think."

"But if you could escape, would you?" I asked. "Would you forget Thomas, if you could?" I wanted, very badly, for him to answer *No*—for him to refuse to abandon love's memory.

He shook his head. "But I don't want him to return to me. In his way Thomas is magnificent, but his heart is not weighty enough to hold down a single sheet. Thank you for listening, Sarah. I feel more peaceful than ever since he left."

I nodded; there was nothing more to say. After a long, silent moment I rose. I left him shuffling through papers in his chamber. Peaceful, he may have been—but it was not a peace without sorrow.

As I worked through the warming afternoon, clearing a weedy hedge out from the courtyard's corner, I thought about love. It is hard to feel that your love is not returned; love can only be satisfied by more love. Too often we offer it to the wrong person, one without the means or inclination to return such a gift.

I wondered if Thomas had any intention of staying with Mary, or if she had only given him an excuse to leave. *Very likely, she'll soon find herself alone again*, I thought.

I hacked at the hedge. I pulled away a final branch of rosemary.

And saw the long stems. The corner, crowded with them. Each covered with tightly closed buds—buds purple with somnolence. *Lethe.*

I ran my fingers under the nearest as though it was a lover's chin. I picked a single leaf. It smelled of stillness; of the hours before dawn. It was the true herb.

Then, nearly weeping, I tore lethe from the earth, failing in my joy to show the plant the proper respect. I clutched at the bounty as though my babes had returned to me. Black dirt fell from suddenly free roots.

"I need your help," I said to Randall.

"You have it."

Now that we had a means of escape, I decided that we must leave that very night. The plague might still surround us, like a black ocean sighing around an isle. When we left, it might drown us in its currents. But I feared that if we stayed much longer, Ridley would be able to smell our plotting; men given to treachery are often quickest to detect it. A careful plan would not do. Our lone hope was to move with reckless swiftness.

So I asked Randall to go to the stream, to help Bill with the fishing. He brought a small cast-net along, for I needed enough fish for a stew, and hooks and lines were too slow and uncertain. Instead the two of them could go upstream, and set the net under a little fall, snaring whatever came tumbling over the ledge.

While Randall was gone I went to the kitchen. Fortunately Heather had not yet begun cooking supper; she might resent me, but not enough to refuse my help. I cut onions to cook down in grease. After a few hours Bill and Randall returned with a basket of perch and trout.

I filled the first pot nearly to overflowing with onions and quartered turnips. "We'll need a second kettle or this one will spill," I said aloud. I took down a small pipkin, and poured in the rest of the vegetables. I divided the fish between the pots and, when Heather turned to fetch the salt, sprinkled a handful of minced lethe blossoms into the larger. Soon cats stood at the door—I tossed fishheads and bones onto the path, and watched the cats wrestle.

The stew was a great success. Lord Renault sent word that he would be pleased to eat the same dish every Friday. When that messenger was gone, Peter stood in the door, scratching his head and grinning. He bowed without dropping his eyes. When he spoke I could tell that he'd been instructed to use particular words, and that their cadence was unfamiliar; he spoke to Heather, but his words were meant for me. "My uncle sends his gratitude for the feast," he said, "and looks forward to the next one you will provide for him."

The candles were damped. I lay in bed, fully clothed, blankets drawn to my chin. My thoughts were restless as bats. For what seemed like hours I imagined everything that could go wrong. Perhaps Ridley had not really cared for the stew; that would not have stopped him from sending Peter to taunt me. Maybe not enough sun had reached the buds of lethe. Maybe they were not as strong as I'd judged; maybe I'd spread them too thinly in the stew.

I rolled and tossed, trying to subdue my mind. But there was a good reason for my thoughts to act like snarling beasts—if our plan failed it would mean death for me, and for Bill. If Ridley suspected that we'd once tried to escape, we would not have a second chance.

But it has been a long time since herbs failed in what I asked of them, I thought. Surely, at that moment, the monastery was beginning to quell under a smothering blanket of slumber. Soon it would be certain; I would feel the place still.

Calm yourself. Fear only makes it more likely that the dangers you dream of will come to pass. I heard Bill breathing, feigning sleep. I stroked my mind, slowly filling it with pictures of what I prayed was happening.

The workman lies in his bed. His house is one of the few remaining in what was once a fair town. The fields about him are all gone to forest; he fears for the future. But tonight he sleeps. Tonight his graying head is dull and misty. When he returned to his home he passed his children carelessly. Already his eyes had begun to blur; he walked, unsteadily, for the bed. It is fortunate he reached it at all. Had he eaten the stew at noontime, he would have lain curled in the field. Mice might have nosed him curiously as dark came, loosing planets to roll along their high roads.

His wife thought he was in his cups. Tomorrow she will think him sick; I hope she will not imagine that he is dying. For now he lies beside his woman.

Often scraps are fed to cats. Now, in the cloister, they drape atop ruined walls like lost scarves. Sleep fogs the night. It dulls the air. It deadens the sight of stars.

Lord Renault sleeps splayed across his bed. He wears lordly clothes, adorned with points of gold. Beside him is a workman's daughter who often sneaks here in evening. Tonight, just as she began drowsing, she jerked upright—feeling curious, and smelling something like thistles. The room was full of horses. Then she was down again, and then she was asleep.

The horses she saw were portraits, shapes made of paint. In all the monastery, only the living horses are still awake. They sniff the night air. Something in the stillness alerts them; this is a strange silence, an absence not only of sound but of its possibility. Even the rats ate fish, chewing on the dregs emptied out of one kitchen window. Now the hay bins do not rustle. The trash in our dormitory is still.

Sam Ridley…

But Sam Ridley I could not see.

A steady tapping called me from my half-dream. Quiet as the night, I crept from bed, and picked up a small, wrapped bundle from the floor. When I reached the door Bill already crouched there, an almost invisible shadow. I motioned for him to move back, then slowly swung the door wide. Randall stood outside, just visible by the light of the stars and slim moon. He cradled four bottles in his arms. When he stepped aside to let me pass, one slipped—it shattered, splitting into a hundred shards, ringing through the night. Randall spun to look behind; beside the birdbath, Peter lay curled like a wolf cub.

"Take more care!" I hissed. But we had nothing to fear from the young sentry. His mouth hung open; spittle dripped to the bare, weeded ground. For once he seemed a child. Our steps crunched broken glass as we picked past Peter and into the gardens.

The moon had shrunk to a bright sliver. Still, its light silvered the world; I saw everything as though in a smoothly hammered mirror.

Herbs, vines, crab-apple trees—every stem, every stone stood out as sharply as though traced by razors. An orange bull of a cat with two torn ears slept as I'd imagined. His legs draped as loosely as yarn.

My heart lightened; I fought the urge to shout. For a moment I placed an affectionate hand on each companion's shoulder. Then I began making for the residence, my bundle tucked carefully into the crook of one arm.

"You're not going to the stables?" Randall whispered.

"You go. I have something to do," I said. "I'll meet you here soon." I crutched through the dark garden. When I'd gone near a dozen steps I paused, and turned back to him. "Do not stay here, when we have left," I said. "Go. Only go."

"There is nothing to keep me here."

The residence had once been used by the monks' chief, who would need a place for quiet study away from the dormitory's sneezing and snoring. It was a square, stone house of two levels, set out of sight behind the church. I picked my way over a fallen wall. My heart thumped like a drum as I neared the residence's arched doorway. If I hesitated, I might waver; without a pause I pushed the door gently open.

I squinted against the dark. There seemed to be little in the room but empty book shelves—and, in one corner, a plain bed. The man sleeping there could only be Ridley. *An honor,* I thought, *to have this level all to himself. He's been quick to endear himself to his new master. Not many men would be trusted enough to serve as the lone guard.* About us the shelving had the vacant, lonely air of a stage after the theatre has closed.

Ridley was clothed. He lay flat on his back, without even his cloak drawn over as a blanket. His breathing was steady as an hour bell, but slower—as slow as freezing, as slow as tanning hides. Still I stepped quietly; I could not know how much Renault had eaten, or his girl.

Standing over the bed, hugging my breath close, I unwrapped my bundle. It was the hollow clock-casing Mary stole from Edward Keaton. Bill had given it back to me without a qualm; now I left it beside Ridley's head. It was partly a taunt, a message he could not know the meaning of. I only hoped that Lord Renault might see it too, and recognize the clock he'd wanted. Then he might insist on learning how Sam Ridley had come by it. The explanation might take an hour. And even an hour, we could use.

Slowly as a stalking cat, fiercely as a mute dog, my hand drifted towards Ridley's head. I watched it lower as though to nuzzle his hair. I pulled back, shocked. If I'd touched him he might have woken. That would have given me a reason to call for help; and that might have led to killing. Some part of me, it seemed, still wanted that.

I clenched my fists. I left him there.

Outside, the night seemed misted with lethe. In the courtyard was Bill. There was Randall. There was the moon. There was a steed. I rubbed my hands together, and set the crutch firmly under my arm. Then I called softly to Bill, that we might begin our flight.

Twenty-three: Peter Turnip

Always
I will watch
and guard her
Always
she will
hide
behind these walls
of swirly night

Twenty-four: Sarah

Downy clouds blew overhead, their white making the sky seem a deeper, truer blue. The field of teazle, blooming pimpernel, and spindle-tree shrubs rose gently. I rode up the last height into a cool ocean breeze. At last I beheld the city.

But I could only bear to look for a moment. Northam had lived for too long in my memory and dreams to take in as a single draught. I looked down past the mare's mane, to where pansies and hearts-ease grew. Sea-birds called their longings—wind filled the world with whispers.

Beside me Bill laughed aloud. "There it *is*," he said. "At last! To it! To it."

I wanted to feel the ground beneath my feet. Bill helped me, so I would not have to drop the last few inches. Once down I gently twisted my good ankle into the sandy soil, feeling the earth. Then I leaned against the gray mare's neck, stroking her as though it was she that needed comfort, stealing only brief glances at the place I'd so long sought and feared.

Beyond the height we stood on, the meadow was all blown sea-grasses, broad and unsettled as a lake. And beyond that stood the staunch gray rocks of the city wall. That much, I had expected; the barrier was solid as a monument, and I remembered it well. But as my glances lengthened, at last becoming a hesitant gaze, I realized that houses had spilled beyond the wall. Beside the Roman stone, the new frames looked light and slapdash; it seemed that the wind might puff them away as easily as pollen.

Atop the walls flew flags of various green: Lincoln, willow, popinjay. No sign of plague's black banners. Though no roofs could be seen within, far beyond the stone fortifications and green flags I saw more pennants, like daffodils growing on a distant hill. *Ships*, I realized. The flags must fly from the masts of vessels anchored in the harbor.

Beyond the flags, beyond it all, was the blue vastness of the ocean.

Bill danced with want. He grasped his cap with two hands, pulling it down over his ears. "Wonderful!" he said. "There will be meat, and a bed, and no need for fear."

Seeing Northam was like hearing the tread of an old friend outside the door—a friend who long ago betrayed me. I girded myself. I lifted a star from my temple; I put it back where it had been. *Flags on the walls, and men whose duty it is to fly them. Ships in the harbor. This is a prosperous place.*

"Perhaps it is wonderful," I said. But my wonder was not a happy one, like that I might feel watching a caterpillar weave a home where it will make its wings. This was the wonder of watching lightning—of waiting for the flash that blinds you even as you see it.

Bill often knew my heart. He fell quiet.

I remember well how he looked that day: the leather vest that Randall had given him, his hat and simple trousers, his wisps of beard like a handful of straw. I remember how his eagerness called the mare onward even before he pulled on her reins. I remember him as clearly as I do the moods that stormed through me on the heights.

"We've come a long way to see this, you and I," I said. "When we first met, I promised you clean ocean fish. Let's find out what's been hauled today."

Bill took my arm, gently as he might a baby thrush's wing. I mounted with his aid. Then he took up the mare's bridle, and he led me to the city.

We had traveled for two days. Our journey was a blur of damp branches flashing across my face after we left the sheep-meadows, and the glare of the sun, and a hole of hunger growing in me as our store of crust and cheese ran out. Being so hungry laid a dark glass over everything I saw. It browned the land, and made every man seem a ruffian. But that was only in my head; in my heart I did not fear. Having seen him, I knew that Ridley would sleep a long while. Though we would not stop except for a few bare nighttime hours, we did not need to panic.

As we made for the outer houses of Northam I gripped the reins, so tightly that it seemed my palms were hot. The houses crowded the wall like a litter of kittens. Most of them were shuttered, their rag-sized dooryards empty except for an occasional chicken or drowsing dog. But I could tell from fresh thatching and newly-sprouted herbs that all were lived in. I wondered where all the folk had gone.

The wall had been built without mortar, each carefully cut stone fit tightly into four or five others, the whole held together by its own weight. As its gray mass rose before us, four cranes flew from the top. They turned and wheeled, swooping down low so their legs nearly brushed the outer rooftops. Finally they rested on one, and raised their beaks for the sky.

We were at the gate. I held my breath; we passed within. A rush of sound rose gabbling about me, as though I'd taken my hands off my ears.

Inside, the shutters of houses were thrown wide open to catch what light they could. The alleys looked clean, perhaps washed by recent seaside rains. And now, at last, there were people, everywhere people. Children played their mobbing ball-games, dodging the wheels of carts. Drovers cursed, and swiped good-naturedly with their crops. Water dripped onto my neck from clothes hung on shutters to dry.

I breathed out. I breathed in.

As Bill and I made for the ocean, we walked a street of airy things—of tailors, their worsted and fustian and linens ballooning gently from their lines. Hardened fingers pinched hooked needles to sew sailcloth. Finished sails hung heavy on their racks, as though held down by the weight of their want for the sea. And there were cages of birds—doves, nightingales, blackbirds hopping between perches and staring balefully. From a rooftop a girl called, *hey hey!* and I thought her lucky, if she desired the makings of a kite.

We passed onto another street, this one filled with ashes and the steam of bread. Ovens lined the sides, just far enough apart to allow for cords of wood. Some of the ovens were open, empty, ready to be swept and rekindled; others burned hot, readying for the day's second baking. Counters held round bread, and sweet bread, and bread twisted into ropes; there were loaves spiked with rosemary, and others freckled with anise-seed. I looked down from my mount at goodwives carrying baskets, and men wearing leather aprons scarred by years of flying sparks. Towards the end of the street, the smell of bread turned to that of metal—we had reached the smelters, and metal-smiths, and others whose trade called for a blast of flame. For a moment I feared that the hot sparks might alight on my sky's black felt, riding as high as I was.

The abundance dizzied me; this had been a such a sad, overlooked place. But even as I wondered at the change, feeling that I was seeing Northam for the first time, there was a darkness before me, like an enchanter's black tunnel that only I could see. I knew it led to the harbor. Bill walked through it heedlessly, head held high.

We passed washers with dripping wool, and leggings, and cloaks. The air seemed cooler around the spilled suds. Further on were the papermakers—Bill paused beside them, and breathed the stink in deeply—and then a forlorn maker of ice-skates. I wondered why he troubled to lay out his wares, since it was six full months before they'd be wanted for play atop the sink-ponds.

At last we came to a pair of fishmongers. "Salmon. Cod. Herrings, and eel," I said, naming every fish I knew from the dozens of kinds arrayed glistening on the shaded table.

"Whatever is wholesome," Bill said. I called for two bowls of bubbling herring stew, thinking that it would be soft on our stomachs after a day without food.

It was more than soft. It was like coming upon a hoard—so rich with fish and milk, and dots of floating butter! My body straightened as though I'd shed ten years. But as we ate, drawing the bones from between our teeth, a fellow walked past with a bag made of fishing-net slung over one shoulder. The bag bulged with black-and-white feathers. *Barnacle geese*, I realized. The sort I had been hunting when I met Henry—and Cudman. Perhaps I'd needed a reminder that this was still the city of my nightmares. Now I felt the ground tilt beneath my horse's hooves; I hoped she would not leap from such a height. I called for Bill to lead on.

As we passed an astrologer's hollow globe and the long-necked bottles of an apothecary, I could smell salt, sharp and immediate, and I knew we were nearing the sea. Still it was a shock when the street opened; before us were masts upon masts—masts like the stripped, black trunks left behind by a swift forest fire.

The sun shone on reefed sails, and taut rope, and flapping pennants, and bright water. It shone on cargo fluyts, ketches, and hoys; it shone on plain fishing-boats, crusted with blood and barnacles and salt. I saw crayers and long-boats; hulls that had sailed every sea. There was even a frigate, the *Swift Suit*, looming among the rest like a castle over rabbit hutches. And everywhere, everywhere, were barnacle geese. Geese thick as beaten flax, so thick that it seemed the ships would struggle to leave their moorings.

There were thousands upon thousands of them, dabbling, diving, and squalling. They croaked and gabbled, ducked their necks, splashed their wingtips, took brief flight. Seeing them was like hearing a lullaby that your mother would use to soothe you after nightmares; the tune may be comforting, but it also reminds you of the horrible dream.

Launches and skiffs plowed between the moored vessels. The boaters cast nets and lashed out with hooks. Other folks waded from shore with clubs, taking all the geese they could to pack into old burlap. They laughed and called, competing to see which household might take the most. A mother consoled her boy—he had a shriveled left arm, I saw, and had dropped the goose he'd labored so hard to catch. Already a few fires were burning on the shore.

Far more, I knew, would flare that night. And though I sat atop a noble mount, I suddenly felt a kinship with the people there. I knew their delight in the hunt, for I had once shared it. I knew the feel of an empty net in my hands, and the satisfaction of feeling the net go heavy and struggling. I knew the smell of the fires, and of the seaweed shriveling and crackling on the burning driftwood, I knew how the fire-pits would blaze and blare in the dark, stretched down the shore like the signals of a victorious army.

I knew what it was to share those things. I had shared them with my husband; he had shared them with me. Whatever happened afterwards, we had met in joy. And afterwards lived with love, love that sustained us when the world tried to break us on its wheel.

This is only a city. Only a city. There is no curse here. The knowledge filled me to the roots, completely as laughter, full as tears. I dismounted, and sat on the seawall. Then I watched the people harvest geese, my head resting upon Bill's shoulder.

Twenty-five: Bill

I sit beside Sarah so she may rest her head on me. I stay there all the afternoon, that she may take her rest. She lays her head down like flowers, as the tide pulls slowly away to leave the pier's legs naked. Then there is the smell of limp green weeds on the shore, and of smoke from fires burning in sandy holes.

The pilings are coated like an old turtle, sheathed in gray and white shells. One boat ties there briefly, tipping in the small waves as its owner empties his nets.

I count three fires. I count four. Wood burns in shallow dug-outs, cracking in the blustery wind off the ocean. As the piles of old boards burn, coals fall from them to pile, glowing, below.

Sarah shifts her head atop my shoulder, and she sighs.

In the last bit of bubbling surf a girl runs, aprons wet to the knees, hair falling carelessly from beneath a brimless hat. When she lifts her aprons there is a quick glimpse of white leg. Then I think of Roslyn. And that makes me think of my lost sisters, Sally and Dory; and the rooms we lived in, when Roslyn used to bring me joy. I miss all of them, all of that. I do wish to see my sisters again.

But I am bound to Sarah, bound as though with chains. And

there is joy in the sight of her at rest. There is more when her breath goes soft and I know that she is sleeping, her lips loose with slumber. I can give this gift, offering a place to rest after the jolting of our fearful flight. And glad, glad! I am glad to do it. She has given me a place of relief.

That place is not one I can walk to; this is not one that must at last be left behind. I carry the place she gave me in my own chest. It is empty and still. Sarah lies with cheek on my shoulder, her stars in a circle, my arm around her back, and I never feel the twinging that seized me in the stormy woods. There is no fear of what the twinging might mean, or what it might make me do.

Should it ever come again, I have a charm to banish it. The charm is the memory of Sarah's hands upon me. Cleansing me built a wall between us; but that wall somehow brings us closer. It makes both of us safer, and thus allows for love. Now she may sleep soundly beside me, whether that is in a hutch or by the harbor's bright shore. I do not wish to leave her while I live.

Men haul nets. They swing sticks like threshers, clubbing their meals of goose.

I gaze at Sarah's face. Never have I seen her sleep so peaceful. Two tips of one star have loosened, like bark peeling back. She licks her lips as though she dreams of geese. Well she might—for now there are geese cooking, staked above the pits to burn their feathers off.

At last she wakes with a soft jolt. She looks up, and for a moment is confused. Then she bids me go to the closest fire, and to ask if I and my old mother might join the people there at their feast.

I do. And we may. And the goose is better even than it smelled—roasted, and dipped into the ocean, then roasted again until crisp. Thus the sea's salt makes the skin fine, like wild bacon.

I eat quickly, and burn my mouth. My Sarah eats slower but more ferociously, tearing wings and legs until grease streaks her arm like rain on tree-trunks. Her eyes are distant, and happy. She sighs with love for the feast.

Those about us smile but they are not comfortable. I think they wish they had not given us leave to join them. One tries to jest with me; he says he breeds bandogs, to fight against other dogs at fair. *Your mother is as hungry as they are before they fight,* he says. *You should keep her better fed than that.*

But his jest has no edge. It clanks from my Sarah's fierce smile—from her shield of stars.

The man laughs, because he must. He daggers Sarah another fowl.

She takes the handle. She gnaws the bird. Its cousins cry on the harbor, blank and blind and unaware.

Twenty-six: Sarah

The root the vendor showed me reminded me of the star-stone that David Merchant once found nestled into burned grasses near the village mill. In spite of its name, the star-stone had been made of iron, its metal gouged and blackened by passage through the sky. David was not the only one to see it fall, but he was the only one to run to it rather than retreat into his house with desperate prayer. Master Stradling soon took the fist-sized stone from the boy, saying gruffly that such a thing had its proper place. Whether that place was tucked into the podium he spoke from, or sunk into the muck of a cow-pond, Master Stradling never said.

The knobby root was like the star-stone's cousin, though brown rather than black, and less pitted than it was shriveled with age. Here and there white shoots had begun to sprout from tiny divots. It lay alone on a folded gray cloth, drawing my eye at once away from the surrounding trays of familiar turnips, carrots, and parsnips.

"A potato," the vendor said when he saw my interest. "A Virginia curio. Some wise wives cut them into squares and plant them. Soon their gardens are adorned with American things."

I bought it for half of what I'd have been willing to pay. Selling the mare had brought me silver like a summer storm; she was a noble mount, and I doubted I had seen so much coin in my life as was now hid in our comfortable rooms. But nothing had made me feel as wealthy as finding that I could afford the strange root with such ease. I squeezed it gently; it had the give of firm moss.

Virginia. Only the day before, I had glanced into what at first seemed the shop of a mad ropemaker, the ceiling covered with hooks that dangled what looked like rough, knotted ropes. Then I saw that the ropes were made of tightly wrapped brown leaves, and walked into the rich, dank smell of tobacco. It amazed me to see so much of it; this was not a curiosity, like the locust-tree, or the potato. The tobacco was grown for use in England. The sight of it spoke to me of broad fields, and wet summers, and the sea.

The shopkeeper was a stoop-shouldered, morose old factor who measured off knots of sot-weed with his knuckles. Almost without volition I asked him what he knew about passage to the Americas. There was no one better to ask; he had often helped arrange for a place on board a returning tobacco-ship. And the price of a berth was well within my means. The colony's leaders must have been eager to have any who were willing to come.

Afterwards, I told myself that asking about passage had been a fancy, a whim like buying a poppy-cake. But I knew that it meant more than that.

I took the potato to the docks and sat upon a barrel. With waves shushing below me I cut the root open. Inside a gray outer ring, the flesh was the color of cream ready for the churn, firm and slick and wetter than a carrot's. It smelled dusky, like foreign clay.

Crewmen hustled about me with clumsy barrows and sacks of freight. During the week we'd been in Northam, the docks had enthralled me more every day. Every man there meant more than he knew; every man was a sign that the world had grown, and changed. Every man was a note in a song I had been deaf to, each laden ship a verse.

I turned the strange root in my fingers as I thought of my old village. Surely some thread ran between the changes in Monkshead and those in Northam. The ruin of one was somehow connected to the prosperity of the other.

Flame can clear a field, making it ready for new growth. It seemed to me, there, that all the world was burning, being consumed and growing anew. Some places, like my village, would vanish. Others would grow and seem blessed. So many new things were coming from over the ocean; so many people were on the road and on the water, traveling hundreds of leagues after a lifetime spent on a single tiny plot. When Henry and I came to Monkshead to stay, our unannounced arrival had been a seven-days wonder; now all the world seemed on the road.

I again thought of Virginia. It might already have changed under the attentions of trappers and traders and tobacco-farmers. I could not know. But I did know, somehow, that without colonial trade the vagabonds would never have come to steal our commons for sheep. Whatever moved them also drove men across the sea; a single wind may shake shingles from a tower and cool a lady's wrist.

The tides, the tides…they hissed over the shore, shifting sand, leaving behind half-circles of weedy wrack. This shore was the one I remembered. It held the same place in the world as the one I'd walked, and dreamed of, and feared. The ancestors of these geese once fed me. This was where I was sinned against, and where I sinned.

But the waves broke, sighing, palming the sand. Could it truly be said to be the same place where Cudman lured me, and where in dreams I saw myself killing him? For scores of years the waves had been breaking up the shore and building it again, every tide shifting the sands like the pieces of a puzzle.

A slim rivulet ran from a cracked clay culvert in the seawall. The culvert looked old—green, mossy, long past ready for repair. But I did not remember it. Maybe I once splashed through that rivulet, wetting my ankles, angering tiny crabs and sending them clicking for their holes. Maybe Henry and I leapt it together; maybe the years had wiped it from my mind. Memory was treacherous. But for that moment, all of me felt clear.

I'd feared that Henry had sinned beyond God's forgiveness. For many years I'd struggled against the thought that Henry burned for a sin that should have been mine—that he drowned in an ocean of fire and damned souls. He should never have endured that for me; he should never have imagined that killing Cudman would bring peace to my heart. I could not pay such a debt, not if I had ten lifetimes to do so. But sitting on the pier, running my thumb over the slick flesh of a root from a thousand leagues away, I remembered my congregation's one wise, unassailable truth: we cannot know God's will or judgments. The congregation might not have honored that truth in their own lives, but it was true. Children on the quay dangled from the bottom of a hanging cage, using it for a swing; peace spread over me, warm as the sun.

Nothing in the world was set. There was terror in uncertainty—but there could also be solace. If Bill could triumph over the pollution that he had believed so solid and leaden, perhaps my Henry had nothing to fear. He had been first among men. Maybe in death he dwelled among the finest. Surely he would deserve their company.

"I would choose you," I said aloud. "I would endure it all again for you. And for the sake of the years we had."

The salt breeze brushed me. I dropped the potato to splash among the swells. Geese swam croaking through the barnacled pilings; their cries affirmed my gift.

Later that day I returned to the tobacco-factor, and paid for passage to Virginia. *I will tell Bill that I am going,* I thought then. *But not where. Better that I disappear, this time—that I vanish as into the sea.*

Twenty-seven: Bill

One eve she leads me to the wharf. Then she points to a signal-flame, her finger stretching like a candle she means to light. The signal-flame is in a stone house on a neck of beach, far past the swaying ships. In evening it glows like the goose-pits; every evening and night it burns. If it were damped, sailing ships might crash together. There would be a tangle of wood and rope, all wound together as they sank, turning, down.

Now Sarah's head blocks the signal-flame. She says she will soon see it from the sea. At that my fingers go cold. My blood rushes from them, to warm my chilling heart.

Our time here has been grand, she says.

She says that I may never know how grand it has been. But I do know. I know the joy of an ocean breeze on my face, and of waking without fear that she will be harmed.

She tells me that being here has made her hungry to see more places. She wants to travel onward, before age leaches flavor from the world. There are many places she wants to go. There are the Low Countries, where congregations like hers have fled. There is Virginia, tumultuous with blooms; she thinks she could fill her life learning of its creepers and vines. There is Guiana—a hot country, where golden snakes hang like a ship's rigging, and monkeys run in tribes.

She names country after country. I know that one of the countries is the one she will go to, when she leaves me. For that reason every name is horrid.

Where would you go, she asks me. She watches me close but I have no answer. I bite my cheek inside, until it bleeds. I do want to seek my sisters, and stand before them as a clean man. But I do not wish to leave her. If she would let me, I would also take ship. I would go.

Though she watches for an answer, I do not give one. Instead I watch the harbor, and the fire-house glinting through the high hulls. There are fewer geese here now. Soon, Sarah has told me, they'll take to their airy trails.

After that I cannot sleep calm. Darkness crams our room, the hours pile high atop my head. Still I cannot sleep. I lay wakeful with my back rigid and my eyes blank, seeing nothing but the black waters beyond the harbor.

Sometimes I stand and go out. I do not care that I have kicked the stool, or that it may wake her. I think she is already awake, watching the blackness where I stand.

Then I walk the quay road until the harbor turns red. The oars of the day's first fishers spin circles on the water. Back and forth I walk, pacing ten steps this way, pacing ten steps back.

One night I weary of pacing. I walk along the road past a man pounding wedges to hold his mast firm. I walk past snailshell shops, and homes like nests. I walk out through the gate of the city wall, and the ragged ring of houses around it. Then I am on a trail of slippy sand, ribboning through brush beneath the growing moon.

The brush has some thorns. Still I take off my boots, and walk on with sand in my toes. When the sun begins to show, it lights the sand as pink as skin. There is less brush and less brush, until there is no trail, for there can be no pathway over blank dunes.

I swirl my feet this way and that way, making a road I will follow back. After a while the ground slopes down. As it does it begins to stiffen underfoot. At last I am on the sandy neck that leads to the squat signal-house. I squint to see it through blowing beach-dust.

I am there when the sun rises. It casts orange atop the toss of the sea. Slowly all the water yellows, all the rolling waves go yellow. I walk through sea-grass whiskering the spit's ocean side, and wash my feet in the foam below the signal-house.

Sarah is right that the city has been a good place. But the thought of her leaving sickens my memories of it. Sarah will leave. We will have had only a handful of days here. And those slip…

I look back at the signal-house. A fellow there watches me, his gaze making me think of a badger. Maybe he does not wish for company, here where the signal fire is his kingdom.

When I begin walking back, something cuts against my foot. I kneel to find the villain. In the spongy ground there is a sharp black shell, pointing upward like a spike in a trap. There is another shell, and another. They speckle the sea-grass.

I pull at the one that cut my foot. It comes away slowly, tied to others by a web of beard. It is a mussel like the ones binned beside smelt at the fishmonger's. I do not wonder that it was the cheapest of all his wares. There is bushel upon bushel here, for any man to take.

I look across the spit, and through the harbored ships at the spread of the city. Then I walk to seek out Sarah, to tell her where to find shelled meat.

She flatters the glue-maker, and borrows his shovel. Its blade and handle are made from a single heavy branch. It stinks from stirring fat. *But it will make our work easier*, she says. *And it won't sully any flesh that's already in a shell.* I sling a bucket over the shovel, and the shovel back over my shoulder. Sarah crutches behind me. We make our slow way over the dunes.

The day began with orange, but it is now blue. The sky is blue, the sea is blue. If the wind had a color it would be blue from love for them. Pelicans come, and gulls. They sweep crying across the neck. Though Sarah never speaks, I know she is there; I know it surely though the wind hides the sound of her clumsy crutching.

A stilt-kneed bird drags one broken wing. It drags and stumbles. I chase it, the bucket knocking against my shoulder, I chase it down a dune towards the shore. But the bird has been mocking me—once she has played enough she spreads her wings, both of them now sound. She flies crying over the harbor. Then she turns back, landing, at last, close to where our chase began.

Sarah is now far behind me. This could be a joyous errand, like the day we went to the butcher man for beef to boil. But I do not feel that. This day is empty.

There is sand in my boots from chasing the bird. It grates there as we near the signal-house. I do not stop there though Sarah is far behind. I do not stop until I am in the shell-beds, amid the meager grass.

Then I dig, prying loosened clumps of mussels from the sand. Here's a knot of four. Here are seven, a fine family held together by a beard. I dig and dig, just above the play of the surf. Sometimes an eager wave licks at my feet, cleaning the shells I've heaped. I never pause nor rest. The pile grows like the coins I dreamed of.

At last I feel Sarah behind me, like a shadow though I see no shadow. I plunge the shovel-blade deep. Already I have more mussels than the pail will hold, but I plunge the blade under a great mass of shell. I lean on the handle until it bends. I do not fear to break it; I fear that I will not break it.

Bill, Sarah says then. *Bill*. She lays her hands on me.

Nothing loosens in me. I shake like a drying dog; her hands fall away. Again I pull the handle. This time it wiggles. Soon the shell will burst forth.

If you were to come with me, she says. Then she is quiet for a time. I jerk the shovel. I jerk and jerk.

If you were to come with me, she says, *I would still have to leave you one day. I don't have so very many years left. Then you would be lost, on the other side of a sea, far from your sisters. They would always long for you, and wonder.*

Again her hands are on me. This time I do not shake them off, but only shudder.

It will be hard for me to leave so true a friend, she says. *But to think of them losing their brother, and never knowing where he is, or if he even lives...I could not bear that. And I know that you could not. You need to find them. You need it as badly as I need to go. But wherever you do find them, you will have my love.*

Then she leaves me leaning on my shovel handle, where I weep to think of being cut from her. She goes to the waves with a clump of sandy shell, and dips it in the ocean until the shells shine black. When all are gleaming she takes a knife from her belt. She pries one mussel off; she opens it with a cunning twist of the blade. She looks at me as she raises the shell to her lips, and drinks from it like a cup. The taste makes her close her eyes. She comes to me and she opens another shell.

Eat this, now, she says. I slurp it down as she did. The taste is that of the crashing ocean, spilled onto my tongue. I toss the curved shell to the sky. The wind blows it behind us and into the harbor. It floats there, a raft, like those used to hunt geese. And then, at last, I can laugh. Sarah can laugh.

We sit in the sand above the beds and eat mussels, tossing shells to float and drift. Once, the signal-man comes to his window to peer at us. But he only shakes his condemning head, and closes the heavy shutters.

Sarah will leave. But for now I rub the silver on the inside of an empty shell—slick as ice!—and I feel blessed to know her.

I throw a shell high, higher than before. It is when I turn to see its flight that I see the man following our sandy path. I see his crimson cloak blowing. He is on the trail we followed; he swings his spear as though it is only a staff.

Sarah is standing. *Bill,* she says. The man walks without hurry but already he is nearing, step after step after step. *Bill,* says Sarah. I have never seen her so without force. She does not know what to tell me to do.

The shovel is heavy. I shake sand loose from its blade.

The man stops a score of paces away, his spear aimed at the heavens. We should have snapped it when he slept but he has it now.

Why will he not leave her alone? The cry is silent in me but it is a scream. My eyes go steamy. There is no path around him. He will not let us be, will not let her take to her ship…

How? she says. There is no hope in her voice. There is no thought of defying him.

His beard is patchwork. *There's only the one gate*, he says. *It wasn't hard to guess you'd pass through it.*

She starts to talk—to ask, I think, how he knew to come to this city of all cities. But all she says is *Did Mary*. Then he does not let her talk.

The boy Thomas told me, he says. *He was quick enough to loose his tongue, after he returned and found my Lord Renault so eager to find the thief of his mare. Thomas will find himself rewarded, as I would if I returned. But now there are my companions in Monkshead to think of. I might still regain my place there, if I return with a trophy of my hunt.*

He draws up his own long hair, as though to lift head from shoulders.

Call your boy, then, Sarah says. *Don't do your murder when only the blind ocean can watch. Coward. Call your boy. Let him see what his master is. Coward.*

As she speaks the man reddens, as though his mind spills dye. The hand on the spear trembles like my body. His eyes blacken like me. At last something cracks and *there is no boy to call*, he says.

Peter, his name was, he says. *My nephew, and now dead. He never woke from your sleep. I never meant to leave you alive. But now if I could I would kill you again every hour for all my life.*

At that I run. I run to him in challenge. These are lies! She never would give something that would kill. His lies are meant as a doorway to murder, giving him a reason and a righteous cause to hurt her. But I will not stand and see Sarah wounded, or even threatened by his raised spear. Before he can raise it and cast it I am on him, swinging my shovel, swinging to kill.

It meets nothing but air. But it does drive him stumbling back. Again I swing with all the force rising through my feet and legs, my back and arms and hands.

But now he has his footing, he is firm and ready. He comes to me. His weapon comes to me, ramming, his siege spear. It finds me and stabs me. It tears me like a saw. There is blood in my vest. His shaft pins my vest to me, tightly as a wineskin.

But I have felt the hurt of cleansing, and this is less than that. This hurt is mine. I know the shaft is there and yet do not fully feel it; that will come.

My arms are strong from dragging lead gutters, my back iron from digging graves. I grip the haft within me with one hand, and with the other swing my shovel as I wrench my body. He steps back and must let go. Thus I am freed, and he is without a weapon. I have his and also mine.

He turns from me and seeks to run. He stumbles. He no longer hopes to find an easy kill.

But there will be no flight for him. There will be no more terror or wandering for us. He stumbles; my third stride brings me to him. On the fourth I swing through Sarah's screaming. The spear is in me but I do not feel it. It does not slow me as I swing to murder.

Once I was polluted by others' sins, and hated those sins until I hated my own flesh. This is different, for though I beat him, beat him down, in the sand I beat him, long after he lies there I beat him steady as his skull breaks and looses its gore, this is no sin, and if it is sin it is one I choose to take upon myself.

At last he lies quiet in the sand. He is a bait crab—a feast for fish.

Then the haft in me grows longer. It is heavy as the bough it was carved from.

It pulls me aside him, to the sandy ground.

At last comes the midnight I have reckoned on. That I have heard of, in old stories.

Twenty-eight: Sarah

The shovel was turned beneath Bill as though someone had tried to lever him from place. He had fallen on the tideline, on a sweep of limp green weeds curving along the top of the mussel beds. Sand-pipers stabbed for sea-spiders, already recovered from their fright. Above Bill, the sand formed small hillocks as though it had been poured out from cups. All around him were the scattered footprints of the combat.

When I knelt beside him, his eyes had begun to teeter and fade. His lips moved, but quietly. The spear kept me from laying him gently on his back. I called to him, I brayed with my mouth beside his ear. I did not care what words he heard me speak—only that he heard me, and knew that I had come to him.

Out of breath, I paused. And in that pause I watched him fall away. He went without a sound, but as absolutely as though he'd stepped off a mountain crag.

What was left of Sam Ridley lay as still as a butcher's shambles. Not even a kinsman would have known his face, so ardently had Bill sought to cudgel the harm from him.

* * *

During the fight I had thought desperately of the signal-house keeper. Maybe he could run for help, or bellow within his house in an attempt to frighten Ridley off. When that hope had been dispelled—when all had been dispelled, and I sat suddenly alone on the shore—I still hoped to give Bill a final gift. The truth about that day would be known. The dogs of the city would worry Sam Ridley's body. The people would raise Bill high in their minds and hearts.

But I did not know the keeper then. I did not know that he would think any man dressed as richly as Sam Ridley an innocent.

If I had been present when the keeper spouted his rotten tale, I might have struck at him, clawing at eyes that were no more trustworthy than crabs. But the city constables brought us to a granary with walls of heavy timber and a floor of fired clay, and I remained there with Bill while the keeper offered his testimony.

The granary had not been used for a long time. The floor was swept clean to discourage rats; there was no window. There was only a plank bench, and Bill, and me.

I did not offer the body any outer tenderness. I offered only the loyalty of my presence, kneeling on the clay beside the bench where the constables had laid him, almost unaware of the pain beginning to grind in my knee. Bill's eyes were still closed, not yet stiff and open with death. Beyond the open doorway I could hear the faint mumbling of the constables.

The world had gone ghostly. In my heart, Ridley yet stalked me. He trod down hard roads and through soft mires, searching for me in filthy horse-stables and in meadows glad with daisies. In my heart Peter still trailed him. And Bill still slept; soon he would wake. When he did, he would see that I had sat vigil beside his sickbed. When he woke he would see me.

The door opened behind me, and a young constable in a peaked green hat came to the foot of the bench. He watched me without looking, examining the rafters as though for cobwebs.

"I wish to see him well buried," I said. Keepers of the law always know who to call upon for a funeral.

He glanced down, as he might at a child who wanted the moon for a bauble. "You would need a curious coin for that," he said.

"I have enough." I wondered if burials had become so dear. Perhaps they had. In a prosperous city, the fees of grave-diggers might rise along with the fortunes of the men they bury. But I did have money, and there was a week left before my passage to Virginia. It was more than long enough to see to a fine burial.

But the young constable's words hung in the silence of the granary. *A curious coin.* He did not mean a curious sum, I realized; he did not mean that I would need an uncommon weight of silver or gold. The necessary coin might be the Lord's forgiveness, or time spent in Purgatory, or the healing touch of Jesus—in any case it was nothing I could offer.

He fingered his green hat and he thought Bill a murderer. The voices of the others rumbled outside; their conference would decide the fate of my friend's body. I thought hopefully of the signal-keeper. Surely they would know him, respect his calling, and believe his word.

"What will you do with him?" I asked with all the resignation I could summon.

"Take him to the boneyard, or else the killer's cage," he said.

"Must you always bear them on a slat?" I asked. When they'd fetched Bill from the beach they'd laid him on a plank with three dowels hammered to the underside as handles.

At last he looked with some pity at me—at the poor grandmother, who only wished to see the boy carried properly. "Most days we have a cart," he said. Then he began to prattle, telling me about how the cart had been lent to one of the constable's cousins. The cousin's daughter was to be baptized, and wanted her to ride lordly on that day…

As he spoke the room seemed to fill with warm feathers; I gasped them quietly, I drowned on down. For there was nothing at all that I could do. These men would do what they believed their duty to be: I would watch.

At last the other constables returned to us with the resigned air of miners. "Stay here, grandmother," one said, though they had not yet given me a reason to protest. My heart ranted at him and the rest, shouting at faces blank as duckweed. But the memory of the scold's bridle leashed me; I could not afford to be punished that day, and thus fail to be witness to Bill's fate. I had more than myself to think about.

They laid Bill's body to their plank. When they left I followed like a shadow, though one quickly lost and left behind. Bill was soon hid from view in the confusion of a market, my crutching easily outpaced by the constables' steady tread.

When I reached the docks, Bill was already in the cage I'd seen hanging from a huge iron wicket over the harbor seawall. When the last constable stepped away, I saw that one bar had left a rusty line on Bill's temple as he settled into place. They had arranged him as though he was sitting, his head slumping loosely forward.

I looked up at him from the street. The bars. Bill's body. Beyond that, nothing but the blue sky of afternoon.

The constables took up position across the street. They looked casual and officious, not wanting to be seen watching. But they would not leave. They needed to see the way their actions affected passing folk, the way that Bill's body altered the street's flow and temper. They tasted the city's changing mood as a cook might sip soup after adding thyme.

The cage was shaped like a pyramid; they'd dropped one side open to make a ramp and doorway, then chained it fast near the apex. Such a cage is said to be for the humiliation of murderers before they're taken to the gallows. But in truth it is more a warning than a punishment. Though Bill was beyond the constable's grasp, they could still use him as a signboard.

The inward angle of the cage kept him from seeming at ease. Had he been alive, sitting so skewed would have been a slow agony. One of the constables had wound wire around his arms and then through the bars, making him lean forward as though choking. They would not even let him seem to rest, lying curled on the cage's floor.

No one troubled to throw fish-bones, or fruits past their prime. Bill's crime was not a celebrated one; his victim had not been high-born, or well-loved. But I felt the eyes of passersby on him. Their glances—so careless, so casual—showed worse contempt than any maliciously-thrown rind. They did not see him with the respect he deserved; they saw nothing but a body.

So I tossed my crutch to the top of the seawall. Then with granite tearing at my fingertips I climbed, reaching and crawling, breaking two nails to nubs. At last I lay gasping atop the wall. I used the sickle handle to pry myself up before the cage. One of the constables called an order to me: *He must hang there two days!* A younger voice—a boy, swinging a rat on a string—called out that I should free the man. He knew the constables would stop me. A boy loves to see a tussle.

But I did not mean to struggle against the cage. The chains were as brawny as a bear's arms; the bars were like musket-barrels; the lock was hard as a duke's heart. I could not break them and would not try. I stood before Bill. Within all that iron he looked defenseless as a sleeping hare.

I faced him only for a moment before turning to the street. I set the crutch beneath my arm and raised a hand as though to shield myself against a blazing light. I had no illusion that I could stop anyone from making light of Bill's misery, or his end. But I could make myself a spectacle. I could make them think of an elder's madness, rather than of a young man's crimes. I could make them see that Bill was not the guilty one.

If the crowds must look at something, they could look at me.

It was late afternoon when I took my station, the stark daylight already beginning to soften. Across the street was a tavern, and beside that a rope-winder's plain lean-to. Next to that was a bleached yellow awning-tent, where a woman sold chipped cups of bone soup to dockmen and chilled fishers.

I stood there as the sun fled, my back to the cage and the rustling, rising tide. I thought of the goose hunt, when so much of the city had plunged into the waters about the quay. Thinking of that made the bustling street seem empty.

People carried slabs of dried cod, clay smoking-pipes, and half-drunk friends. When a face turned to me I would hold its gaze, steadily and without expression, until it flashed away as quickly as a moth's wings. *Later,* I thought, *they can tell their friends about the old woman who stood with a dead man. I will be the oddity then. When they think of murder, they will think of me; that will be just.*

Heaven purpled, going black. A star began to glint, then a few more. Tendrils of fog stretched from the ocean; past me, around us, down the seawall, into the street. Soon all the city was encompassed. The coming darkness could have been as much from the crawling cloud as from the vanishing of the sun.

Fog masked the few stars. The tavern-keeper lit four candles around his doorway; the rope-maker had long since finished his twisting and weaving. The soup-cook rubbed her old arms, torn between eagerness for the business the cold evening might bring her and desire for her bed.

The wind died to nothing. But the creak of the cage and the rusty grind of ship-chains seemed all the louder for that.

The battle on the sandy neck seemed clearer in memory than it had in life. I had become like Randall, drawing the world more precisely than I truly saw it. Again and again Bill ran from me, away from my arms and calls. Each time he did I saw something new: the sprays of sand behind his booted feet, the shovel held down and to his side, even the place I'd mended his shirt along one shoulder. And every time Ridley faded, until Bill was running down an empty beach. Until he was running from me for play.

He'd never spoken after I reached him. Already he was almost gone. He'd lain on his side, crazed by the agony of the killing shaft.

But he'd gone quickly. I remembered Ridley's words in the church, and was grateful that fear had forced him into a stroke that would kill so quickly. I was glad that Bill had not had to wait for long. Though I had not found good words to offer him, I knew that I could not have found the right ones in a thousand hours.

Peter is dead. Ridley had not gamed with me in that, trying to burden me with guilt before sending me screaming from the world. *Peter is dead.* The knowledge came like an ogre rising gnashing from the ocean.

For Bill hung behind me, blind, and mute, and forever senseless. The grief in Ridley's face had not been a playact. It was my own feelings made flesh.

The street had long since emptied. Still I would not go. I had been a sentry; now I stood vigil.

The tavern's second story had four dormer windows, each one thatched with a curve like an eyebrow. In the first, a candle made a pale yellow ring in the fog. Every two hours a woman would come to the front door with two dripping candles, and replace the guttering stubs around the entrance. If she ever glanced at us I never saw it.

She had replaced them three times; it was midnight. But the tiny flame in the upper window never wavered. It glimmered behind the glass without pause.

It was not possible; surely it had been replaced. I had only missed the change and I resolved I would not miss it again. It seemed important; a measure of my devotion. I wanted, for one night, for the street to be mine—to be ours. To know everything that happened there, and to remember it.

The tide was low again; the night filled with the stink of barnacles. When I closed my eyes—already forgetting, in my weariness, the candle I'd resolved to watch so closely—it seemed that I walked the mud beneath the harbor. I squinted against the water's sting.

Once, redness passed across my eyelids. Then I saw the watchman's torch as though it glinted in veins and half-circles atop the harbor's ripples.

* * *

Bill should never have left me with such a burden. It should have been me that struck out at Ridley, and died under his spear. Bill should have run, plunged into the harbor, swum to the city, saved his own life.

The crutch was rubbing me raw, I feared that any movement would make my knee collapse from under me, and for a time I hated Bill. I hated him for killing, and for dying, and for leaving me in his debt. I hated him because all I could offer was a vigil on a seawall.

I remembered our first meeting. I remembered how he had faced the gray weather without clothes. In the fever of night, it seemed that both of us had been naked.

The woman came to change the candles. Once again I'd missed the change behind the dormer glass. Maybe it had happened when I closed my eyes, imagining that I had sunk without drowning. *Strange that she still replaces the lower candles*, I thought feebly. *It's been long hours since any have gone in looking for a drink or a hearth.*

Under the soup-cook's awning, two rats skittered like spiders—but more warmly, thus more evil.

By that hour Bill's eyes were surely open. I had seen enough dead to know that his eyes had opened.

One by one I stripped the stars from my face. Wearing them had been the most ridiculous of all my useless acts; they were a game in a country that knew nothing of play. Without them my face felt empty, as though I'd lost my teeth. I cast them behind me. The sea could have my sky; this tide would take it, or the next.

Night mulled its stubborn way; phantoms came to me. Humors I had long forgotten caressed me in the gulf between the living world and that of dreams. I tasted pepper, I felt the moisture of love. I smelled rosemary, I heard Henry's chuckle. I wavered; if not for the pain I would have thought my legs had died beneath me. There is nothing so long as a night that one must drag through when grieved.

The phantoms tried to coax my mind from the wall, and from Bill. The flavor of Henry's straining shoulder, the flash of light in a cowslip tossy, the satisfaction of seeing an apple branch readying its fruit—all tried to tempt me from my task. They offered to soothe me if only I would follow, and forsake my friend.

But I would not be called from vigil, no matter how my legs might gnaw me, no matter how I was tempted. I tore from my memories, from old voices and old tastes; I struggled against them fiercely as Jacob with the angel. Still, for long hours the phantoms battered the fog about my head, begging me to sleep so that I might dream of better days.

But even the longest night must end. Even the most muscular darkness weakens. Slowly, slowly, the deep black of the fog began lightening to gray. The huffing, muddied figure of a fisher slogged by, a net rolled and slung over one shoulder. Soon after there was a pair of them, like cats who resent each other's company. Another, singly. They carried their nets like soldiers bringing guns from a bloody field. Not one looked up; I do not think they saw me. From far offshore I heard the muffled thud of crates being groggily loaded. A bell rang thrice.

I drew a palm across my bare face. Even while walking unwillingly to another bitter day of hauling mackerel, the fishers showed an easy strength I could never recapture. There seemed no blood left in my legs; only habit and my crutch kept me upright. Surely I would soon slip. I would fall. Bill's cage creaked gently behind.

Figure after gray figure passed, the city's earliest risers, on their way to fish and bake and stand guard. I hated and envied them. Then one stopped by my feet. For a long, appalled moment, I thought I saw Melode below me—Melode, my young friend from the village. She gazed at me, earnest and familiar.

But it could not be Melode. Melode was gone. She would not return to me. With that realization, the figure below me contorted, and became Mary.

Through my bleariness I could see only that she held an elm switch, and wore a shawl. The shawl was the blue one she'd worn riding from the cloister. She was alone.

The long night had left me turning in a whirlpool of delirium. My legs and back cried for release; I fought against grief, and fought to embrace it. Against all of that, Mary was nothing to me. She had long since passed out of our story; I cared not at all that she had entered it again, nor whether she had done so by accident or design. Now that she was there, it seemed as inevitable as though we'd appointed the meeting place. Thomas had not stayed with her for long; she could not be alone. It seemed as predictable as winter that she'd come looking for my help again.

The morning was a filthy gray. Tides licked the wall's lowest stones. Mary looked away from my silence; she saw Bill. She bit her knuckle, damming any words.

I was wearily glad for it. I had seen what true malice was, and she had nothing like that in her; I could not summon rage at her carelessness. Even if she had told Thomas where we were going, I knew she had done so without hatred; it was only a slip. It was Thomas that did us intentional harm. And in the end Ridley seemed fated to find us, whether we had a horse or a donkey or lethe or nothing. No, I could not hate Mary then. But she had surely not earned any account of what had happened to us.

She knew enough not to ask. She turned, and began walking away. Then she stopped as suddenly as though halted by a bed of nails. Without a word she returned to the seawall. When she leaned against it the edge blocked her from my sight.

The tavern-door candles had long since burned to drippings. Even the dormer-light had at last gone dark. I could not see whether it had been blown or simply melted away, for the foggy light made the dormer-glass as opaque as slate. When the door opened a red dog came out and stretched. The soup-woman trudged under her awning with a heaped basket of mutton-bones, ready to begin the day's broth. From behind us came the soft thumping of fishers rowing for the open sea.

I had little force left. Pain had bloomed in places I'd never have foreseen—the tops of my feet, the rims of my shoulder blades, the point of my right hip. I knew that all of it would converge in the end, growing into an agony that would defeat the strongest will.

For a while I tried to use the pain; it might help keep me awake, and also take my mind from Mary. Her appearance made everything feel like a dream; and if it was a dream then I need not grieve, nor stand vigil beside my friend.

Dawn became morning. Slowly the quay awoke, filling with drowsy heads and questing bellies.

I did not notice that Mary had gone until she was returning to me. She stretched to lay a folded cloth at my feet, then again took her station. Yeasty steam rose from the makeshift pouch. I smelled onions, cooked in butter. A pasty's brown lace showed between the folds of linen. I girded myself on the crutch, and flipped the pouch with one toe. It fell from the wall with a clatter of pebbles. I did not care if Mary would eat it herself or toss it to some grateful hound.

Later, when the city was at full gait—even the gulls spreading their wings on crates seemed to be hawking wares—Mary went again. She returned with a simple oaten loaf, a thumbs-worth of butter melting on top. This time I kicked the loaf from the wall before her hand had vanished.

The third time was less than an hour later. But in that time I had begun to sweat; salt drained from me, taking the little force I had left. My arms hung slack. At first the crutch had been a corner-post; now it was the foundation, the only thing keeping me up.

Mary came from the soup-woman with a brimming bowl. It was slightly cracked, and dribbled rich broth. Two poached eggs floated in the juice.

I felt a fountain of anger. I planted my legs as surely as I could. I lifted my crutch to knock the bowl. It would soak Mary, perhaps burn her.

Let me bear my own burdens. The voice might have been imagined, or remembered, or heard in a waking dream. I did not know. But I did hear it.

Below me the street murmured on unabated. Each townsman walked his regular route, each wife her habitual path. Every one sought a good meal or a night's love. In so little a time, I had gone from being an oddity to being simply odd; the city must see many things more curious than an old woman standing like a signal-post. None of them, I saw clearly, cared at all what dangled over the wall. They only cared that it was day.

Let me bear my own burdens. Bill had done what he had chosen to do; he had a right to that. There was nothing I could do but thank him, and let him go.

I rubbed my eyes. Then slowly, slowly I lowered myself down, keeping the crutch planted firmly, using it like a ladder. As I reached the stone my joints released, then locked again, ensuring that I could not stand to torment them further. I bowed my head; I moaned, quietly. At last I called down hoarsely to Mary. "Come. Sit aside me."

As she climbed I picked up the bowl. The first sip spread through my veins like honey. The bowl was warm and a few drops from the tiny crack moistened my fingers.

Mary watched as I split an egg and bit the yolk. "You should rest," she said. "I'll stay."

"Such generosity," I said. "But I won't leave him yet. I want to see him laid in the ground, or burned. Whatever they intend to do with him."

"I'll stay," Mary said. "I owe him much."

"You know that?" My question was short and sharp. But I listened.

She stammered a bit in answering. "You would not have brought me with you, had it been your choice alone."

"Maybe. It's true that he was the first to say that you shouldn't be left there. Who's to know, now, what I'd have done?" I heard my own question and knew how much I meant by it.

I finished the first egg and washed it down with a swallow of broth. The woman knew her work; the soup was wholesome, with a whisper of nutmeg.

It is such a pleasure to live. To eat eggs, and the broth they were cooked in.

Mary smiled sadly, or wryly. I knew she would soon ask what had happened. Before she could, I spoke again: "Thomas." Then I waited.

"Unfaithful fellow," she spat. "We had been together scarcely three days when he tired of me. He had such words of blossoms and love, of devotion and birds on the wing…" as she spoke I felt disappointment grow in me, stronger than I would have expected. Then she stopped, sharply as she had on the street. "I should never have gone with him."

"You could not have known his heart," I said, more gently than I felt.

"I shouldn't have gone, no matter how it was to end with him. I should not have left you without a word, or my mother. I've no right to spill out words now, telling you what Thomas did, asking for your pity." She shook her head disgustedly.

She did not have to ask about Bill's fate, then. I told her.

Not everything. There were many things I could not speak of. There was Peter; that was a sin I would carry on the day I stood before the Lord. Perhaps we cannot know His will. But surely He is not so forgiving as that. The days I had left to me felt more precious still; when they ended, I was sure the Lord would grant me no peace.

But first among the things I would not say was this: that as Bill waited for death to find him, the surf pounding on the weedy beds below, for a bare instant I thought I saw him calm. In the midst of his anguish there was a tiny, fleeting moment of peace. *I could not have seen that*, I told myself. *Do not tell yourself comforting lies. Do not tell yourself tales to heal your own guilt.*

But it had been there. Some joy, some peace had filled him. I knew it; and it wrenched me to the heart.

The world teems with life and the living, so richly that it sometimes seems impossible for any life to be lost. But all are. To save some bit of life, if only for a while, to offer breath and blood to another, if only for a little time…that is such a gift!

And a greater gift still, to give what little life you have. I would not speak of it.

"I will stay," Mary said.

"You should go," I said flatly. She began to protest, but I bore on. "I am not trying to be rid of you. I need you to do something. Whether you do it is your choice. But I hope you'll go to Sidley for me."

She pushed out her upper lip with her tongue, questioning.

"Bill was from there," I said. "When I first met him, he called the stars on my face the Anvil, as people from those parts do. He had sisters there. Sally, and—and Dory, I think. I hope you will go, and find them. That's more important than seeing to his body."

I waited for her questions—where was Sidley? How would she know the sisters? How would she sustain herself?

But she asked nothing. Watching her, I felt that a glass had been lowered over the three of us, giving us solitude beside the busy street. Before me I saw a woman who had…not grown, that was too kind. She had much living to do before she could be said to have grown. But perhaps she knew how she might begin to grow; there was perhaps a seed there. It might sprout—who could know? Faith can do a great deal, and I could not offer her any greater faith than trusting her with that task. I prayed I was doing right. "Please," I said.

She laid a hand on my shoulder. At times, she was a well-looking girl. "I will. God keep you, Sarah." Then she was down from the wall, and walking for the alleyway beside the rope-winder.

That evening the constabulary came, and took Bill's body. They threw it in a general pit, with criminals and those feared diseased.

Four nights later, having begun to heal from the aching wounds that seemed to span the whole of my body, I climbed the ramp of the Jamestown ship. I clung tightly to the hand rope to aid me until I was on the level deck. Though I asked the hired boy to place my chest in the hold with the rest of the colonists, I refused to go there myself, saying that I wished to watch my old country vanish behind me. The captain indulged me, for I was old, and alone.

The rest of the passengers were third sons and fortune seekers, the chary and the chaff. Even if permitted, few would have chosen to join me as the last stars were humbled under the light of the coming day.

I still had stars of my own, in the little box I'd kept since

Monkshead. Standing by the bow, close to the figurehead's grand headdress, I picked out a new sky. I touched them with sap and set them on my face. This time I did not mean to make a pattern. People could see what they wanted in the angles. Below me the harbor water was still; only a vague throb showed that it was joined to the living ocean.

At dawn the harbor master came with two long launches, and towed us from our anchorage. We passed through the first stirrings of the moored ships. The sun rose over the harbor mouth, lightly as blown glass.

Even beyond the sandy neck, there was no breeze to blow us on. The swells rocking the ship had been blown to us by distant gales.

Then I leaned to one side of the figurehead, less from fatigue than eagerness. For at last there came a hint of air on my skin; and from that rumor of breeze grew a sure, steady blow. A blessing of wind that spread our sails, fiercely as a falcon's wings.

THE END

Acknowledgements

Among my first and most important readers were Neela Vaswani, Robin Lippincott, Julie Brickman, and Kirby Gann, all of whom provided critical help and guidance as the story took shape. Close and generous readings by my sisters Michele Byrnes, Jenny Beahrs, and Suzanne Beahrs, as well as by Angela Hobson, were also vital and much appreciated.

Thanks to Sena Naslund for the Spalding MFA program she founded and sustains, which provided great inspiration and companionship. Thanks also to Crystal Wilkinson for her friendship and support, and to all the Spalding students who read and commented upon various drafts. There are too many to mention each by name, but special thanks to David Brasfield and Elizabeth Slade.

Many thanks to Matthew Miller of Toby Press for his patience and faith, to my editor, Deborah Meghnagi, for her generosity and insight, and to my agent, Leslie Daniels, for her steady confidence and guidance.

I'm forever grateful to my parents, Richard and Carolyn Beahrs. Thanks also to their old friends Terry and Lynn Myers, and John and

Suzanne Manners, all of whom helped to cement my early and abiding interest in the colonial period in both England and America.

I can never adequately thank Elizabeth Windchy and Erik Beahrs for their constant, inspiring, and humbling presence.

Finally, thanks to my grandmother, Virginia Beahrs, for sharing her large, unforgettable spirit.

About the Author

Andrew Beahrs

Andrew Beahrs is the author of *Strange Saint*, a companion novel to *The Sin Eaters*. His fiction and essays have appeared in *Gastronomica*, *The Writer's Chronicle*, *Virginia Quarterly Review*, *Alligator Juniper*, and other journals. He lives in Berkeley with his wife and son.

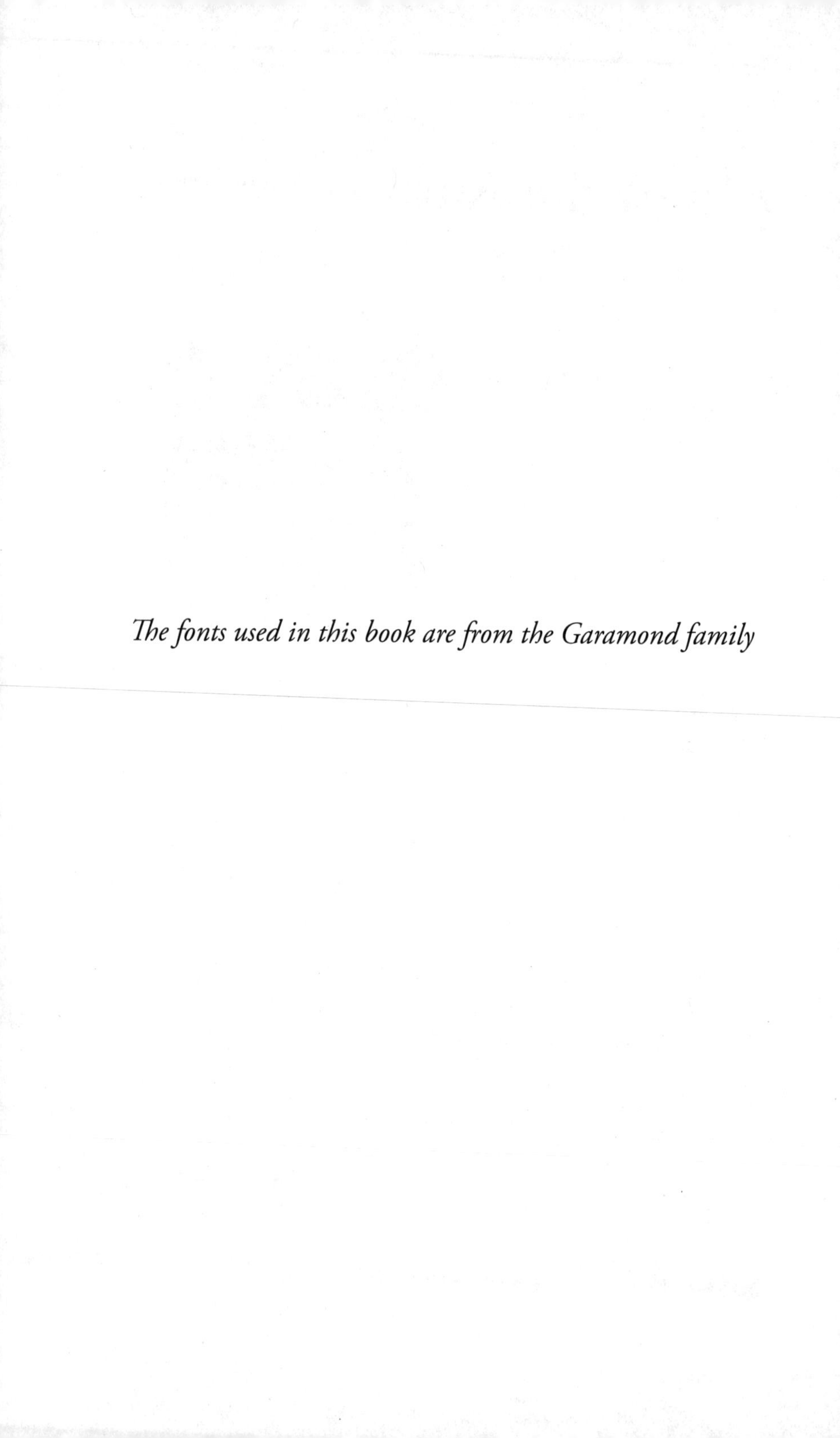

The fonts used in this book are from the Garamond family

Other works by Andrew Beahrs
available from *The* Toby Press

Strange Saint

The Toby Press publishes fine writing,
available at leading bookstores everywhere. For more
information, please visit www.tobypress.com

Chevy Chase Library
8005 Connecticut Avenue
Chevy Chase, MD 20